HIDE
AND SEEK

Books by Fern Michaels

Sisterhood Novels:

Tick Tock
19 Yellow Moon Road
Bitter Pill
Truth and Justice
Cut and Run
Safe and Sound
Need to Know
Crash and Burn
Point Blank
In Plain Sight
Eyes Only
Kiss and Tell
Blindsided
Gotcha!
Home Free
Déjà Vu
Cross Roads
Game Over
Deadly Deals
Vanishing Act
Razor Sharp

Under the Radar
Final Justice
Collateral Damage
Fast Track
Hokus Pokus
Hide and Seek
Free Fall
Lethal Justice
Sweet Revenge
The Jury
Vendetta
Payback
Weekend Warriors

Men of the Sisterhood
Novels:

Hot Shot
Truth or Dare
High Stakes
Fast and Loose
Double Down

Published by Kensington Publishing Corp.

FERN MICHAELS

HIDE AND SEEK

ZEBRA BOOKS
Kensington Publishing Corporation
www.kensingtonbooks.com

HIDE AND SEEK

Chapter 1

If you had known the seven American women of the Sisterhood of Revenge *in their other life*, the women sunning themselves might appear completely familiar. But upon a second look, you might turn to your companions and say, "No, it's not the American Vigilantes; it's not the Sisterhood. These women have a serenity, a certain jocularity about them. Would vigilantes on the run be painting their toenails and lathering each other with suntan lotion? No, no, these gals must be rich Americans on holiday. The American Vigilantes are somewhere else, playing hide and seek with the authorities, waiting to strike again. . . . Who knows where?"

It was a glorious day with golden sunshine and balmy breezes. At first glance it looked like a luncheon party of chattering young women sitting poolside, sipping fruity drinks with little umbrellas. From time to time the women stopped talking just long enough to rub more suntan lotion on as they waited for a lunch none of them would eat.

From their perch high on the mountain, their eyes were on the sparkling Mediterranean where District Attorney Jack Emery and martial arts guru Harry Wong, mere dots on the water, were tussling with a catamaran.

Kathryn Lucas, former long-distance truck driver, sat up and wrapped her arms around her knees. "I still can't believe there's a price on our heads. We're wanted fugitives back home. Every bounty hunter in the world will be coming after us one of these days, and here we sit relaxing at the pool."

"Aha! But first they have to find us. What do you think the odds of that are?" Alexis Thorn adjusted the wide-brimmed straw hat over her dark hair. "Even if one of them gets lucky, we have sanctuary here on this mountaintop."

Nikki Quinn squirted coconut-scented lotion into her hand. "We're only granted sanctuary as long as we *stay* on top of this mountain. The moment we go down the mountain, we're fair game for anyone who thinks they're smart enough to take us down. Padre Messina will do his best to make sure that never happens, but mistakes happen from time to time. As we all know."

"It's such a small village, not even a thousand people," Isabelle Flanders said. "Any stranger will stand out like the proverbial sore thumb. According to Charles, most of the villagers are related to the padre. Annie, and her husband before her, have always taken care of them. She sends the older children off to university, she keeps the church going, buys new fishing boats for the residents. She makes sure all the houses are maintained, she sees to their health, pays the schoolteachers to teach the little ones. She even hired a constable, a third cousin of the padre. The people love her. They won't let anyone up this mountain. That fact you can take to the bank. Plus, the padre will ring the bell if a stranger appears in the village. There's no way a stranger or anyone can get up this mountain without help. I think we're as safe as we can be." Her voice turned ominous sounding when she said, "At least for now."

Former flower shop owner Yoko Akia looked around at her sisters. She was brown as a berry and almost as tiny. The others referred to her as a 90-pound stick of dynamite because of her martial arts expertise. "There are hundreds of electronic monitoring devices scattered around the mountain. I feel very safe here, safer than I felt back in the States. I have enjoyed being here so much, and so has Harry, my love. I think paradise must be like this," she said, waving her arms at the profusion of sweet-smelling flowers, the meadows of green grass, the umbrella-like trees and the pungent scent of pine from the forest that carried on the breeze from time to time. "We have everything here . . . a tennis court, this pool, gardens, excellent food from those gardens and from the villagers. We will be learning new survival methods starting tomorrow. And"—she wagged one of her tiny fingers—"we will be expanding our minds, although I know I will never be able to speak German. It is too guttural sounding and my tongue will not work for the words."

The others laughed.

"Guess you aren't going to sleep, then," Kathryn said. "Charles is going to crack the whip." Her voice dropped to a whisper. "Do any of you think there's a change in Charles?"

Isabelle whispered in return. "Of course there's a change in him. He's blaming himself because we got caught. Thank God he had the presence of mind to prepare this place for us ahead of time or we'd all be sitting in the slammer. Let's just say Yoko's mission was a bit out of the ordinary and let it go at that. We're here and we have to make the best of it. By the way, Annie has me designing a new schoolhouse for the village. When I'm finished, I'm going to design a small library."

Annie de Silva—who owned the monastery as well as the actual mountain—and her longtime friend Myra Rutledge climbed out of the pool. Both donned terry robes as they made their way across the terra-cotta patio that surrounded the Olympic-sized pool.

"Did I hear my name mentioned?" Annie asked as she towel-dried her hair.

"You did. We were talking about the villagers and all you do for them," Alexis said.

"I love helping them. They're like my family. I want you to believe me when I tell you those villagers will protect us with their lives. Are you girls homesick?"

As one, the young women said, "No!"

Myra sat down next to Nikki and reached for her lotion. "I'm so glad. Charles, Annie and I have been worried that you might want to go back and . . . and face the music."

Always the most verbal of the group, Kathryn said, "Not in this lifetime. I do miss my truck at times. On the other hand, think about it, what's to miss? You're all here. I have Murphy," she said, patting the German Shepherd that was always at her side.

"Plus, the eats are great!" Kathryn was a lover of all food; fine food, bad food, any kind of food.

"Where are the boys?" Myra asked.

"Playing with the catamaran," Nikki answered. "They wanted to check out the speedboats and the Jet Skis. Jack volunteered to keep everything in shape. He likes Fernando, the young guy in charge of the upkeep of all the watercraft. He'll be going off to university in Madrid in the fall, so Jack asked him to teach him about boats. He's loving the experience. Harry is . . . what he's doing is outfitting the boats with a few *special devices*. They can hardly wait for those cigarette boats to be delivered." Nikki beamed as she peered over the top of her sunglasses.

Annie leaned back in her patio chair. "That was Charles's idea. He said a cigarette boat can outrun any boat except another cigarette boat. Drug runners use them all the time and the authorities never seem to catch them. Fernando is going to teach all of you how to operate the boats. He's a wonderful young man and he grew up on the water."

"So, girls, what's on your agenda for the rest of the day?" Myra asked.

Myra Rutledge, heiress to a Fortune 500 candy company, had formed the Sisterhood a few years ago, back in the States, with the help of her adopted daughter, Nikki Quinn, after her own daughter, Barbara, was killed by a drunken driver with diplomatic immunity.

Myra had thrown caution to the wind and enlisted Charles Martin's help in finding ways to help women who had fallen through the cracks of the justice system. Charles, an ex-MI6 operative in service to Her Majesty, the Queen of England, had gone to the United States to head up security for Myra's company many years ago.

In their youth, Myra, on a trip to England with her family, met and fell in love with Charles. But duty called and Charles went on assignment, and so Myra returned to the States . . . carrying a baby in her womb. What with the world as uncertain as it was at the time, the lovers lost contact. Decades later Charles showed up at Myra's corporate offices in Virginia and they fell in love all over again.

Given his vast covert knowledge, his many contacts in the spy arena throughout the world and his political savvy, Charles was able to make the underground organization of the Sisterhood run like clockwork. Long ago, the sisters had ceased to question his methods, knowing only that if they followed his orders to the letter, things would work out the way he planned. Among themselves they continually said, "Charles can do anything." And they believed it.

Myra had once told them, in secrecy, that Charles often called a friend—in the middle of the night, stateside time, early-morning time in England— and referred to the person on the other end of the line as Lizzie. As in Queen Lizzie. That alone had been enough to convince the sisters that Charles was invincible.

They knew they were breaking the law but they didn't look at it that way. If justice wasn't served the first time around, then the second time around they served up the justice, Sisterhood-style. They'd done that seven times—seven missions, one for each of them, before the authorities closed in on them.

Now they were fugitives from justice with a bounty on their heads. But, in the proverbial nick of time and with exquisite planning, Charles had whisked them away to this mountain hideaway in Spain where they were afforded sanctuary.

Now, Charles had a plan.

Tomorrow that plan would go into effect.

With two new additions to the Sisterhood: Jack Emery and Harry Wong.

Each man would bring his field of expertise to the table.

At least that's what everyone thought.

behind his back as Dimples. No one was sure if he knew about the nickname or not. The consensus was that he did not. He was not loved, nor was he even liked by the people who worked with him. No one in his personal life liked him much, either. AD Mitch Riley was all about Mitch Riley and his desire to become the director of the Federal Bureau of Investigation.

Riley perched on the end of the ugly metal table and said, "Let's look alive here, people. You all know why you're here so let's get right to it. The Bureau has become a laughingstock this past month. That means I'm a laughingstock. I will not tolerate that. Each of you," he said deliberately, looking at each member, "was handpicked by the director for this special task force. For some reason he seems to think you have the chutzpah to bring those female vigilantes to justice. Me, now, I don't think you can do that, so your job is to prove me wrong. If you can't do it, your collective ass is out of here.

"For starters, I don't want to see any more demonstrations in front of this building. Get rid of those vigilante supporters. Get rid of those international camera crews. Arrest them if you have to. I want to see this crap relegated to page 42, not page 1 of every goddamn paper within a fifty-mile radius. Call in the heads of all those shitty women's groups and sweat them. I want the television coverage to stop. The media is glorifying those goddamn women. Let them see what a Come to Jesus meeting is all about. In short, do whatever the hell you have to do to put a cork in this mess. If I hear one more late-night talk show host bashing the Bureau for letting them get away, I'll personally fry all your asses. Last night they called us the Jackass Brigade, saying we couldn't find our own asses even if we had a searchlight and the best proctologist in the business was holding the flashlight. Do I have to tell any of you what the director thought of that little tidbit?

"Seven goddamn women took the law into their own hands and wreaked havoc on this fine institution. It has to stop. The only way it can stop is if you find all seven of them and bring them to justice. No one drops off the face of the Earth without leaving a clue. Are you listening to me? They're women, for Christ's sake. You're *men!* And one woman," he said as an afterthought. "Whatever you need, whatever you want, it's yours as long as you bring those women to justice. Warrants are yours for the asking. If you have any questions, ask them now."

"It would help if we had a file, a dossier on the women," one of the agents said. "Do you expect us to go out there blind and hope for the best? You indicated this is not a Mickey Mouse operation. We need to know who we're hunting, not the crap that's been published in the newspapers and what we've been seeing 24/7 on the tube."

Riley looked at his people again. He didn't like what he was seeing. They might be good agents, but they didn't have fire in their bellies. He truly believed that all of them, especially the female one, were secretly rooting for the vigilantes. Hell, even Alice, his own wife, was rooting for them, and so was his daughter. He couldn't believe it when his defiant wife told him she'd contributed a thousand dollars to the defense fund set up by the women's lawyers. Christ, his wife and daughter even had T-shirts that said GO, SISTERS, GO! Two days ago he'd waited until they were asleep, confiscated the shirts and burned them in the fireplace. The next day both Alice and

Sally sported new ones. There was a war going on in the Riley household, but there was no need for anyone but him to know that. One way or another he'd make sure Alice toed the line. A shiver of something akin to fear skittered up his spine. She hated his guts. Maybe it was finally time to do something about that wife of his.

"In due time," he answered. "Right now I want you all to meet two people who know more than we do. Did you hear what I just said? There are two people out there in the hall who know more about those goddamn women than we do. We're the fucking FBI. We're supposed to know everything and we don't. I'm going to call them in here and I want you to listen to them. Then I want you to pick their brains."

Feet shuffled. Someone coughed. They all squirmed. Riley let them squirm. He managed to weave his way through his people and opened the door. He jerked his thumb in the direction of the small room.

Maggie Spritzer and Ted Robinson entered the room. Both reporters looked like they had just backpacked in the Appalachians for a month. Actually, what they'd been forced to do was hitchhike from Boise, Idaho, stopping at times to earn enough money washing dishes to pay for food. The Gold Shields—whose only loyalties were to the President of the United States and Charles Martin—had closed down the reporters' bank accounts, canceled their credit cards, confiscated their cell phones, their money and their identification, then drugged and dumped them after they had interfered in the Sisterhood's last caper in California where the infamous group of women had been captured.

Maggie and Ted smelled really bad and they knew it.

Mitch Riley introduced the two reporters. "Talk," he said.

They did, ending with the trek from Idaho to the present moment. It was Maggie who looked around and laughed in the agents' faces. "It's a joke, right? You can't possibly think you're going to catch those women. I don't care if you bring in the CIA and the rest of this crazy Alphabet City. They are untouchable, so get used to it. They have the most prestigious address in the world on their side: 1600 Pennsylvania Avenue, to be precise. You guys . . . oops, you guys and *one* woman, are no match for those special Gold Shields. You know it, and we sure know it. You might *think* you're the best of the best but those women *are* the best of the best. They proved it. They got away right under your noses. The media is on their side. Hey, you might even have to shut down and turn everything over to the CIA."

Riley eyeballed the reporter. Her voice was so bitter, so hateful sounding, Riley could hardly believe his ears. No woman, except maybe his wife, had ever stood in front of him and talked the way this reporter was talking to him. His eyes narrowed to mean slits as he let them bore into hers.

"That will never happen, Miss Spritzer. We're the FBI and we always get our man. In this case, women." Riley was proud of how cool and professional his voice sounded. Inside, his guts were churning. J. Edgar's famous words ricocheted inside his head: *Never let them see you sweat.* Never! "That's a goddamn fucking order, gentlemen." The AD's slight to the female agent was deliberate.

"How come you let Jack Emery get away? And that crazy lunatic who kills people with his bare hands? Huh? Huh? Answer me that, Mister FBI," Maggie said, not caring that she was screeching.

"We have no reason to arrest or talk to Jack Emery. Or the lunatic you just mentioned. Both of them have impeccable credentials and, yes, the Bureau is aware of Emery's past engagement to one of the vigilantes. As to the martial arts expert, we have no just cause to haul him in here. They're probably on vacation. Emery is probably livid that the women got away. He's undoubtedly off somewhere licking his wounds. For all we know, Wong could be in Japan or some Third World country."

Ted Robinson started to laugh and couldn't stop. "You must be some kind of Neanderthal, Riley. You don't fucking get it, do you? *Emery is one of them. So is that martial arts guy.* Those two guys have been helping those women all along. We had the hard proof until that guy Martin took it away from us. Are we the only two people in this town who know what's been going on? You are never going to catch those women or Emery or Wong. They've got it going on. They have money blowing out their asses, they have 1600 Pennsylvania Avenue on their side and they have that guy Charles Martin, whose best friend is the Queen of England, calling the shots. You don't have clue one, you're flying blind. Go for it. There's nothing we can do to help you. Can we leave now?"

Mitch Riley couldn't wait to get rid of the two reporters. So much for picking their brains. With attitudes like theirs he didn't want to do a Q&A. In the space of fifteen minutes, they had managed to make the FBI look like a rinky-dink operation with agents no better than shotgun-toting bubba rejects trying to maintain law and order. His strong jaw clenched as he noted the smug looks and smirks on his agents' faces. "Stay in touch, and don't even think about leaving town," he said, determined to have the last word.

Ted Robinson was a nanosecond behind Maggie when she offered up the universal single-digit salute on the way out the door. Riley knew he was being petulant when he returned the salute but he didn't care. He didn't take kindly to people who thought he and his beloved Bureau were incompetent.

A light mist was falling when Maggie and Ted exited the Hoover Building. Spring had arrived in Washington. Maggie wondered if the cherry blossoms were blooming along the Tidal Basin. She said so. Ted shrugged and mumbled something Maggie didn't hear. Like blooming cherry blossoms were important. Right now they had to walk a good thirty blocks to their apartment to get cleaned up. Then they had to go to the *Post* to get an advance on their pay just so they could eat, thanks again to the Sisterhood and the Gold Shields who had taken matters into their own hands, kidnapped them and dumped them in Idaho.

Midway down the block, Ted stopped dead in his tracks. "We know something those agents don't know. They don't know about Mark Lane. I suggest we keep it that way, too. Of course we have to take into consideration that those cruds back there will have a tail on us. When we get to the paper, let's give Mark a call and arrange a meeting."

"You arrange a meeting. I'm going home and I'm taking a five-hour bubble bath. When you get some money, buy some food and bring it home. I'm not meeting anyone until I get about five days' sleep. If we're fired, don't tell me until I wake up. I mean it, Ted."

"Okay," Ted said, his step lighter, his eyes sparking. "We aren't out of the running yet."

"Ted, you are an asshole. We *are* out of the running. The FBI is in charge now."

"Those guys can't find their dicks unless they have a diagram showing where they're positioned. That guy Riley is on a short string. Scuttlebutt in town is and has been for years that if he flops one more time, he's out. Not demoted. OUT!"

Maggie thought about Ted's assessment for a few seconds before she burst out laughing. "For once, I think you're right, Teddy boy."

The two reporters high-fived each other as Maggie went one way and Ted went the other.

Chapter 3

At any other time Jack Emery might have enjoyed the Montana sunrise. Not today, though. At this early hour he was trying to come to terms with a drug-induced hangover and the fact that he was now back in the United States in some godforsaken cabin in what looked like the wilds of nowhere. He cracked an eyelid to see Harry Wong sitting next to him, looking as befuddled as he felt.

"How the fuck did we get here, Jack? Where the hell is this place? The last thing I remember is drinking that beer Charles gave me. It seems to me we both put up a hell of a fight. Do you remember it that way?"

Jack decided to open both eyes. The early-morning glare of the sun seemed to burn his eyelids. He groaned. "Yeah, that's pretty much the way I remember it. The Brit drugged our beer. I don't remember going down the mountain in the cable car or getting on a plane and yet, here we are in Montana. I know this is Montana because Charles said that was our final destination. Somewhere, someplace, there is a deed saying this dandy little piece of real estate belongs to me. How weird is it that I can remember that shit? That son of a bitch doesn't miss a trick. I'd kill for a cup of coffee."

Harry stood up. "So, somebody brought us here and dumped us on these steps and took off. Is that what happened?"

"How the hell should I know, Harry? What's in the backpacks?"

Harry shrugged. "Probably a shaving kit and toothbrush. Who cares? I'm going to see if there's any food inside. Come on, Jack, this is your abode. Help me out here."

Jack struggled to his feet and swayed sickeningly until he got his bearings. He followed Harry into the tidy cabin and was surprised at how comfortable and clean it looked. He headed straight for the compact kitchen. He wasn't surprised to see the stocked refrigerator or the coffeepot with a can of Maxwell House standing next to it along with a can opener. By the time he had the coffeepot going, Harry was pouring orange juice and had a half dozen eggs boiling.

The stringy, hundred-pound martial arts expert put his hands on his hips and spat out, "I'm going back to get Yoko."

Jack shook his head and was instantly sorry. "Back where? You don't even know the name of the damn mountain. They'll kill you, Harry. Don't you get it, we're on their radar screen! The only place we're going is back to Washington. *They* agreed to Charles doing all this," he said, waving his hands about. "I don't like it and you don't like it but there's nothing we can do about it. Nik and Yoko didn't put up a fight to let us stay. Digest that and let's figure out how the hell we're going to get back to DC. Where are those backpacks?"

"I left them on the steps. If you're lucky there won't be a bomb inside. I can just see that crazy nutjob blowing us up here in Big Sky Country. Think about it, Jack, who the hell would ever know, since this place is in the middle of nowhere? Toddle along there, Big Guy, and if I hear an explosion, I'll eat these eggs all by myself."

Jack's middle finger shot in the air as he stomped his way through the living room to the rustic front porch.

He looked around uneasily as he picked up the two backpacks. They were heavy. Way too heavy for just a change of underwear, shaving gear and a toothbrush. A gust of wind blew across the steps carrying the pungent scent of pine. He inhaled deeply. The clearing in front of the cabin drew him toward it. Still carrying the backpacks, he squatted down to look at the tire tracks. Big tires. Heavy tread. They had been brought here in an SUV or maybe a Hummer. A mess of footprints. Two or three people. No clues there.

He was disgusted with himself. As a detective he was sorely lacking. He had allowed himself to be drugged and transported to this place, and he didn't have a clue as to how far he was from civilization. For all he knew he could be days away from a town, which meant he and Harry would have to hoof it to wherever they were going. "Shit!" he said succinctly.

"Coffee's ready, Jack!" Harry called from the open door. "Do us both a favor and open one of those bags while you're down there."

"Wuss!" Jack squatted down again to unzip one of the bags. His teeth clenched, he started pulling stuff out of the bag as though there was a priceless prize at the bottom. He looked up to see Harry standing next to him. Harry reached for the other bag and did the same thing Jack had done.

"There are two letters in mine and a cell phone. What's in yours, Harry?"

"One letter. It's Yoko's handwriting. Pretty fancy-looking cell phone. Never saw one like this. Five bucks says if we click it on, it will blow us up. Wanna bet?"

Jack shook his head as he licked at his dry lips. He fingered the letter from Nikki. He thought he could smell her perfume on the paper. He ripped at the envelope with Nikki's scent on it. He wanted to cry at the short paragraph.

> *My darling Jack,*
> *It is so hard for me to write this because I know you won't understand, but I love you too much to keep you here on the mountain. You love the law, it's your life. I don't want you to be a fugitive. I thought I could live with it but I can't. I want you to be safe. That's what will make me happy and in the end it will make you happy, too. I want you to get on with your life. I will always love you.*
> *—Nikki*

His vision blurry, Jack looked over at Harry, who was looking at him blankly. "Yoko said she loves me and this is for my own good. What kind of love is that? Jack, what kind of fucking love is that?"

Jack struggled to find the words. His voice was rough and raw when he responded. "The kind of love where the person who wrote the letter puts you first and thinks only of your well-being as opposed to her own." He cleared his throat and asked, "Are those eggs ready?"

In a daze, Harry responded, "Yeah, they're ready. I even peeled them but couldn't find any salt. I don't understand. We gave it all up, we walked away knowing what it meant. I thought we were part of *them*. What the fuck went wrong? I need to know, Jack."

"I don't know any more than you do. I have to assume Charles knows something and sending us out here is for our own protection. Maybe they want us to help them from here. Christ, I don't know."

The birds overhead started to chitter as two capricious squirrels raced up and down one of the pine trees nearest the clearing.

"Open the other letter, Jack."

Jack was already opening it. It was neatly typed, unlike the handwritten note from Nikki. He read it through twice and then stuffed it in his jacket pocket.

"Well?" Harry demanded.

"The cell phones are encrypted. We can call the girls or him anytime we want. The phones have been programmed. Charles said even the CIA doesn't have phones like these so we are to guard them with our lives. We're to go back to Washington and someone will eventually—that's what he said, eventually—get in touch with us. He said all of them are depending on us. Us, Harry. That means we aren't out of the loop.

"Now, as to how we get out of here and back to DC. We're to follow the path to the bottom of this place and there will be a black Chevy Suburban complete with all the paperwork, insurance, title, etcetera, in my name. Guess it's my vehicle now. We're to drive back to DC and leave a trail—stay at motels using credit cards, buy gas using credit cards, which, by the way, are right here in the envelope."

Jack snapped his fingers under Harry's nose. "Hey, Harry, look alive here. Let's eat and hit the road. Go on, call Yoko. I'll call Nikki in the house."

"I'm not sure I want to call her now," Harry grumbled as he started to stuff his gear back into the backpack. "That little lady broke my heart. You don't get over a broken heart in two minutes." As he spoke he was punching in the numbers that he hoped would mend his broken heart.

Inside the cabin, in the cozy, knotty pine kitchen, Jack stuffed two of the hardboiled eggs into his mouth, one after the other. Then he gulped down a glass of orange juice. With trembling hands he called Nikki, who picked up on the first ring.

"It's Jack, Nik."

"I know," came the whispered reply.

"I thought we had a deal. I gave it up, didn't look back. Just tell me it wasn't your idea. If you can tell me that, I can live with this."

"It wasn't my idea, Jack, but I understand the reasoning. I love you too much to put you at risk. In the beginning . . . It . . . I was just so happy you were with us. I didn't look beyond that. I cannot be a part of taking away your life as you knew it."

"Without you, Nik, I don't have a life. I thought we were clear on that."

"I'm going to hang up now, Jack. This is ripping my heart to shreds. Call me anytime. Just remember, I love you more than life itself."

"Nik, wait . . ."

"I want to kill someone," Harry barked from the doorway.

"Join the club," Jack snarled. "Eat those damn eggs and let's get out of here."

An hour later, Jack fixed his gaze on a shiny black Chevy Suburban. "I was hoping this was all a bad dream. Guess not. Get in, Harry, and let's go home."

Chapter 4

Charles Martin sat at the round table in the newly constructed war room in the old monastery—a room that was reserved for the members of the Sisterhood. His head was in his hands and for the first time in his life, he was second-guessing his latest decision. He wondered if he was losing his edge.

Maybe he'd had too much caffeine this morning. Just the way he'd had too much yesterday and well into the night. He'd consumed pots and pots of coffee, and could feel his nerve endings twanging. Right now if someone came up behind him and said, "BOO!" he'd probably jump out of his skin.

His problem, and he knew it was a problem, was that he was dealing with women's emotions, and it was an alien feeling, well outside his field of expertise. These women of the Sisterhood were like daughters to him and who was he to tamper with their feelings? What gave him the right to make the kind of decision he'd made in regard to the women he'd taken responsibility for?

They did. They had literally entrusted their lives

to his care and agreed to abide by any and all of his decisions, no matter how opposed they were to those decisions. They said they understood that there could be only one person in total, absolute charge.

Charles raised his head and shook it to try and clear away his morbid thoughts. It was time to enter the lioness' den and beard them all. He risked a glance out of the window. All of his chicks, minus his two roosters, were sitting poolside fully clothed in athletic gear. They'd just returned from a five-mile hike. They all looked surly, and they appeared to be in intense conversation. He rather thought a revolt was imminent. One look at his beloved, Myra, who was in the pool with Annie, told him he was probably on the money, and Annie looked like she was chewing on lemon rinds. No help there.

The vibration of the cell phone in his shirt pocket brought him up short. He clicked it on, identified himself and listened. As he continued to listen, a frown built itself between his brows. He found himself clenching his jaw as he paced the confines of the state-of-the-art kitchen.

His face was grim when he clicked off the special phone and returned it to his pocket. Time to get on with it. Whatever *it* turned out to be.

The women looked whipped. He'd put all of them through the wringer. Then he'd done what they referred to as the unthinkable: he'd banished Jack and Harry from the mountain to protect them and the women. And this was just the beginning. At this moment in time with what he was seeing, he wouldn't want to meet up with any of these women in the dark, and that included Myra. He wasn't sure but he rather thought he would be sleeping alone tonight and for many more nights to come.

Few things in life frightened Charles Martin, but the thought of carrying out the huge silver tray with drinks and munchies to the women sent chills up his spine. He sighed as he did his best to paste a smile on his face before he picked up the silver tray.

Poolside, the women groaned when they saw Charles approaching with his laden tray.

"Go away, we're too tired to eat and drink," they said as one.

Charles's voice was cool and firm. "The word *tired* is no longer in your vocabulary," he said. "Take your pick, food and drink or a three-mile run." He set down the tray.

Kathryn got up, her expression totally blank, and pushed Charles into the pool. "I know, I know, now it's a *five*-mile run. It was worth it! Okay, okay, we're going. It was worth it, Charles," she said again, starting off at a full trot.

Myra and Annie peered over the side of the pool. "I'm not running five miles even for you, dear," Myra told him. "If you say one word, I will push you back under the water. Right now I do not like you, not one little bit."

"And I'll hold you down. I don't like you, either," Annie said. She got out of the pool, reached for a handful of chips, and then washed them down with a glass of tart lemonade. "Even my hair hurts. We're too old for this."

"Nonsense, you're in fine shape," Charles said, climbing out of the pool. "All you have to do is pace yourself. Your body will tell you when it's time to quit. It's not time."

Myra stood over Charles and said, "My body told me to quit nine days ago." She pushed him back into the pool, then joined Annie and reached for the chips. She held up her hand and whispered, "He's not drowning, is he?"

Annie grimaced. "I wish. He's swimming to the other side. With his shoes on. I can't believe you love that man! He's cruel! He's a sadist! He hates us! And don't forget for one minute what he did to Nikki and Yoko by sending Jack and Harry away."

The two women watched as Charles dripped his way back into the house.

"Trust me, I am not forgetting about that. Right now I'm too tired to go there, Annie. He's right about one thing, though, and we both know it. If we can't keep up with the others, what good will we be to them? We have to do our share. You said you wanted to belong to this little group. Well, this is what it's like. I love him no matter what. Let's double up on our vitamins."

Annie looked around to see if anyone was in sight who could hear her. "Are you sure we're up to this, Myra? I don't know what I thought but whatever it was, it wasn't this. I thought we'd be using our *minds. Supervising,* if you will. Contributing money, that sort of thing. I have to tell you, dear heart, I am not fond of rolling around in the mud and belly-crawling under barbed wire. We're *old,* Myra. That man you love is going to kill us."

Myra's eyes snapped open. "Age is a number. Sixty is *not* old. Ninety is old. That means we have thirty more good years. Don't you get it, Annie? Charles wants us to quit. He wants us here so he can hover and protect us. He thinks we can't keep up with the others. Well, I'm here to tell you he's wrong. We can . . . uh . . . cut it."

Annie grappled for a Kathryn line and said, "That's pure bullshit and you know it. I am so damn tired I can't keep my eyes open."

"Get untired right now. Charles is watching us from the door. I can see his shadow. Do you want one of those ugly checkmarks next to your name? He can't wait for us to fail, so get your tush up off that chair and let's do our run. Trot? Fast walk? Okay, a slow walk, but we have to do the five miles. Let's go."

Annie heaved herself off the chair and joined Myra. "I hate you!"

Charles stood at the door and watched the two women. He laughed silently as his beloved and her best friend started off at a slow trot. He felt like cheering and beating his chest. His girl was all woman. Still smiling, he cleaned up the puddle by the door where he was standing.

In a million years he never would have believed Myra would push him into the pool. Then again, he never would have believed Kathryn would push him into the pool, either. He made a mental note not to cut either woman any slack.

The following weeks and months passed slowly. While the sisters labored over French and German verbs, firearms lessons, karate classes and endurance trials, Charles worked at the computer trying to stay as up-to-date as he could with what was going on back in the States.

He started off each day knowing he'd misled the

group he'd taken responsibility for. Each day he tried to justify it to himself. Some days he succeeded. Other days, his gut churned with fear.

The days of sanctuary were long gone. He, Annie and the padre were pushing the envelope and they all knew it. If the authorities descended on the village, intent on reaching the top of the mountain, the only things the padre and villagers could do were delay the proceedings and ring the bell at the foot of the mountain in warning. The padre had issued Annie a scroll, on ancient parchment that looked authentic, saying he'd granted the inhabitants of the mountain total and complete sanctuary. The padre said the Spanish courts would take over if he and the villagers took a stand and refused to allow any and all strangers access to the mountain. The padre had gone on to say the Spanish courts always favored the priests in these types of matters. Charles, Myra and Annie had talked it over and agreed to trust their safety to the padre and the villagers and to take their chances . . . and to leave the others out of the loop.

Charles stared at the screen in front of him as he called up his e-mails. Each morning since he'd come here he'd gotten an e-mail like the one he was now looking at. It was from a fellow covert operator named Pappy Kolar, who ran an operation much like his own. Pappy, his cover blown, had been relocated to a mountaintop in North Carolina. Those in the know said the people at NORAD had set it up. While all the e-mails were important, there was only one that Charles printed out—the one that was encrypted and from Pappy.

Charles studied the e-mail. So far, so good. In

four months' time, the assistant director of the FBI still had no clues as to the disappearance of the seven vigilantes. The sender went on to say there was speculation that the CIA would be taking over the special task force within days. Charles frowned. There was only one explanation for that decision. The authorities now thought he and the so-called vigilantes had left the country, hence the CIA. A black mark for the FBI, since they were domestic. More bad press. The word *ineffectual* came to mind when he thought of the Fibbies.

The second e-mail, one he wasn't expecting, caused him to suck in his breath. He printed it out and read it. He felt the first stirring of alarm. *Think, Charles.* Tell the women or not tell them? Sooner rather than later, Jack and Harry would be on the encrypted phone. Unless . . . unless he rendered Nikki's and Yoko's phones inoperable. But, did he want to do that? Prior to coming here to Spain he would have made a snap decision and walked away.

"You aren't God, Charles. It has to be their decision."

Charles whirled around. He would know that soft, gentle voice anywhere. His voice was hushed, a bare whisper. "Barbara?"

"Yes, Charles, it's me."

Charles grappled for something to say. This was the first time his dead daughter had spoken to him since they were in Pinewood. Myra said she conversed with Barbara on a regular basis. "Why now, dear child?"

"You haven't needed me lately. I want to help if I can."

"From the *other side*?"

"Yes."

"What do you want me to do, dear girl?"

"The right thing, Charles. Whatever you do, don't turn Mom into your enemy."

"I would never do that."

"Too bad you didn't hear the conversation I just heard on that five-mile walk."

Charles combed his hair with nervous fingers. "Should I go after them and bring them back in the golf cart?"

"I don't think I would do that. It's time for you to make nice. Bye, Charles." His daughter's tinkling laugh seemed to ricochet around the empty room.

Charles was a deer caught in the headlights. He whirled around as his whole body started to tremble. He tried to steady himself as he looked down at the printed e-mail in his hand.

His darling daughter was right. This wasn't his decision to make. He squared his shoulders as he made his way to the terrace to wait for the women he loved with all his heart.

Chapter 5

Jack Emery leaned back in his swivel chair, propped his feet on the desk and rubbed at his tired, aching eyes. He made a mental note to make an appointment to get his eyes checked to see if he needed reading glasses. A real no-brainer there.

Since his return to DC from Spain via Montana four months ago, he'd settled into a routine of sorts. The end of the day was the worst for him emotionally. This was when he had to pack up his briefcase, leave the building, go to his car and head out to Georgetown, where he was living in Nikki's house, thanks to a quitclaim deed she'd had the foresight to draft up. He now owned the pricey, high-end piece of real estate.

His mind drifted to what he was going to eat for dinner. Leftover pizza or leftover Chinese? Or maybe some toast with the dried-up orange and wrinkled apple he'd seen in the fridge this morning when he'd used up the last of the cream for his coffee.

He hated shopping in supermarkets. Hated it with a passion. Nikki had always done the shopping and the cooking. Christ, how he missed her.

His eyes were burning, so he closed them, felt the tears on his lashes. He rubbed at them mercilessly. When he finally opened them he saw Harry Wong standing in front of his desk.

"Jesus, Harry, you have to stop doing that. You move like a damn cat and never make a sound. How the hell did you get into the building, anyway?"

"Hey, I work for the police department. See this badge! It says I can come up here to see you anytime I want. I wanted. I'm here to take you out to dinner. One of those big, juicy porterhouse steaks, a twice-baked potato and a big salad with everything but lettuce in it. A couple of beers and then I'll even drive your sorry ass home. What say you, oh mighty District Attorney?"

"Best offer I had all day. You paying?"

"Unless you want to open up that wallet of yours and let the mothballs out. Yoko isn't answering her phone, Jack." Harry waited expectantly to hear what Jack had to say.

"The last time I talked to Nikki was three days ago and then it was hello and good-bye."

"Does it mean what I think it means, they're weaning themselves away from us?"

Jack's feet dropped to the floor. He rolled down his shirtsleeves, buttoned the cuffs and slipped into his jacket. The end of the day also meant he could remove his tie, which he did. He stuffed it in his pocket and followed Harry out to the hall and the elevator.

"Squire's Pub okay, Jack?"

"Yeah. You okay, Harry?"

"Hell, no, I'm not okay. I want to kill someone. Give me any shit and you might go to the top of my list."

Jack stepped out of the elevator. "Take your best shot, Harry. Right now I don't give a good roaring fuck about anything and that includes you. Put me out of my misery if that will make you feel better."

Harry sailed through the revolving door. "I'm too tired. I just needed to vent."

"Well, vent somewhere else, okay?"

The walk to the Squire's Pub was made in silence for the most part, each man busy with his own miserable thoughts. If either one of them had been up to speed they would have observed the parade of people following them as they tried to be invisible.

Ten minutes later, they shouldered their way through the bar area—Jack clapping some colleagues on the back and shaking hands with others—before heading to the back of the pub. The owner had established a smoking room there for his regular customers, with a state-of-the-art exhaust system, after a hard-won, long legal battle, with favors called in from every corner of the Beltway.

Jack preferred the back room because it was usually empty; smokers were rare these days. It was a great room to hide in to avoid the crowds in the main part of the pub, to actually hear what your companion was saying, and for some reason the service in the back room was far superior.

They settled into a booth and Jack raised his hand to the waitress. Two bottles of Heineken appeared as if by magic. He drummed his fingers on the wooden tabletop as he gave his order.

Harry rattled off his order and then tipped his beer bottle toward Jack's. "What should we toast, Jack?"

Jack was saved from a reply when the cell phone

in his jacket pocket started to vibrate, since the ringer was turned off. He whipped it out, his eyes hopeful.

Harry slumped back in his seat when he saw the frown on Jack's face. He listened intently.

"Jack Emery." As Jack listened the frown deepened between his brows. "I think the Justice Department would have something to say about a meeting. You're the enemy, Lizzie. I can't be seen with you." He listened again, aware that Harry was eyeballing him. He kept his voice to a whisper, not that anyone appeared to be listening, but you never knew who was who these days. Suddenly Jack laughed, a bitter, angry sound. "That has to be the funniest thing I've ever heard. The great Lizzie Fox needs *my* help! Get lost!" The cell phone clicked shut and went back in his pocket. It started to vibrate almost immediately. Jack ignored it and eventually the cell phone ceased.

"Guess you heard, huh?" Jack asked Harry.

"Well, yeah. I couldn't help but hear your end of the conversation. What's she up to?"

Jack looked around the back room to see who was there. A lobbyist with someone who wasn't his wife, chowing down on a steak. Two paralegals he recognized, puffing away as they talked intently, probably discussing their boyfriends. Four lawyers swigging Amstel Light from the bottle, their eyes already glassy. He strained then to see into the back of the room, at which point he almost fell out of the booth. Judge Cornelia Easter, a cigarette in one hand, a tumbler of bourbon in the other, looked right at him and wiggled her cigarette in his direction. Jack nodded and then slumped down in his seat. "Don't look now but that's Judge Easter in the back of the room. I didn't want to stare, but I think she's sitting with Judge Stephens. That's as in, 'Hang 'em High Stephens.'"

"And this all means . . . what?" Harry hissed as his plate of food was set in front of him.

Jack picked up a knife that looked like a bowie knife and ripped through his steak. "How the hell did Lizzie Fox know where to find me? Yeah, yeah, she called my cell phone. I could be anywhere and pick up. It's just too damn coincidental. I've been coming to this pub for ten or more years and I've never, ever seen a judge in here. This is working lawyers' turf, where they come to cut loose, to vent, to gossip. It's also a favorite hangout of reporters hoping for a morsel of something they can blow up into a page-1 byline."

"Speaking of reporters, I saw your old buddy Ted Robinson out front when we came in."

"And you're just telling me this now! What the hell's wrong with you, Harry?"

"You told me never to mention his name to you. I'm not really up on all of this spy stuff like you are. You want me to waltz back in there and take him out for you?"

"No, I do not want you to take him out for me. One of these days I'll do it myself. He's the main reason we're in the shit we're in right now. Was Spritzer with him? I think she's the brains of that duo."

Harry looked at the chunk of steak on his fork. "I didn't see her but I wasn't looking for her. I just saw Ted out of the corner of my eye. I don't think he saw us."

"Oh, he saw us all right. He doesn't miss a trick. Do you think his being here is a coincidence?"

Harry wiggled his fork around. "Jesus, Jack, I don't have a clue. Is there a class or something I can take to get up to speed on all this crap? Or do I just hang out with you and hope for the best? You're like a fucking magnet that draws this stuff to you. You should maybe think about changing your profession. Why aren't Yoko and Nikki taking our calls?"

Jack blinked at the change of conversation and tone. His mouth full, he simply shrugged. He looked down at the food on his plate and then pushed it away. He wished he had a dog so he could take his dinner home in a doggy bag. He looked over at Harry, who was mouthing words to him. He seemed to be saying, *"Here she comes."* Who? Maggie Spritzer? He jerked upright when he felt a hand touch his shoulder.

"Mr. Emery, how nice to see you out for the evening. I always say you DAs work way too hard. You know Judge Stephens, don't you?"

Jack mumbled something as he struggled to slide out of the booth, then nodded and mumbled again. He shook hands with both judges and then jammed his hands in his pockets. He had never been more uncomfortable in his life.

"This establishment is . . . quaint. I've never been here before. I'm told it is the only place in the whole District that allows smoking. Since Judge Stephens and I still indulge in that nasty habit we thought we would grab a bite before heading home. I found the food to be delicious. How about you?"

"I agree, the food is very good." He couldn't help but notice the way Judge Easter was looking at his and Harry's plates. "Our eyes were bigger than our stomachs," he said.

"You should have been here earlier. Lizzie Fox was here sitting across from us and cleaned her plate. And she has that smashing figure."

Jack shuffled from one foot to the other. Where the hell was this conversation going? Harry looked like he was in la-la land. Jack thought he was being brilliant when he said, "Sooner or later, every lawyer in town finds their way here. Very popular watering hole."

"Well, good night, Mr. Emery. I miss your entertaining ways in my courtroom."

Jack stood with his mouth open as he watched the two judges leave the back room to fight their way through the happy hour revelers.

"This is probably a very dumb question, Jack, and I don't even mind asking it of you, but was that judge talking to you in some kind of code? Is this how you people in the spy world communicate? Something is going on, isn't it?"

Jack sat back down in the booth and raised his hand to wave his empty beer bottle in the air. "That would be my guess, but I don't have a clue as to what it could be. Maybe Ted and the judge being here on the same night is just what it seems, a coincidence. The call from Lizzie Fox tonight, and her eating here, another coincidence? No one knew we were coming here. This was a last-minute, spur-of-the-moment invitation on your part, right, Harry?"

"Yep. Maybe we have a tail. A professional tail, the kind who blends into the scenery. Neither one of us is very observant these days."

Jack upended the new Heineken bottle that had just arrived. "Coincidence, my ass."

"Come on, Jack, let's get out of here. Suddenly, I don't trust this place."

"You know what, I think you might be right." Jack shrugged into his jacket and picked up his briefcase. He waited until Harry dropped some bills on the table before he followed the martial arts expert out of the pub.

Together, Harry and Jack weaved through the happy hour customers. His eyes narrowed to slits, Jack eyeballed the room for any sign of the reporter but found none. He offered up a shrug and followed Harry from the pub, his mind swirling, his heart heavy.

Chapter 6

Jack Emery awakened from his dream, then groaned aloud as he smashed down on the snooze button of his alarm. Damn, it felt like he'd just hit the pillow, but it was 5:45 AM. Time to get up and head for the gym for his hour workout. It was the only thing that was keeping him sane these days.

Normally, he was a morning kind of guy—get up, shower, shave, eat a robust breakfast and slog his way to work—but since returning from Spain via Montana, his life had taken a 90-degree turn. And not for the better.

It was 5:55 when he locked the door of Nikki's house. It would always be Nikki's house to him. He looked up and down the street. It was still dark, the sodium vapor lights glowing eerily on both sides of the street. At this time of day he was always alert, always watching to see who might step out of the shadows. Seeing nothing to alarm him, he jogged for a block to where he'd parked his car the night before on the skinny, overcrowded cobbled street.

At 6:10 he slammed through the doors of the gym, his garment and duffel bags in tow. He went straight to the locker room, jammed his belongings into his locker and headed to the workout room. He didn't bother to look around. He knew everyone, if not by name, then by what they were doing on their workout. He waved airily as he headed for the treadmill and got started. He was sweating profusely, his speed at 7.0 on an incline when he saw her. He almost lost his balance when Lizzie Fox waved to him and sauntered over.

She looked good. Better than good. Actually, she looked good enough to eat. The sheen of perspiration on her high cheekbones made her face look like satin. He could see the strength in the muscles of her upper arms. The middle of her tank top was soaked with sweat. Lizzie Fox took exercising seriously. He wondered why he didn't feel attracted to her. Actually, he knew the answer: he was a one-woman man and there was no one but Nikki for him.

"You hung up on me last night," she said.

"Yeah," Jack said, not missing a step on the treadmill.

"That wasn't very nice, Jack. I need to talk to you."

"Get off it, Lizzie. You and I have nothing to talk about. I have no clue where your clients are, but I think *you* know. I don't even want to be seen talking to you. You're bad for my reputation."

Lizzie's incredible blue eyes sparked angrily. She looked like she was about to say something when a tall, handsome man appeared out of nowhere.

Without the government-issued sunglasses, gold shield and power suit, Agent Bert Navarro could have been a power broker or just another health nut. Jack's eyes almost bugged out of his head. Harry was right, something definitely was going on.

"Jack, aren't you going to introduce me to your friend?" Agent Navarro asked.

"She's not my friend. Lizzie Fox, this is Bert Navarro. Now, if you'll both excuse me, I'm not here to socialize. It's too damn early in the morning to get pissed off. You're both pissing me off." Jack hopped off the treadmill and walked across the room to a rowing machine, mopping the sweat from his neck and face.

Lizzie followed him. "Jack, I *really* need to talk to you."

"Yeah, Jack, she really needs to talk to you," Navarro said coolly. "You should always listen to a lady when she says she really needs you."

Maybe it was Navarro's tone, maybe it was the jittery way Lizzie sounded or maybe it was his own curiosity, but he turned around and asked, "What do I have to do to get rid of you? All right, all right, spit it out."

"Someone is trying to kill me, Jack."

Whatever he expected to hear, this wasn't it. Jack's gaze flashed to Navarro, who was eyeing him carefully. "So call a cop. Report it. Where do you get off thinking I'm your personal 911 outlet?"

"Maybe you should listen, Jack," Navarro said.

"Aren't you way off your beat, Bert? I don't have to do anything I don't want to do. Go ruin someone else's day, okay?"

The rest of his workout was a lost cause so Jack headed for the locker room and the shower, Lizzie and Bert dogging his every step. When he reached the locker room and it looked like both Lizzie and Bert were going to follow him, he stopped in his tracks. "Enough already! What? I'll listen to you for two minutes so talk fast."

"Someone's trying to kill me," Lizzie said.

"You already said that. Do you mean someone besides me?" Jack asked flippantly. Then the words really dawned on him. "Okay, okay, let me shower and dress and I'll meet you in the coffee shop downstairs. I have to be in court at eight so it will have to be quick. If that doesn't work for you, I can spare some time around five o'clock. Well?"

"I'll see you in the coffee shop in fifteen minutes," Lizzie said.

As the door swung shut behind him, Jack took a second to realize he'd never before heard Lizzie sound anything less than calm and forceful. Maybe someone really *was* after her hide. Probably a jilted lover. Courthouse gossip was that she changed boyfriends like other people changed their underwear, which really was none of his business, anyway.

The special cell phone in the pocket of his sweatpants started to vibrate. Jack's heart soared. Nikki. Jack clicked it on and sighed so loud he lost his breath.

"Jack. It's me."

"I'm at the gym. Why haven't you taken my calls lately?" he blurted angrily.

"There's a reason for everything. Things are . . . well, things are . . . Listen, I'll call you later today. Will you be around?"

"Well, hell, yes. I will be in court till four and then I have a couple of hours of paperwork. Is something wrong?"

"Something is very wrong, Jack. I'll call you later."

"Listen, I have something to tell you, too. I think it might be important. Nik? Nik, are you there? Ah, shit!" Jack shoved the cell phone back into the pocket of his sweatpants. He had to call Harry to see if he'd gotten a call, too. Just as soon as he showered and shaved. Lizzie Fox could wait.

Twelve minutes later Jack was knotting his tie and trying to talk on his cell phone to Harry. "Nik just said something was wrong and she would call me later. Sorry you haven't heard from Yoko, pal. Listen, come by the office around five. Right now Lizzie Fox and that Gold Shield Navarro are waiting for me in the coffee shop downstairs. Do me a favor and call Mark Lane and tell him to run a check on Lizzie Fox. She seems to think someone is trying to kill her." Jack listened for a minute and grinned. "Yeah, I pretty much thought the same thing. Better yet, let's meet at the Dirty Dog at six o'clock. That will give me a chance to play catch-up with some paperwork."

"Six it is," Harry said.

Jack looked around to make sure he had all his gear before he slung his empty garment bag over his shoulder. He took the elevator to the lobby where he fought his way through the crowds of health nuts trying to race to the gym to get in a few laps before going to jobs where they sat around all day.

The coffee shop was a joke. It served everything *but* coffee. Oh, they served something that *looked* like coffee but tasted like burned popcorn. Juice, tofu, sprouts and carrot juice were the heavy hitters. Bran muffins that ripped your stomach apart were piled up on the counter. In another hour they would be all gone. Navarro and Lizzie were each picking at one of those muffins and had a glass of something that was a shitty green in color.

Jack sat down and said, "Well? By the way, Navarro,

what the hell are you doing here, or does this concern you in some way?"

"It's too early in the morning to be so testy, Jack. I just happened by this morning and you introduced me to this lovely lady. She invited me to have coffee with her. I'll not cramp your style." He got up, waved airily and was gone.

Jack studied the young lawyer. She was dressed for the day in a formfitting navy blue suit with a white blouse. Her blond hair was piled high on her head, every hair in place, adding another inch to her already six-foot stature. She was perfectly made up or else she had flawless skin and didn't need makeup. Either way, she was beautiful. And she'd accomplished it all in under fifteen minutes. Her legs were crossed, the short, tight skirt hiking up to midthigh. Jack looked but wasn't enticed. "I'm waiting, Lizzie," he said irritably.

"Look, Jack, I know your history with Nikki. I'm sorry things went to hell for you both. Don't take it out on me. I was doing my job and you were doing yours. Let's have a little mutual respect here, okay?"

"You're a good lawyer, Lizzie, I'll give you that. Who is trying to kill you?"

Lizzie squirmed in her seat, her skirt hiking farther up her legs. "I might have . . . uh . . . exaggerated a little in that regard. Although I know someone is following me. Hell, maybe stalking me. It's not my imagination."

"And you're telling me this . . . why? Go to the police, file a report. Hire a private detective or get yourself a bodyguard. Why come to me?"

Lizzie stared off into the distance. "*Because you're one of them, Jack.* Don't bother to deny it. I'm not stupid and neither are you."

Jack was glad he hadn't had breakfast because he would have lost it at that moment. He wondered if he could bluff his way through the rest of this meeting. "I don't know what you're talking about. You're just pissed that your clients bailed on you. Not good for the Silver Fox image. Lawyers are supposed to control their clients. You failed to do that and the Sisterhood escaped, leaving you to deal with it. Rumors are you aided and abetted it all. Like I said, Lizzie, not good for your image. Hell, you could even lose money on the deal, right? No one wants a lawyer they can't trust." He hoped he sounded properly outraged. *Because you're one of them.* His stomach did a hop, skip and a jump. He had to get out of here right now before he gave it all away.

"Spare me the sermon, Jack, and listen to what I'm saying. I *know* you're one of them. I want to . . . I want to . . . *join up.* I've been doing my homework. I might have opened some cans of worms that would have been better off left unopened. I also suspect, and I can't quite prove it yet, that Judge Easter belongs to your select little group. Now we both know I'm especially smart and intuitive, but there are people who are dogging me. I'm one hundred percent sure that I am being followed. I've had a couple of things happen that could be simple accidents or someone trying to . . . do me harm. I deliberately didn't go to the police because I want to . . . protect my clients. They're still my clients, Jack. Don't insult me now by trying to con me. I want to help. I want you to trust me. I took a big chance coming here today to talk to you, just so you know."

Jack reached for his bags, his head swimming

Chapter 7

Thunder rolled across the mountain in sonic blasts as torrents of rain sluiced down over the ancient monastery. Age-old trees swayed in the vicious wind as bolt after bolt of ugly lightning ripped across the dark sky. The members of the Sisterhood cowered in the kitchen, their eyes glued to the water dripping into the twelve-cup coffeepot. A jug of fifty-year-old homemade brandy, compliments of the padre at the foot of the mountain, was just waiting to be poured into the exquisite china cups.

Myra paced the confines of the kitchen; the clicking of her heels on the old brick floor sounded ominous. "The first night we all met, the weather was like this. Charles and I were so sure none of you would be able to make the journey out to the farm and then there you were, Kathryn plowing down the gates with her big truck. Then the power went out. I don't think I'll ever forget that night." The others nodded as they clustered close together.

"That was the beginning of something for all of us. Now, here we are facing the same sort of obstacles again. Only this time they are much more serious. Do any of you think this is an omen of some kind?" None of the women responded. "I'll take that as a yes, then," Myra said.

Isabelle reached for the coffeepot as Alexis poured brandy into the waiting cups.

"Where's Charles?" Nikki's voice dripped ice.

"Where he always is at this time of the day, in the command center," Yoko said, her voice as icy as Nikki's.

It was obvious to everyone in the room that neither woman had forgiven Charles for sending Jack and Harry back to the States. This frigid state of affairs had been going on for some time now, unnerving all the women.

Kathryn, always the most brash and outspoken of the group, looked around.. "There isn't much to command these days. Isn't it obvious that he's hiding from us? He only appears for meals or when he wants to issue an order. This whole thing is taking a toll on all of us. We have to make some decisions or it's all going to fall apart and then where will we be?" She tossed down the coffee-laced brandy in one long swallow and held out her cup for a refill.

"By the way, Myra, where are you sleeping these days? Whose side are you on, anyway?" Kathryn continued to bluster as she downed her second cup. Murphy threw back his head and howled at his mistress's tone of voice.

Myra flushed. "On my side of the bed, dear. I'm on *our* side. Charles is *not* our enemy. Yes, he made a decision none of us liked, but he is . . . uh . . . running our little show. It wasn't Charles's fault that we got caught. I ask you all to please remember that. We willingly put our lives in his hands and he did the best he could under unbelievable circumstances. Emotions have been running high among us all and it has to stop. Charles sent Jack and Harry away for good reason, mainly their safety, and who better on the scene than Jack and Harry to keep us all up to speed. We have no other choice but to accept our circumstances. If any one of you feels you want to leave, that's your choice. I, for one, trust Charles and I feel terrible that we're treating him like a pariah. I would be remiss now if I didn't tell you I am getting a little sick and tired of tiptoeing around all of you, weighing my words and trying to make things work. I really don't mind telling you I dislike your . . . your . . . ."

"Pissy attitude," Annie chirped as she came up with what she thought was one of Kathryn's favorite words. She took a healthy gulp from the padre's brandy jug to seal her statement.

"Ah, yes, that pretty much sums up what I was trying to say." Myra reached for the jug and took not one but two belts of the fiery homemade brew. Tears rolled down her cheeks but that didn't stop her from taking a third swig. What little coffee that remained in the pot was ignored as the jug made the rounds and the wicked storm outside continued to rage.

Two hours later, when the storm had abated a little, the sky had grown light and the padre's jug was bone-dry, the women made their way to what in happier times they had called Charles's Lair, or the command center, to make peace with their fearless leader.

Charles looked up from the keyboard where he was typing out an encrypted message. He flinched at the sorry look on his beloved Myra's face. He was certain she was the ringleader of this little expedition to the command center. A niggling voice warned him, *"When in doubt, say nothing."* He waited.

Kathryn offered up a sloppy salute of sorts before she flopped down on one of the padded swivel chairs. "We're reporting for work," she said, slurring her words.

"Yes, dear, we're . . . tired of studying and training. We want . . . we need—" Myra stammered.

"Action!" Annie said. "Where we"—she bent over to whisper in Kathryn's ear and then said triumphantly—"kick ass and take names later."

The women all giggled and clapped their hands.

Charles mustered his courage and finally found his tongue. "So, am I to understand you all came down here to apologize for your surly attitudes for these past months?"

Nikki tried to focus her gaze on Charles. "Don't flatter yourself, Charles. We are not here to . . . ap . . . *a-pol-o-gize.*"

Kathryn waved her arms about as Murphy whimpered under the table. "What that means, Sir Charles Martin, is this. We are done crawling under razor wire, we are done with French and German verbs. We are *NEVER* going to go on another five- or ten-mile hike. Never, never, never. We decided . . . What did we decide, Isabelle?"

"To go our separate ways and take our chances with the authorities."

"After we kill you," Yoko said simply.

"Oh, my dear, that is so harsh. Do we really want to do that?" Myra asked, hiding a smile.

"Hell, yes," Annie said spiritedly. "We're more than capable of running this operation ourselves. We're women."

They hooted their pleasure at their newest recruit's words and high-fived each other.

"Well, Charles?" Alexis demanded.

"Might I make a suggestion, ladies?"

"Suggest away. It doesn't mean we'll follow your suggestion," Kathryn said.

"It's obvious none of you is in any condition to absorb what I want to tell you at this moment. What I suggest is this . . . Take a nap. Come to me when you are clearheaded. I have our next mission in the works. It will mean we have to covertly sneak back into the United States. And, yes, you will see Jack and Harry, and I understand there is a gentleman who is most anxious to meet up with you, Kathryn. Agent Navarro. It seems when he met up with you in California, your eyes mesmerized him. He also said you were *'all woman.'* Very refreshing in his line of business. It seems he is enamored of you. Now, that's all I'm going to say. Run along, girls, and let me get back to work."

Myra forgot how angry she was with her true love. She asked, "Are we really going to go home again? Is it safe?"

Charles didn't respond to the question. Instead, he made shooing motions with his hands as the women formed a single-file line and left the command center, mumbling among themselves.

"He better not be blowing smoke up our butts," Kathryn said. "Would you really kill him, Yoko?"

Her curt response sent shivers up Kathryn's spine. "Yes."

On the other side of the world, Judge Cornelia Easter was doing what she always did on the first

Monday of every month for years and years: take her two younger sisters and two cousins, all of them Benedictine nuns, to lunch at the Dog and the Duck restaurant near the courthouse. Two priests from St. John's parish would join them shortly. She always made sure her court calendar could accommodate this private time that she cherished.

As she ushered her guests through the wide double doors, she smiled and waved to friends and colleagues. The hostess made small talk with the nuns as she led the way to the reserved table at the back of the restaurant.

These four nuns had opted to retain their black "penguin habits," preferring them over the modern dress that was now optional for nuns. A practicing parishioner, Judge Easter approved of their decision. She held court now, catering to her guests, asking them what was going on in their lives and what if anything she could do to help them. She encouraged them to order shrimp, scallops and lobster, knowing they didn't eat such luxurious foods at the convent.

The "penguin parade," as Judge Easter referred to her little party, was a staple in the nation's capital. It was not at all unusual to see all of them at the movies, at the ice skating rink, visiting art galleries, shopping in the malls, and taking long walks and picnicking in Rock Creek Park. Often, if time and everyone's schedule permitted, it was not unusual to see twelve or so nuns and four or five priests enjoying the judge's hospitality and generosity.

The perfect cover.

Two hours later, the judge presided over the departure of the religious folk, making sure the nuns were safely settled in a taxi that would take them to

Catholic University where they were attending an afternoon seminar. The priests from St. John's said they were stuffed and would walk back to the parish house. There were fond hugs, kisses and arm waving before the judge walked in the other direction, back to the courthouse.

All were oblivious to the presence of the *Post*'s roving reporter, Maggie Spritzer.

Two hours of hearing motions and Judge Easter could head out to the farm. She could hardly wait, knowing a phone call from across the world would be forthcoming.

Tomorrow court was dark, so she would have a day off to do nothing or to do *something*. The phone call would let her know which.

Chapter 8

Jack Emery eyed the numerals on his watch as he willed the special cell phone in his hand to ring. At two minutes past five, the phone buzzed. He immediately clicked it on, knowing it was Nikki. "God, I miss you!" he blurted.

"I miss you more," Nikki said sadly. "This is so hard. We're coming back, Jack, but not for good. Something is going on. Charles is on top of it but he hasn't shared the details. A week from tomorrow. I'll be in touch again to arrange things before we leave."

"Jesus, Nik, is that wise? I want to see you so bad, but if you're going to be in danger, don't even try for a comeback. I was going to try to make it over there at the end of May for a few days. Is there something I should know? Don't keep me out of the loop."

"Charles hasn't seen fit as yet to tell us. All I know is it has something to do with Lizzie Fox."

"Well, this is your lucky day, Nik. Lizzie tracked me down at the gym this morning and told me someone was trying to kill her. I thought she was pulling my leg but I did listen to her. Special Agent Bert Navarro just happened to be at the gym at the same time. What do you suppose *that* means? Lizzie called yesterday but I didn't return her calls. I played the game. She *said* she knew I was one of you and pretty much said the same thing about Judge Easter. She scared me, Nik. What the hell is going on?"

"The FBI has been watching her. That means they now know she was talking to you. For all any of us know, she could be one of *them*. Watch your back, Jack. Listen, as you know these calls are limited so I have to hang up. I love you, Jack, more than you will ever know."

Jack wanted to cry when the line went dead.

A week and he would see her. Seven days. He wished he were a mathematician so he could compute the hours, minutes and seconds in his mind. Maybe he'd do that tonight when he got home. With a calculator. That was later, though; right now he needed to call Harry.

He picked up the office phone and called Harry's dojo. "Hey, short stuff, can I come by and get a workout? I got sidetracked this morning and only got a few minutes on the treadmill. I'm kind of stiff. See you in fifteen minutes."

Jack raised his right hand and flipped the bird to anyone who might be watching him. Go ahead, you bastards, listen to my phone calls, follow me and then kiss my ass.

In the middle of the lobby, his garment bag over his shoulder, his gym bag in hand, he ground to a stop when he saw a woman approaching him.

Jack glared at Maggie Spritzer. "You!" he spat.

* * *

Judge Easter, a double bourbon in hand, two of her four cats in her lap, leaned back into the easy chair that hugged and caressed every bone in her arthritic body. The chair had been a gift from Myra, made especially for her. There were many nights when she slept in the chair to wake more refreshed than if she'd slept in her own bed. She looked at her watch and then at the special phone that had come in the mail months ago. A gift from Charles.

Nellie Easter leaned back and closed her eyes. Never one to doubt herself or her decisions, she let her mind wander. Since the death of her daughter in a fatal head-on car accident, she'd barely managed to get through the days. Now, though, she had a purpose, a reason to get up in the morning. When Myra recruited her, over a year ago, she'd agreed willingly to join the Sisterhood, agreed to try to right wrongs, agreed to break the law, all in the interest of justice. She'd also willingly agreed to delay her retirement so she could keep her hand and ears in the game. So far, it was working out perfectly.

She had been stunned the day Myra and Charles had brought her here to what was then called the Barrington Farm and told her it was all hers. Myra had handed her the deed tied like a scroll with a bright red ribbon. How she'd cried that day.

She'd always been the poor one. Myra and Annie both had fortunes of their own while she'd had to work for everything. A judge's salary didn't necessarily allow for a life of luxury. Still, she'd managed to put her only daughter through college and law school without incurring any debt. She had a savings account that was far from robust but enough to let her live comfortably.

Nellie knew that her financial situation never entered either Annie's or Myra's mind. They were friends. That was all that had to be said. Both women had been such a comfort to her when her daughter was killed. Without their help she knew she would be in some mental hospital. Yes, she owed Myra a lot, and Annie, too.

The special phone buzzed to life and Nellie's eyes popped open. The cats in her lap stirred and began to purr. Myra sounded like she was speaking from the next room, not from the other side of the world.

"It's good to hear your voice, Myra. Has something happened?"

"We're coming back home. Just for . . . just to . . . You know what to do, Nellie. Make the arrangements, perhaps a special birthday surprise, something along those lines."

Nellie's gnarled hand that was stroking one of the cats started to shake. The cat stopped purring and jumped off her lap. His partner followed suit. "Are you sure, Myra?"

"Charles is sure. One week from today. He said you were to go to the farmhouse and turn on the computer if you aren't there now. Be careful, Nellie. Please tell me you aren't having second thoughts."

One of the cats leaped back up on the chair and then to the headrest where she nuzzled her little head on Nellie's shoulder. The judge calmed almost immediately. "No second thoughts, Myra. How are things over . . . ? What I mean—"

"Tense. A little stressful. Annie, bless her dear

heart, is having the time of her life. The girls are . . . Well, what they are is—"

"Pissed to the teeth?"

"Well, uh, yes, that would about sum it up. Have you seen Jack, Nellie?"

"In a restaurant. We said hello but not too much more. Did something happen that concerns him?"

"In a manner of speaking. He was seen talking to Lizzie Fox. It's my understanding she followed him to the gym where he works out in the morning."

Nellie sucked in her breath. "And you know this . . . how? Never mind, I don't want to know. Why would I even ask such a silly question? Living on top of a mountain thousands and thousands of miles away in Spain should be a walk in the park as far as gathering information in the United States goes. Are you all right, Myra? I worry about you. At night I find myself looking out the upstairs windows hoping to see lights on in your house. I miss you, old friend."

"I'm fine, Nellie. I will admit I am worried about the girls. They're cranky and they're picking at each other. A revolt is imminent. I tried to tell Charles you can't tamper with young love but he didn't listen. I'm sure we'll be able to deal with it all. Let's go over it all one step at a time. This is what you have to do and you cannot deviate one little bit. Tomorrow you will . . ."

It was a slow day in the *Post* newsroom. For some reason spring didn't bring much in the way of news. Maggie Spritzer swivelled around to eyeball Ted Robinson. "I hate this inactivity. It's your fault, too. I hate everything today, Ted, even you."

Ted eyed his running shoes. Not that he did much running these days. These days he was relegated to the position of gofer. All the good assignments were going to more senior reporters, his boss's way of punishing him and Maggie for screwing up the scoop on the Sisterhood's capture.

Ted raised his eyes to stare at the woman he loved and hated. He didn't bother to respond. He'd said it all before, just as Maggie had said it all before. He wasn't about to rock any more boats. He needed this job. If he had to suck wind for a few more months, that's exactly what he would do. Sooner or later he'd get downwind of a big story and he'd go back to being a *real* reporter again.

"Did you hear what I said, Ted? I hate you." When there was still no response, Maggie countered with something she knew would drive him nuts. "Have you heard from Jack lately?" She waited and was disappointed. "C'mon, Ted, talk to me." She nervously picked at her cuticles and her nails that were bitten to the quick. No response.

Maggie swivelled around, her eyes full of tears. Their relationship was going to hell and nothing she did or said was helping them get back on their old footing. Maybe it was time for her to move on. The thought saddened her unbearably.

Her slumped shoulders jerked upright when Ted said, "Jack used to be one of my best friends. I should have given him a heads-up that we were going to scoop the arrest of the Sisterhood. I owed him that much. But, you said no. Everything went sour after that. When you play fair, things work out, and if for some reason they don't, you at least know you did it the right way."

"And this is all my fault. Is that what you're saying?"

Ted sat up straighter in his chair, his gaze circling the newsroom. He hoped to see a friendly face, but no one would look at him. No one wanted to associate with a loser, and he and Maggie were both losers in his colleagues' eyes. He cursed under his breath.

"Yeah, Maggie, I'm saying it's your fault."

Maggie was glad she wasn't facing her roommate, her lover, her best friend. Tears rolled down her cheeks. She didn't bother to wipe them away. Somehow or other she managed to make her head bob up and down to show she'd understood. As soon as she could get herself under control, she'd head back to the apartment she shared with Ted and his two cats, Minnie and Mickey. She'd gather up her stuff and move back in with her parents until she could find an apartment of her own. She wondered if Ted would even notice that she was gone.

Maggie looked down at her weekly schedule and wanted to barf: covering the local Brownie cookie sale, the Boy Scouts' dog show, checking out a new brand of peat moss the garden club swore was the reason for the bumper crop of azaleas this year. Real heavy-duty reporting. Ted's schedule was worse than her own. She wiped at her eyes, blew her nose and turned around to offer up a smart-ass response, but Ted's chair was empty. She blinked away more tears as she reached for her backpack and jacket. She wished now she had told Ted about seeing Judge Easter the other day. She didn't know why she thought it was worth repeating to Ted. Maybe it was her reporter's instinct kicking in. All she could remember was a shiver of excitement at seeing the judge in such a civilian situation.

As Maggie made her way back to the apartment she let her mind wander to her finances. How long could she stay afloat on her own? If she cashed in her 401k she could take a leave of absence, try to make things right for Ted, for Jack, for everyone involved. As long as she stayed with her parents, she could exist for about eighteen months. Maybe in those eighteen months, if she hunkered down, she could try to figure out what and how things had gone wrong. Maybe there was a chance for her to get her scoop after all. Maybe, maybe, maybe.

All she needed was a plan, but before she did anything she had to talk to Jack Emery. To clean her slate. Only then could she move forward. Ted's rule of "play fair" rang in her ears. Okay, she'd play fair and see what it got her.

Maggie called her mother and within seconds her hopes of moving in for eighteen months were dashed. Her parents were hosting friends from Switzerland for six months and all the bedrooms were taken. Three additional calls to friends dashed any hopes of bunking with them. Never a fool, Maggie realized she had no other choice at the moment but to stay with Ted. Unless he decided to kick her out.

Maggie did a quick turnaround in the middle of the sidewalk and headed for Jack Emery's office. If the district attorney was in court, she'd simply wait around for him and do her best to make things right between him and Ted. If that turned out to be an impossible task, she would be able to live with it knowing she'd at least tried to do the right thing.

Chapter 9

If Maggie had a tail it would have been between her legs as she slinked out of the building. She'd given it her best shot but District Attorney Emery had threatened to call Security if she didn't leave the premises immediately. His ugly words rang in her ears and she knew in her gut it would be a very long time before she would be able to tune them out. The same ugly words Ted had said time and again: It was all her fault the women got caught, her fault that she'd told Ted to forge ahead because this was Pulitzer material. She was the one who'd pushed the SEND button. And, in the end she'd failed even that. She'd seen the hatred in Jack Emery's eyes. As far as she knew, no one else in the world actually hated her. Oh, they might not like her abrasive, in-your-face style but they didn't *hate* her. It was clear that Jack Emery hated her with every fiber of his being.

As she trudged along, Maggie's mind raced. If she told Ted she'd gone to Jack to try and make things right, he wouldn't believe her. She wished there was a bench somewhere so she could sit down and cry. Instead, she made her way back to the *Post*'s locker room, where she changed into her running clothes. Maybe she could run off some of the misery.

Fifteen minutes later she was running around the Tidal Basin, the scent of the cherry blossoms so sweet she felt lightheaded.

It was a beautiful, sunny day with runners, joggers and sprinters working their way around the Basin. From time to time she passed a nanny or a new mother pushing a pram or walking a toddler. She adjusted her wraparound sunglasses so they would be more snug around her ears. At the same time she yanked at the bill of her baseball cap to lower it farther so her forehead wouldn't get sunburned.

That's when she saw Lizzie Fox and the person she was running with. Maggie slowed and dropped back so two high-speed runners could pass her. What was Lizzie Fox doing running around the Tidal Basin at this hour of the day? And who was the guy she was with? Her imagination ran wild. Running along the Basin was a perfect way to meet someone for a private conversation, but Maggie remembered reading a profile on the high-powered defense attorney where she said that she didn't believe in exercising. And yet, here she was, running with some muscle guy who had the body of Adonis.

Maggie's reporter's instincts kicked in as she wiped at the sweat on her face. She increased her speed a little, aware that by the end of the run she would be crippled with shin splints.

With two other joggers ahead of her and behind the lawyer, Maggie wasn't able to hear a thing, and the joggers appeared in no hurry to speed things up. There was no way she could wiggle her way in between them. She could pick up more speed and get in front of them, but she knew she couldn't continue to run at that speed; her body simply wasn't up to it.

She studied the man running with Lizzie Fox. There was something familiar about him. The crew cut, his height? It wasn't the clothes because they were the same as everyone else's who was running and jogging. Maybe it was his thick neck? When he'd turned a moment ago she'd seen that he was wearing aviator shades. Government issue, she was sure of it.

He was running but he was checking out things as he did so. Only cops did things like that, but Maggie knew in her gut the guy wasn't a blue-suit cop.

A boyfriend? Lizzie Fox was known to play the field with a different man every week, if the gossip columnists were accurate. No, she decided, it wasn't a boyfriend or a cop. The body language wasn't there.

It hit her then like a bolt of lightning. Mitch Riley. The assistant director of the FBI. The same guy who had grilled her and Ted on their return from Idaho. She congratulated herself on her phenomenal perspicacity.

Maggie's heartbeat quickened. She was witnessing something important but what was it? Was he some kind of Deep Throat? Was Lizzie Fox some kind of female Deep Throat? Was Lizzie on the FBI payroll? Wooeee, what do we have here?

The joggers in front of her suddenly broke away, walked over to one of the cherry trees with a canopy of blossoms and slid to the ground. Maggie took advantage of the moment and picked up her speed slightly, staying far enough behind her quarry so as not to arouse suspicion.

She could hear their voices but couldn't make out what they were saying. They appeared to be arguing. Riley turned slightly and noticed the two joggers had disappeared. He gave half a glance at Maggie and turned back to Lizzie. He said something as he steered her to the side. Maggie had no other choice but to keep running.

What to do? Collapse onto the grass or keep going? If she stopped, Lizzie and Riley would eventually jog the rest of the way around the Basin. Should she stop now, or finish up the run and wait at the starting point in the hopes they would pass her to go to their respective cars? She finally opted for finishing. Her legs were killing her when she sat down to massage them. Tonight she would be walking like a ninety-year-old crone. But if she was onto something, and she suspected she was, it would be worth it.

Maggie strained to see the two runners, who were now jogging toward where she was sitting. She watched as they parted company without even saying good-bye or waving to one another. Lizzie Fox looked like she wanted to kill someone.

Pleased with herself, Maggie hobbled off. The big question was: Was this something she kept to herself or should she tell Ted in her quest to bring their relationship back to its old footing? She would have to think about that long and hard.

Charles stood at his computer as he waited for the women to take their seats at the round table.

He tried to gauge their respective moods but gave up when he saw Myra's stony gaze on him. If Myra was still unhappy with him, then so were the others. The truth was he was more than a little tired of the women's attitude and he was on his last nerve. He tilted his head to the side as he watched and listened to the irritation that was rampant among them. He made up his mind to wait them out.

It took all of eleven minutes for the women to realize nothing was happening. One by one they straightened up in their chairs, their shoulders thrown back, their gazes reflective. Charles nodded as he stepped down to the main floor. He held papers in both hands. When he was sure he had everyone's attention, he spoke. "I have here, in my left hand, my resignation. In my right hand is the game plan for your next mission. Let me also say that I am very disappointed in all of you. I expected you to act like the professionals you are supposed to be. I'm taking your attitudes as a personal insult. Because of your sloppiness during Yoko's mission in California, you got caught. We worked, at the time, with the only means available to us. You all knew the plan was short-term at best. When plans don't work, they have to be changed. You've been acting like children whose lollipops were taken away. You seem to have forgotten that you not only failed me, you failed yourselves. I will not single out anyone in particular. You worked as a team and you failed as a team. That's your bottom line. From day one I told you I have zero tolerance for failure."

Charles's left fist suddenly slammed down on the round table. "Here is my resignation. Accept it and you are on your own. Survive any way you can." His right fist hit the table with the same ominous sound. "This is your next mission. I'm going to give you precisely fifteen minutes to make your decision. My bags are packed should you choose to accept my resignation. It's your decision, ladies."

Without another word, Charles left the war room. The women looked at one another, their mouths open, their eyes filled with tears. Myra was openly sobbing as Annie tried to comfort her.

Then the others went at it, screaming and yelling at one another.

"Stupid bitch!"

"It's your fault!"

"I didn't sign up with this group to get caught!"

"Shut that damn dog up!"

A long leg shot out and Kathryn fell flat on her face. The screaming led to a pushing match that ended up on the floor as all hell broke loose. Strands of hair flew as grunts and groans ricocheted against the old stone walls of the monastery. Accusations spewed from the women's mouths at the speed of light. A chair smashed against the wall and splintered.

Then the vicious sound of a second chair crashing into one of the walls finally got to Myra, who looked around in horror. A metal thermos sailed through the air to land at Yoko's feet. She stomped on it and it crushed as easily as a tin can.

"I'm outta here. I don't need this crap!" Isabelle screamed.

"Me, too," Alexis said just as her fist landed on Nikki's jaw.

"Do something," Annie hissed.

Myra stood up on wobbly legs and called for quiet. The women ignored her. She looked at Annie and shrugged.

Annie rushed to Charles's workstation on the raised platform. She knew there was a gun in the cabinet because she'd given it to Charles. Her hands were shaking so badly she could barely lift the heavy pistol. She slid off the safety and fired three quick shots at the ceiling. She was rewarded with instant silence.

"We have three minutes until Charles gets back here. I am a terrible shot so don't make me angry. Myra, call this damn meeting to order and let's get on with it." Annie took her seat, the gun still in her wobbly hands.

"I'm ashamed of all of you. I'm ashamed of myself, too," Myra said in a voice none of the women had ever heard before.

"I'm not ashamed," Annie said loudly. "We did what we were supposed to do. We caught a bad break and things went south. It's those reporters who brought us down. So if you want to blame anyone, blame them. As for Jack and Harry . . . Get over it, girls. There's no room or time to go all sappy. We're talking about our very survival here and I for one am not worried about your love life. If you can't stand the heat, leave the kitchen." She leaned over to whisper in Myra's ear. "Did I say that right?"

"You did," Myra whispered back.

Kathryn looked over at Annie as she massaged what was soon going to be a black eye. "You sounded just like me. Oh, God, I have a clone."

"Did I, dear? I'm going to take that as a compliment. We have one minute, girls."

"Girls, raise your hands if you wish to accept Charles's resignation. I want you to know if Charles leaves, I will be with him," Myra said.

"Me, too," Annie said.

At these declarations, five hands shot downward.

"This is going to call for a major attitude adjustment, girls," Annie said. "As in immediately. Five seconds. Ah, the door is opening. Two seconds."

Kathryn leaned across the table to pick up Charles's resignation letter. She tore it into shreds.

Charles observed the byplay as he made his way to his workstation. He eyed the gun in Annie's hand but said nothing. He did his best not to stare at the disheveled sisters, who all sported bruises, bumps and lumps.

He flicked a switch and the wall-to-wall plasma television screens came to life. All were tuned to the American 24-hour news channels. The sound was muted. He waited patiently. He hoped he looked calmer than he felt.

Myra stood up to face her longtime lover and spoke. "We do not accept your resignation, Charles. We've agreed to mend our ways and we in no way blame you for our current situation. We are again entrusting our lives to your care. We're ready for our next mission whatever it may be. In closing, we offer you our sincere apologies for our . . . for our—"

"Shitty attitudes," Annie chirped.

"Ah, yes, our . . . our shitty attitudes," Myra said.

Charles straightened his shoulders before he slipped a CD into the CD player. "I accept your apologies. Right now I want all of you to pay attention to what you are about to see. We'll discuss your observations at length when it's finished."

When the CD came to life, the women collectively gasped in shock.

Chapter 10

It was a beautiful evening with twinkling stars and a gentle breeze that was just strong enough to make the new leaves on the tree-lined street whisper to one another. Even though the hour was growing late, Jack could make out his neighbors, none of whom he knew by name, walking their dogs. He longed suddenly for a golden retriever. Maybe one day when his life returned to some kind of normalcy, he would get one.

Sitting on the stoop of Nikki's town house, Jack glanced down at his watch. Almost midnight. The witching hour. He wondered if anything would happen at the stroke of midnight. Probably not. He knew *they* were out there waiting for him to do or say something. The infamous Gold Shields, the president's special agents. The same special agents he'd managed to trick more than once. The same special agents that had beaten him to a pulp and almost killed Ted Robinson. Top-notch, answering to no one except the president and Charles Martin, those guys with the special gold shields had been dogging and tailing him longer than he cared to remember.

Just for the hell of it, Jack whistled and then shouted, "Come out, come out, wherever you are, you son of a bitch!" He had to continue to play the game, according to Charles. Now that was a crock of crap if he ever heard one. Still, if it meant the safety of Nikki and the other members of the Sisterhood, he would do whatever Charles told him to do.

Jack nonchalantly fired up a cigarette just as a dark figure stepped out of the shadows.

"Do you want to say good night, Mr. Emery?" The agent didn't advance past the sidewalk but continued to remain in the shadows between two parked cars.

"Well, hell, yes, Mr. No Name Special Agent to the President and Charles Martin. I wouldn't dream of going to bed unless I said good night and extended an invitation to tuck me in, at which point I will tell you to kiss my ass and to get the hell out of my house. So, you want to go for it or not?"

"Testy this fine evening, aren't we, Mr. Emery? If there's any ass kissing to be done it will be by you. Listen up, mister. I have you by the short hairs and don't you ever forget it. You're running on the debit side and we who carry these special shields have not forgotten what you did to one of ours. Or should I say three of ours? Three of the president's most loyal are now without their spleens, all thanks to you. Don't think for one minute that I've forgotten that gold shield you stole. I'll get it back with your hide stuck to it. You're on shaky ground, Mr. Emery."

Jack whipped his sport jacket to the side to let

the agent see the gun nestled in the holster under his arm. As district attorney, he had every right to carry it. He drew it out, clicked off the safety and pointed it at the man standing in the shadows. "Did I tell you I qualified in the gun trials and came out number one? Uno! That means my draw is a tad faster than yours. And I now have a black belt so I can whip your ass nine ways to Sunday and not break a sweat. What do you have going for you, hotshot?"

"A deep-abiding hatred for you. That's all I need. Anytime you want to bring it to a test, say the word."

Jack almost laughed aloud but caught himself in time. "There's a time and a place for everything, asshole. Fortunately, this isn't the time or the place. When I decide to take you on, it will be on my time and I'll pick the place. Write that down so you don't forget, you asshole. Good night, Special Agent Asshole." Jack clicked the safety on the gun and then shoved it in the holster under his arm. Without another word, he walked into the house. When the door was closed and locked, he swiped at the sweat dripping down his forehead.

Jack turned on the alarm, knowing it wouldn't save him for one minute from a guy like the one he'd just threatened. It had been all bravado on his part. If push came to shove, he'd be a lamb going into the lion's den with those guys with the special gold shields. All he *really* had going for him was his new martial arts expertise.

Jack climbed the stairs to the second floor on tired legs. His shoulders drooped, and not even the thought of seeing Nikki in a few days could lift his spirits. He hung up his jacket, stripped down and then pulled on the bottoms of his pajamas. His cell phone rang, startling him. He looked down at the little window that announced his late-night caller. Mark Lane, good friend, ex-FBI computer programmer. Mark Lane, who knew everything about the Sisterhood except the fact that his good friend Jack Emery was a bona fide member of the clan. Jack intended to keep it that way.

Mark's voice was cheerful when he announced himself and asked, "You weren't in bed, were you, Jack?"

"Not yet. What's up?"

"I think I'm onto something. I tailed Lizzie Fox just like you told me to. The only thing she did out of the ordinary was to go running along the Tidal Basin."

"So she likes to run, so what? With those long legs of hers she'll get to wherever she's going before she starts." Jack laughed at his own witty response.

"That's just it, Jack. Your colleague doesn't believe in exercise. Guess she gets enough of that between the sheets. I saw a profile of her a while back. She said she abhors exercise and eats a lot of oysters. For her libido, I guess. Anyway, she went running. She had a partner."

Jack's tired shoulders straightened. "Anyone I know?"

"If you don't know him, you've heard of him. Mitch Riley. He's in charge of the Fibbies. I met him a few times when I worked at the Bureau. Trust me when I tell you the guy is a ring-tailed son of a bitch and not loved by the people who work under him. The guy eats, sleeps and drinks FBI. He's married but he cheats like hell on his wife. Everyone in this whole damn town knows it except his wife. At least that's the rumor. He's got aspirations of being the next J. Edgar Hoover but that's never going to happen. He's got too much baggage. I called a few of my buddies who are still at the Bureau putting in their time, and they told me Riley was in charge of a special task force to find the Ladies of Pinewood. He's on a short leash these days and unless he comes up with something concrete the task force is going to be shut down. That will go on his record. Failure is not something Riley can deal with. The scuttlebutt is that the quest to arrest the so-called vigilantes is going to be turned over to the CIA. That means someone knows they've left the country and it's no longer domestic but international. That's where the CIA comes in. The guy's meaner than cat shit, Jack. Just so you know."

"Your point is . . ."

"Like I said, he was Lizzie Fox's running partner," Mark said triumphantly.

"No fucking shit!"

"And there's more. Guess who was dogging both of them?"

"Who? You gonna make me drag it out of you, Mark?"

"Nope. Just saving the best for last. Maggie Spritzer, intrepid newshound reporter."

"Tell me this is the truth, Mark. Swear on your mother!" Jack all but squealed.

"It's gospel. I got the photos to prove it, too. You owe me, buddy. My bills go out the end of the month so please pay promptly. A big steak dinner would not go unnoticed, either. With, say, a six-pack of Heineken."

"You got it! Thanks, Mark."

"Anytime, Jack."

Jack closed his cell phone and sat down on the edge of the bed. He kicked off his slippers and stared at his bare feet.

Sleep was now out of the question.

Jack started to pace the confines of the bedroom Nikki had decorated in different shades of lavender, her favorite color. He sniffed. Even after all this time, the room, the whole house, for that matter, still smelled of Nikki. He looked around at the furnishings. How happy they'd been when they shared this house. His eyes burned unbearably when he thought about the day the deed had arrived in the mail from one of the leading law firms in the city. How like Nikki to think of him when her own life was in jeopardy.

Maggie. Lizzie. Mitch Riley. What did it all mean? Who the hell were the good guys and who were the bad guys? When no magical answers appeared, Jack hitched up his pajama bottoms and headed downstairs to the kitchen where he opened a beer. He turned on the television on the counter to watch the midnight broadcast of the day's news. He hooked a foot on one of the chairs to bring it closer, he propped up both feet on the chair and proceeded to let his mind race, his eyes on the little screen on the counter.

Jack mentally ticked off the things he didn't understand: Lizzie and Navarro coincidentally showing up at the gym where he was working out. Why? Lizzie said someone was trying to kill her. Probably a gross exaggeration. Navarro just happened to be at the gym at the same time. Why? Jack shrugged as he finished off his beer. He looked at the empty bottle. Did he really want another one? Yep.

Mitch Riley. Well, damn. Some kind of wild card? Mitch Riley and Lizzie Fox. Was she carrying tales? Was it possible she was a snitch or was it possible that she was working with the Fibbies? If true, what did she get out of it? Was it possible she had tried a federal case and cut some corners? Knowing Lizzie Fox the way he did, he was sure she would never leave herself open to any kind of blackmail. That left only one explanation. The Bureau promised her something. Something she wanted more than her career . . .

Jack's mind flashed back to the day Nikki had told him Lizzie always went to the wall for her clients, did whatever it took, whatever she could legally get away with. The key word here was "legally." Lizzie did things outside the box but always covered her ass. It was one of the things Nikki liked about her. Nikki had always been an astute judge of character. That *almost* had to mean Lizzie was one of the good guys. Almost. Sort of. Kind of. Shit!

On the other hand, maybe Lizzie had a hate on these days for her seven clients because they'd bailed on her and left her holding the bag. She'd taken a lot of abuse from TV reporters during those first days—he'd watched the coverage on the 24-hour news channels nonstop while he was on the mountaintop. Lizzie had done her best to carry it off but you could hear the anger in her voice, see it in the set expression of her face. The worst thing she'd said as far as he could remember was that she was duped.

Duped?

The Lizzie Fox he knew would never be duped. No way, no how.

Could it be that Nikki, or Myra, or maybe even Charles had somehow gotten to Lizzie and this was all part of some master plan? The more he thought about that, the more stupid the idea sounded. Scratch that completely.

A ripple of fear raced up Jack's arms. Was it possible Lizzie was onto Judge Easter? If so, did she volunteer that information to the Fibbies? Entirely possible. That would certainly put her on the map in Alphabet City. He shivered when he thought about Judge Cornelia Easter doing a stretch in the federal slammer.

His head swimming, Jack let his feet bounce down on the floor. He rinsed out his beer bottles before he put them in the recycle bin in the laundry room. It really was time to go to bed. He felt like crying as he made his way up the steps to the room he'd once shared with Nikki.

Maybe during the night something would come to him in his dreams. Tomorrow was another day. A day that would bring him closer to seeing Nikki again.

Jack crawled into bed and again wished he had a dog to sleep on the bed with him. A nice, warm, furry body who would look at him with adoring eyes. His last conscious thoughts before drifting off to sleep were that he was going to get a dog sooner rather than later, and first thing in the morning he was going to find a way to talk to Judge Easter. On the sly.

Chapter 11

Jack Emery fought his way through the early-morning crowd at the courthouse coffee shop in his quest to find a way to talk to Judge Easter. If he managed to "just happen to be in line" he could say what he had to say and beat feet. There would be many eyes watching, not to mention the security guards; lawyers simply did not fraternize with judges.

Jack hated this coffee shop because the coffee was awful, the bagels hard as rocks and the cream cheese an inferior brand. By eight-thirty they were always sold out. On more than one occasion he'd left the coffee shop with a bag of stale chips for his breakfast.

His gaze swept through the lines of lawyers, court reporters and judges waiting to pay for the food and drink that would give them heartburn all day long. He saw Judge Easter, her court-assigned bodyguard next to her with her tray as she waited patiently, money in hand. Jack jostled and elbowed his way until he was just one person away from Myra Rutledge's longtime friend. He did his best to make eye contact, willing the judge to look his way. All he had going for him at the moment was clumsiness, so he pretended to stumble and dropped his briefcase. When he bent down to pick it up, he apologized profusely and then whispered, "I need to talk to you, ASAP."

The judge looked down at Jack. "Mr. Emery, this is not a good way to start the day. Are you all right?"

"Right as rain, Judge. Just a misstep," Jack said, loud enough for the others in line to hear him. "I think I'll forgo this fine cuisine, find a place to smoke and grab some coffee in the office. Nice talking to you, Judge."

"That was brilliant, really brilliant," Jack mumbled to himself. Old people usually had hearing problems. Did the judge hear him? He hoped so. He looked at his watch. He had fifteen minutes before it was time to report in. Maybe a cigarette would calm his nerves.

Instead of heading for the elevator, Jack walked down the hall to a door with a huge red EXIT sign overhead. This was the door they usually brought high-profile clients through. At any given time during the day there would be clusters of people outside smoking. Hell, even the judges who still puffed away stood outside with the masses. He'd seen Judge Easter out here a few times swilling the hateful coffee and searing her lungs. Maybe she'd take his hint and come this way.

Jack wondered if he was making a mistake. If he was, it wouldn't be the first time. He shouldered through the door and joined the dozen or so smokers. He fired up and leaned against the wall to wait. He had two more puffs on his cigarette left when Judge Easter walked through the door, her bodyguard right behind her. Following protocol, the other smokers moved away. Jack stayed where he was.

"Good morning again, Mr. Emery. A fine spring morning, don't you think?"

She was getting it. Good. "It certainly is, Judge." Jack looked down at his cigarette. He dropped it to the ground, stepped on it, then picked it up and threw it in the trash container. He fired up a second cigarette. "I'm trying to quit."

The judge smiled. "Me, too."

Jack drew a deep breath. "I like to run and if you smoke it doesn't help. I like to run along the Tidal Basin. I'll tell you, you see everyone out there pounding the ground. I always try to figure out if they smoke or not. You know, by how fast or slow they run or jog. Just yesterday I saw Lizzie Fox and that guy from the FBI, what's his name? Oh, yeah, Riley. Running side by side. I don't know if they smoke or not. Probably not. Well, nice talking to you, Judge. Sorry about bumping into you back there in the coffee shop." Without another word, Jack tossed down his unfinished cigarette, and again stepped on it, picked it up, threw it out and was out of there before any more words could be said.

As he waited for the elevator, Jack told himself the judge was sharp and intuitive. He was almost certain she had gotten the meaning behind his words. What she would do with the information, he had no clue. He'd given her the warning, the rest was up to her.

No one had come right out and told him that the judge was actually involved with the women from Pinewood. Not even Nikki. While they all agreed Jack belonged to the group, he knew he was out of the loop on a lot of things, thanks to Charles Martin.

Jack stepped into the elevator with six other lawyers who were moaning and groaning about their coming day. They were all carrying the hard-as-rocks bagels and cups of the awful swill that passed for coffee.

For now he needed to concentrate on the day ahead of him. He was thankful he had only this one court appearance, just to oversee how one of his underlings performed for his evaluation report. If things went well, he'd be back in his office in an hour. With any luck, if he managed to clear his desk, he could spend some time thinking about Maggie Spritzer and how she figured into whatever was going on. He might even be able to work in a phone call to Nikki. She needed to know about these latest developments.

In the end, Jack did none of those things. Within minutes of entering his office, his boss dragged him out of the building and across town to a meeting with four new hires for their understaffed office. The interviews lasted all day with only a twenty-minute lunch break.

The special encrypted phone in his jacket pocket buzzed twice during the day but he was unable to answer it because he knew he wouldn't be able to carry on a conversation with Nikki. He had to fight with himself not to put his fist through the plate glass door.

The minute Jack walked into Harry Wong's dojo, Harry turned his class over to one of his assistants.

He walked behind the juice bar in the corner to pour Jack a cup of green tea and one for himself.

"You here to work out or is this a social call?" Harry asked.

"Let's go outside. I need a cigarette."

"No, you don't need a cigarette. I thought you quit." It was an old argument and neither man had the desire to go at it other than to mouth words.

"Three cigarettes a week is quitting. I had one and a half today. Just shut up, Harry, and listen to me."

Harry concentrated on his calloused bare feet that could kill a man with one well-placed kick. He shifted his mind to another place as he tried to make sense out of what Jack was telling him.

"What's it mean, Jack?" he asked when his friend wound down.

Jack wrinkled his nose as he started to breathe through his mouth. He looked around the dimly lit alley behind the dojo as he inched closer to the door. "This place stinks. You should clean it up, Harry."

"Tell it to the landlord. Explain to me what it all means."

"That's just it, Harry, I don't know. I've been trying to call Nikki but she isn't answering the phone she swore to answer 24/7. I've been dicking around with the idea of calling Charles but I wanted to run it by you. I don't want to do anything unless we're both in agreement. Just so you know, on my way over here I made up my mind that I'm not going to do another goddamn thing in regard to those women, and that includes Nikki, unless and until Charles tells us everything. *Everything*, Harry."

"That works for me. Do it."

Jack waffled. "It's not that easy. It's a given that he isn't going to tell me anything on this superspy cell phone. My gut tells me to threaten him and I'm not sure that's a wise move."

"Then why are we having this conversation?"

"You know why, Harry? I'm scared, that's why." Jack fired up his fourth cigarette of the day. Harry knocked it out of his hand. Jack withdrew another one from the pack and lit up. Smoke spiraled upward. "Nellie Easter is a federal judge. Mitch Riley is FBI. I have no clue what the hell Lizzie Fox is. The CIA is waiting in the wings. Do you *really* think either one of us is a match for all of that?"

"Nope."

Harry's bare feet scuffed at the dirt on the ground. Jack looked down at the trenches the man's bare feet were digging. His toes must be like daggers, Jack thought inanely.

"*They're* coming here. That has to mean *they* aren't scared. What's that say about us, Jack? Think about it."

"It means they know what's going on, whereas we are in the dark. If I knew what the hell was going on I might not be so apprehensive. We're flying blind here, Harry."

"What can we do?"

The hole in the dirt was now deep enough that it was up to Harry's ankle. The man of no nerves wasn't so steady right now.

"Well, for starters we could pay Lizzie Fox a visit. *If* we knew where she lived, that is. Mark might be able to come up with an address. Or, we could start following Maggie Spritzer since she seems to have the inside track right now. The woman is like a bulldog. Or, we could take out Mitch Riley. Barring that, we could sweat him if we could find a way to do it."

Harry started on a second hole, digging with just his big toe. "Seems like a lot of maybes and ifs to me, Jack. Jesus, I hate that Martin guy. He's the one we should take out," he grumbled.

"I'm going to call Mark to meet us here. Maybe we can hatch a plan that takes in all the parties in this little drama."

"What about the judge?"

"Yeah, she's the wild card here but I know in my gut she's in this up to those bushy eyebrows of hers. Five will get you ten she's going to be the one to host this little get-together. Don't ask me how she'll do it because I don't know. Charles is the brains of that outfit. He's got it worked out nine ways to Sunday. You gonna fill those holes back up, Harry?"

"What holes?"

Jack rolled his eyes. He fished for the special phone in his pocket. He pressed buttons until the number he wanted came up. He hit speed dial. He closed his eyes, a vision of Charles in the war room looking down at the number. The voice from the other side of the world was crisp, clear and very British sounding.

"It's rather late for a call, isn't it, Jack?"

Jack sucked in his breath. What happened to *Hello . . . How are you? . . . What can I do for you?*

"Shank of the evening, Charles. I'm here at Harry's dojo. We want to know what the hell is going on. Now in case you wonder why I'm asking you this question at this hour of the evening, let me tell you what has been transpiring." Jack quickly related his findings, leaving out Mark Lane's name. "I want to know what's going on, Charles. For all I know, Harry and I are sitting ducks. I want the poop on the judge, too. And while I have you on the phone, Charles, I want to know why Harry and I have been kept out of the loop. I thought we had an understanding. Now it looks like you used us and then dumped us because we weren't of any use to you on top of that mountain. I'm pissed, Charles, and so is Harry. No, scratch that, we're *really* pissed. Another thing, what the hell am I supposed to do with that house in Montana?"

"Enjoy the house, Jack. This is not a good time to explain everything to you. It was important that you didn't know what was going on so that . . ." He paused for a moment and then went on. "Nikki will fill you in when she gets there. Trust me."

Jack glowered at Harry, who now had two holes in the ground that were up to midcalf. "Those days are long gone, Charles. I gave you your chance and you flunked the test. Harry and I will do what we have to do. Nice talking to you, Charles," he snarled. With a flick of his wrist, he snapped the special phone shut.

Jack extended his hand to pull Harry out of the two holes he was standing in. "You heard my end. He volunteered nothing. The way I see it, we're on our own. Or, we can walk away and pretend everything is normal and we're just two dumb working schmucks who don't have enough sense to come in out of the rain."

"Screw them all. I'm with you, Jack."

Jack nodded while he scrolled down on his cell phone to find Mark's number. He called the number and extended his invitation to meet at the dojo.

He slapped the phone back into his pocket as he followed Harry inside.

"This isn't good, is it Jack?"

"No, Harry, it isn't good. Good old Charles has hung us out to dry. Do you agree or disagree?"

"Do you want me to kill him, Jack?"

Jack made a sound that could have been laughter. "Don't think I haven't thought about it."

Harry's shoulders sagged. "When Yoko gets here, I'm going to try and talk to her about going away with me."

"Get real, Harry. It ain't gonna happen."

"Yeah, I know."

Chapter 12

Nikki twirled the twig in her hand before she snapped it in two and then snapped the pieces again. She looked over at Yoko, who was wringing her hands. Neither said a word.

Directly in front of them, but off the path, two little brown birds were pecking in the dirt. Both women watched them intently, waiting to see what would happen. When nothing happened and the birds flew off, Yoko finally spoke. "I'm not coming back."

Nikki nodded but said nothing. Some instinct told her Yoko just wanted to talk without comments from her.

"All my life I hungered for someone to love me. Really love me. I almost gave up thinking it would happen and then Harry came into my life. He is everything I ever dreamed of. My life was complete for the first time ever. He gave up everything to join us just the way I gave up everything. As you did and all the others, too. And then it was all ripped away. I can't do this anymore. I want to marry Harry and have a family. Someplace far away. Maybe Japan."

Nikki nodded again as she watched the birds, who suddenly were back but this time they perched in the middle of the path. She wondered if they were hungry.

"I thought you felt the same way about Jack. You must be stronger than I am. But then I hear you crying in the night so I think to myself you are not that strong. Then I told myself you had a lovely childhood with people who loved you and still love you. You have experienced something I never had. True love is putting the other person first. That's what you and I did when we agreed with Charles to send Harry and Jack away to keep them safe. We agreed, Nikki, because we don't want the men we love to be outcasts the way we are. In addition, Charles said they would be able to better help us back home. We were willing to suffer the pain, the loss, so that they would be safe. But that was then and this is now. I don't care anymore."

Nikki knew it was now time to speak when Yoko reached for her arm, her wet eyes imploring her to say what she wanted to hear. "You have to care, Yoko. You have to be strong. Harry's a wonderful man. He's safe now, thanks to Charles. You don't really want to turn him into a fugitive, do you? It doesn't matter where or how far you go, you can't erase what we've become. No, I'm not stronger than you. And, yes, I cry at night. I love Jack too much to . . . I just can't, Yoko. Maybe in time—"

"Time is always our enemy, Nikki," Yoko said sadly. Her tone turned defensive. "We could get lost in Japan."

"And in time Harry would come to hate you just

the way Jack would come to hate me. Living on the run would get real old real quick. I don't want to risk that. I don't think you do, either. Charles is right, we're thinking with our hearts and our emotions. It's hard to turn it off but we have to do it. The bottom line is we committed to the others and we have to live up to that commitment. I know that's not what you want to hear."

"No, it isn't what I want to hear. It's not the same. At first it was such a relief to be safe, to be here in this paradise on top of this beautiful mountain. We were all happy. No one is happy these days except Myra and Annie. What is it Kathryn says? Oh, yes, both of them could be happy in a bubble. Charles is angry with all of us. We're snapping and snarling at each other. It's a terrible situation. I don't know if we can make it right again."

"I don't know, either, Yoko. What I do know is we have to try. We don't have a Plan B. This is what we have for now."

Suddenly the small cluster of birds in the middle of the path took wing. Voices could be heard on the path below the rise. Nikki cocked her head to the side to hear better. "It's Myra and Annie."

Huffing and puffing, Myra was the first to emerge at the top of the little rise, Annie right behind her. "Darling girls, what are you doing out here?"

"We decided to go for a walk since it's such a beautiful day. Now that we don't have to do those horrible runs anymore it's a pleasure to walk and enjoy the environment. Is that what you and Annie are doing?"

"Yes and no. Oh, dear, isn't this the place where I threatened to push you off the cliff, Annie?"

"I believe it is. I was so stubborn that day. So

wrapped up in myself, in my own misery, I let the world go right by me. I'm so glad you talked sense to me. It's such a tranquil spot, so perfect for contemplation. Are we interrupting anything important, girls?"

"Yes," Yoko said.

"No," Nikki said.

She patted the huge rock she was sitting on. Myra and Annie perched on it, their legs out in front of them.

"Is it possible you want some of Annie's and my aged wisdom?

"Yes," Nikki said.

"No," Yoko said.

Myra threw her hands in the air. "Which is it, girls?"

Yoko looked away. Nikki shrugged.

"Well, whatever it is, girls, get over it and get over it quickly," Annie said briskly. "Charles sent us out to find you. He's ready to announce our mission and our travel plans. If there's one thing I cannot abide in this world it's a moody female. We're sisters and it's time to start acting like it. Don't make me think I made a mistake by joining up and giving you all a blank check. We're alive, we're well and we're safe. Keep that in mind the next time you get your panties in a wad. Now, let's go. Charles is waiting for us."

Nikki looked first at Myra and then at Annie before she got to her feet. She stretched out her hand to pull Yoko to her feet, and then took off at a dead run, Yoko hot on her heels.

"Well, that went well, Annie," Myra said sharply.

"I thought so," Annie replied cheerfully. "You

did notice neither one of them had a comment. That means I won the debate."

"Shut up, Annie. I'm worried."

Annie's voice was still cheerful. "Yes, I know. What will be will be."

"I can still push you off this cliff and no one would ever know," Myra snapped.

"No, you can't do that. Today I would fight you. Have you really looked at all of my muscle mass these days? It's awesome."

"Shut up, Annie."

"Did anyone say what we're having for dinner?" Annie called over her shoulder as she sprinted ahead.

Myra sat on the moss-covered rock a moment longer, her heart aching for the two young women running ahead. How well she remembered the day she'd sailed from England, leaving Charles behind. She remembered the pain, the deep sense of loss, the tears that never seemed to stop. And yet, somehow she'd survived and had been reunited with Charles later in life. She couldn't help but wonder if Nikki and Yoko would be that lucky.

Her thoughts turned to her daughter and how much she missed her. "I miss you so much, darling girl."

I know, Mom. I'm always with you. Just call me when you need me. Right now Nik needs you, Mom. I mean she really needs you. She cries herself to sleep at night."

"I know, Barbara. I'm trying. I'll try harder. Charles needs you, dear. Do you think you could—?"

"I'm on it, Mom. Rest easy."

Myra blinked away her tears as she swabbed at the perspiration dripping down her neck. She ignored Annie's dinner comment as she got to her feet. She let loose with a long, tortured sigh as she struggled to keep up with her long-legged friend.

Charles stood at his workstation five minutes longer than planned. He needed to gauge the women's attitude. While he put on a brave face, he was worried. Women as a rule were unpredictable. Seven unpredictable women made him itch in places he couldn't scratch. At least in public.

They looked alert. They even looked interested. But, he could see the simmering anger underneath the façade they were presenting to him. For some reason he thought of Adam and Eve at that moment and for the first time in his life he felt real fear. He felt a shiver ripple down his spine. He told himself there was nothing to fear but fear itself. Then he looked at the seven women seated at the round table. If the occasion warranted, they'd turn on him in a heartbeat. He knew it, accepted it. It went with the territory. He squared his shoulders before he picked up his stack of colored folders. One for each of the women. He stepped down off the dais and handed the folders to Myra to pass around. He was back at his workstation within moments.

The plasma screens came to life, with Lady Justice in the center of the screens. As always, the women took a moment to salute the lady with the scales of justice and the blindfold.

"As I stated earlier, you're all going stateside. I'm going to present the pros and the cons and let you make the decision if you wish to get involved in this particular mission. You will be in danger, make no mistake about that. Personally speaking, I think all of you are up to this mission, but ultimately the decision rests with all of you.

"As you know, our last mission was a bit of a fiasco. That's why we're all sitting on this mountaintop hiding out from the world. There are special people who helped us survive and now one of those people is in danger of having her world ripped out from under her. I'm speaking of Judge Cornelia Easter. Or, Nellie, to all of you." A picture of a smiling Judge Easter in her black robe appeared on the screen. Myra gasped as Annie reached for her hand.

"The assistant director of the FBI, Mitch Riley, and his special task force have ten more days to solve the case of the missing vigilantes or it will be turned over to the CIA. That will give AD Riley a black mark on his record, one that will not go unnoticed in his quest to become the youngest director of the FBI in history. In short, he's under the gun. My information is that he is so desperate he's trying to frame Judge Easter to take the fall for a faulty arraignment and your escape. Your lawyer, Lizzie Fox, is about to be tarred with the same brush. Jack and Harry have been under FBI scrutiny since their return to Washington. A trifecta, ladies. In addition to that bit of information, your two old nemeses, Maggie Spritzer and Ted Robinson, are hot on everyone's heels, although at the moment, Miss Spritzer appears to be going solo. There seems to be some kind of personal . . . uh . . . tiff between them. Any questions so far, ladies?"

"Just one, Charles," Isabelle said. "I want to make

sure I understand what you just said. Are you saying this mission is about taking on the assistant director of the FBI and shutting him up or . . . or what, Charles?"

Charles beamed. "That's what I'm saying, ladies. Are you up to it?"

Annie's arm shot in the air like a laser beam. "I am. Ohhhh, this is soooo exciting. Female power against male power. All we have to do is figure out what his Achilles' heel is. It's sex. I just know it's sex. Do you have any idea how many men have been brought down by . . . ? Well, you know . . ."

Isabelle reared back and said, "You better not be telling us we have to have sex with someone like that. That's not what you're saying, is it, Charles?" Her voice was so shrill with indignation that the others cringed.

"Of course not, Isabelle. But that is indeed the man's weakness. He thinks he's been discreet, but everyone inside the Beltway knows about his women. He's a bully, just like his idol, J. Edgar Hoover."

Nikki's face was grim. "Where does Lizzie Fox come into this? Is he framing her, too? What does he have on her?"

"Well, for starters, when they were in law school, they had an affair. We think he traded on that to meet up with her again, since she was your attorney. We aren't sure what he promised her. Whatever it was, I'm sure she didn't fall for it. She's playing the game and reporting back to me when she can. That's one of the reasons I wanted Jack and Harry back in the States, so they could monitor the situation. Lizzie already made contact with Jack. He's playing the game just the way he should. Everyone is on edge. No one knows who to trust and who knows what. Just for the record—Nellie, Lizzie, Bert, Jack and Harry are the good guys. Those that are left are the bad guys."

"And if we get caught?" Kathryn demanded. "The FBI that I've read about is not a friendly organization."

"No, it isn't. If you get caught, there won't be a friendly judge or lawyer to save your hides this time around. I think you should consider this the ultimate challenge. You will be on your own and there won't be a thing I can do to help you. You need to know that."

"It's the damn FBI, Charles. Are we a match for them?" Kathryn demanded.

"I don't know. Are you?"

"Well, I am," Annie said confidently. "So is Myra."

Bug-eyed, the others looked at Annie. Murphy howled and Grady, Alexis's dog, barked shrilly at the tension mounting in the room.

"He's just *one man*," Annie said disdainfully. "There are seven of us. I think we're capable of taking on the whole task force. We're so in shape it's mind-boggling. Girls, I repeat, *he's just one man.*"

Alexis weighed in. "I agree with Annie. I owe those Feds a few things for that stretch in the slammer I had to endure for something I didn't do. Just point me in the right direction and tell me what to do."

"Assuming we're successful, what happens afterward?" Nikki asked.

"You come back to the mountain unless you want to take your chances in the States. I hate to keep saying this to you, but I'm going to say it one more time. You have to start thinking of this mountain-top as your home," Charles said.

"What about Jack and Harry?" Nikki asked.

"You know the answer to that," Charles said quietly.

Her eyes full of tears, Yoko asked, "How are we going to get there unnoticed?"

"With Alexis's and the padre's help. The padre is on his way up the mountain as we speak. He's bringing monks' robes for some of you. It seems that a rather large religious ceremony on the Mall in Washington is about to take place. It's not just for Catholics but for all religious sects. My details are a little sketchy but will be firmed up by the end of the day. You will be traveling as monks. Alexis will alter your appearances. I have it all worked out. I will put the finishing details to our plans once you give me the go-ahead. Your window of time is very short. I want all of you to be certain that you're up to this mission before you sign on. If you have any doubts, now is the time to voice them."

"Won't seven of us traveling to the States look suspicious?" Kathryn asked. "Especially if we all leave from the same place."

"I have it worked out, Kathryn. Four of you will travel together. Alexis, because she is African American, will stand out among the seven of you, just as Yoko will. Bearing that in mind, she will be traveling with Yoko, who will be dressed as a child because she is so tiny. Alexis will be her nanny and Isabelle will be her mother. I think it will work once Alexis works her magic with her Red Bag of Tricks.

"I'm going to leave you now so you can make a

decision one way or the other. I'll be in the kitchen preparing dinner if you need me."

The women looked at one another as they opened the folders in front of them. They started to mutter among themselves, but it was Annie's cheerful voice that dared them to say no.

Chapter 13

With her usual in-your-face style, Kathryn narrowed her eyes as she challenged Annie. "You're pretty gung ho about this mission, Annie. Do you know something we don't know, or are you just getting off on the danger of it? We're talking about the assistant director of the goddamn FBI. Those guys chew you up and spit you out just for kicks. That's before they kick your ass to the curb."

"I'm more than confident in my capabilities. I paid attention all these months to what Charles was training us to do. I might be old in years but my brain is just as good as yours. We can do it if we work together. Now, if you aren't going to . . . uh . . . cover my ass, I don't think you belong here. Stay here on the mountain and contemplate your belly button. I'm up for this and so is Myra. Read my lips: We . . . are . . . not . . . afraid!"

Myra squirmed in her seat. When did Annie become her spokesperson? After she felt a kick to her leg under the table, Myra stepped up to the plate. "I agree with Annie."

"I'm with them," Alexis said, raising her hand.

Isabelle's hand shot in the air. "Me, too."

Nikki looked at Yoko, who was staring intently at Kathryn, her idol. It bothered her that Kathryn had doubts. She voiced her thought as a question.

Kathryn took a deep breath. "I don't like to fail. It's that simple. We failed the last time and here we are. It's those reporters. They damn well bother me. Now, if you said, 'Let's go after *them*,' I'd be the first one in line. No one has said that. None of you seem to realize how dangerous they are. *Dangerous to us.* I want to know what the plan is, the plan about taking on the assistant director of the FBI. How are we going to get close to him? And if we do, what are we going to do with him? Those are the answers I want and need before I say yes to any of this."

Annie folded her hands in front of her. "Now, you see, we're having a dialogue. What you say makes perfect sense. Let's . . . uh . . . bat it around and see what we come up with. We can make this—what's the expression, Myra, when you do a double?" When Myra rolled her eyes, Annie turned back to the others. "It just came to me. It's called a *twofer.* We are, after all, in charge. That means we plan it, map it out and then do it. With Charles covering all of our respective . . . asses."

"When did you turn into this know-it-all monster, Annie?" Myra demanded, her tone sour and a shade miffed.

"On one of the best days of my life, the day you recruited me to join the Sisterhood. We should have brought some popcorn down here. Munchies always help me to think in high gear."

"If you don't stop talking, I'm going to muzzle you. This is serious," Myra said.

"I know that, Myra. I was simply trying to lighten things up a bit. I have no desire to spend my remaining years in jail. So, let's bat it around and see what we can come up with that will be beneficial to all of us and allay Kathryn's worries and fears."

Isabelle spoke first. "I say we take out the reporters first. All we have to do is call either one of them and tell them we have information on the vigilantes. Some dark alley or a sparsely populated area. We converge and . . ."

"And what?" Kathryn snapped.

"I guess we kidnap them," Isabelle said. "Have Charles arrange to send them *somewhere*. Where they are never seen or heard of again. We won't harm them physically. I think it is definitely doable. Can you live with that, Kathryn?"

"If we can make that happen, then, yes, I can live with that."

Nikki spoke next. "It says right here on Lizzie Fox's sheet that she lives in Kalorama. Four doors down from where the ex-national security advisor lives. Remember him? We're all familiar with that neighborhood. I think we could get in and out of that area pretty easily. Jack and Harry know the neighborhood as well as we do. We can have Lizzie call Riley on the pretext that she has information on the vigilantes. Of course, she'll have to tell him to come alone without his posse."

"What will we do with him if this all comes to pass?" Yoko asked.

"Good question," Alexis said. "I know you don't want to hear this but the man is doing his job. Sure, he has his own agenda. We can't really fault him for that. However, having said that, if he is really planning on framing Judge Easter and blackmailing Lizzie Fox, that's what we're dealing with. Just so we're clear here. Do we all understand our motives?"

"I think we do, dear," Myra said.

Annie smacked her hands together in glee. "Now, let's discuss those horrid newspaper reporters and their bad behavior and how we can one-up them. I'm sure we can come up with a suitable punishment for all the angst they caused us in the past."

Maggie Spritzer, armed with a roll of quarters, headed for the courthouse. Twice she looked over her shoulder to see if Ted was following her. Satisfied that she was in the clear, she made her way up the steps, threw her backpack onto the screening machine, waited, and then walked through the security line behind two lawyers who were grumbling about their clients and the jail time that was anticipated. She flinched at how close she might be to needing someone like those two men in front of her.

It took barely fifteen minutes to copy everything she needed. Her next stop was her own newspaper and the archives where she again photocopied everything she could find that pertained to Judge Cornelia Easter. Back at her desk she went online and pulled up profile after profile of Lizzie Fox, going back as far as her high school days where she was voted prom queen and the Girl Most Likely to Succeed. The lady was indeed colorful, no doubt about that. Beauty, brains and guts. She printed everything, even if it didn't look important or newsworthy. She was jamming it all into her backpack when Ted Robinson plopped down at his desk directly behind hers. She turned off her computer, waved airily and left the newsroom.

The moment Maggie was out of sight, Ted beelined to her desk and turned on her computer. Did she think he was stupid? Using her password, Daisy Duck, Ted logged on and within minutes was printing the same information Maggie had printed out just minutes ago. What was she on to?

Lizzie Fox. Attorney at law. Best damn defense lawyer in the District, bar none. Her looks didn't hurt, either. Attorney to the Ladies of Pinewood aka the Sisterhood, aka the vigilantes. What did Maggie hope to do with this information? The arraignment? Jack Emery and the guy who sat second chair, Spiro something or other. Who else? The judge of course. "Ah, shit!" Ted muttered under his breath as he raced out of the newsroom to head to the courthouse the minute the printer spewed out the last sheet of paper.

Forty minutes later, Ted looked like he'd lost his best friend as he exited the courthouse. She'd beaten him to the punch. He forgot about the love-hate relationship he had with Maggie. "Bitch!" he seethed as he walked along, trying to figure out where he was going and what he had to do when he got there.

He still had Mark Lane. Mark was in Jack Emery's corner, but still, it wouldn't hurt to let Lane know he was on his scent. That should shake a few nuts out of the tree. Yeah, yeah, a call to Mark Lane was definitely in order.

As he walked along with no firm destination in

mind, a plan began to form. More than pleased with himself, Ted reversed his steps and headed for Squire's Pub. All he had to do was sit at the bar and order lunch. He'd drop his little bombshell to the first person who sat down next to him. By mid-afternoon, everyone in Alphabet City would "know" the vigilantes were back at work. Right here inside the Beltway. Right under everyone's nose. By six o'clock the high-tech world they all lived in would announce a sighting of the infamous seven, a message that would go around the world at the speed of light.

"And that's why they pay me the big bucks," Ted mumbled to himself.

Ted was wrong about one thing, though: it was just four o'clock when Jack's assistant repeated the rumor to his boss, word for word, along with a few embellishments.

"Tell me that's just some cockamamie rumor you're spreading just for the hell of it, Spiro?" Jack snarled.

"Got it straight from the hot dog guy on the corner, Jack. That guy knows shit before the president does."

"This is probably a stupid question but who are *they* after?"

"Some bigwig. The smart money is on *them*. Every politician who so much as spit on the sidewalk is cringing. So says the hot dog guy. What say you, boss? You were opposing counsel. Maybe they're after *you*." Spiro laughed as he made his way down the hall.

Dumbfounded, Jack could only stare into space. What in the hell was going on? He looked around to be sure no one could hear him, then hit the buttons on the encrypted phone. Charles picked up on the first ring. Jack started to babble.

"Are you sure, Jack?"

"I'm sure, Charles. What's it mean? Turn on the news. There's sure to be a special bulletin with the *full story* at six o'clock that will go around the world. Is everything still on track?"

"Yes. I could be wrong but I think this might work to our benefit. Thanks for the heads-up."

Jack wondered why he didn't feel any better after the call to Charles. He did call Harry, though, to meet him for a drink after work.

Somehow, Jack managed to get through the next two hours cleaning up his desk and ordering a new pair of running shoes online. At five minutes to six he grabbed his gear and left the office.

Harry was waiting outside Twizzlers, one of DC's more popular watering holes for the fine legal minds that ran the nation's capital.

"It's a zoo in there," he told Jack. "I stuck my head in just to see what's going on. All four TVs are tuned to the 24-hour news channels and all they're doing is talking about the vigilante sightings everyone is claiming. They're going to run with this *for months*. What the hell is going on, Jack? Is this karma coming to bite us on the ass or what?"

"You know what, Harry, I don't have a clue. C'mon, let's beard the masses and pound a few beers. Our night's entertainment will be listening to the bar conversation. Five bucks says the sisters are the main topic of conversation. Lookie there,

Harry, front and center at the bar. Lizzie Fox," Jack said, shouldering his way through the crowd to come up behind the defense lawyer.

Harry used his elbows and people moved out of the way to clear a path.

"Two Heinekens!" Jack shouted to be heard over the television and the loud crowd.

Lizzie Fox turned around on the bar stool to reveal an expanse of leg that made Jack's mouth water. Harry jabbed him in the ribs.

"Well, hi there, Jack!"

Jack reached for the two Heinekens and tossed a twenty-dollar bill at the bartender. He upended the bottle. "Here's lookin' at you, Lizzie!"

Lizzie squirmed on the bar stool, the short skirt hiking farther up her legs. Her eyes narrowed to slits as she held up the squat glass of scotch on the rocks. Then she smiled, showing teeth that were so white and shiny, Jack felt like he needed sunglasses. She whirled back around to face the bar but not before she hissed, "Pay attention to the TV, Counselor."

Chapter 14

Maggie Spritzer eyed Ted over a plate of Chinese takeout. Was it her imagination or did he know how she'd spent her afternoon? She speared a succulent shrimp, stared at it a moment and then popped it into her mouth. Play it cool, she warned herself. Ted can't read your mind. The thought did nothing to relieve her nervousness. She almost jumped out of her skin when Ted turned up the volume on the little television set on the kitchen counter.

Maggie swallowed the shrimp and glared at the small screen. Her insides started to churn at the news anchor's excited words. She risked a glance at Ted out of the corner of her eye. How calm he looked. Like he already knew what the anchor was going to say before he said it.

The moment the anchor switched to the local weather, Maggie eyeballed her partner. "What say you, Ted?"

Ted shrugged. "I heard it all earlier today. Went to Squire's Pub and that's all they were talking about.

I'm not sure I believe it. Those women would be fools to come back here."

Maggie pushed her plate to the middle of the table. Suddenly her appetite was gone. She did notice that Ted had cleaned his plate, but that was nothing new. Something wasn't right, she could feel it in her bones. "The one thing those women aren't is fools. We both know that. It's probably some stupid rumor someone dreamed up on a slow news day. They're fugitives, for God's sake."

"You said they were smart so that would make them smart fugitives. Rumors have been floating around this crazy city for months now. Who are we to say they aren't here? If they have us in their sights, we, as in you and I, could be one of their targets. Think about that, Maggie Spritzer. It was you that clicked SEND that day in California. Think about that, too, Ms. Smart-ass Reporter."

"You know what I think, *Mr.* Smart-ass Reporter? I think you're up to something, and you aren't including me. After all we've been through. If that turns out to be true, I would have a very hard time forgiving you. Why don't we do a show-and-tell, Ted? Remember how we used to do that and then we'd go to bed and have ass-kicking sex?"

Ted jumped up so fast his chair toppled over. "I knew it! I knew it! You're just using me for sex!" *Like he could be so lucky.*

Maggie thought about it for a moment. "I suppose we could have sex first and then do the show-and-tell. But . . . I might be more . . . *energetic* and *exuberant* if we did the show-and-tell first. It's your call, sweet cheeks."

Ted was no fool. At least he didn't think he was. "Define 'energetic' and 'exuberant.' "

"Look them up in the dictionary. Make up your mind by the count of three or the offer goes off the table. One . . ."

"Okay, I'll take it." Sweat beaded the reporter's forehead. "Sometimes I don't trust you."

"Well, guess what, sometimes I don't trust you, either. Can we call a truce here for a few minutes? Tell me what you have and I'll tell you what I have. Then we'll have sex, and after the sex, when I am energetic and exuberant, plus . . ." Maggie mouthed a word that made Ted throw his head back and howl. "We'll talk."

Together they ran to the bedroom, the two cats streaking ahead of them.

Two hours later, Ted would have admitted to being Saddam Hussein's second-in-command if that's what Maggie wanted. Instead she leaned over him and cooed, "Now, Teddy boy, tell Maggie everything."

While Ted and Maggie were billing and cooing, Jack Emery was trying to figure out what Lizzie Fox was up to. The moment the bar stool next to the good-looking attorney became available, Jack sat down and propped his elbows on the bar.

"Can I buy you a drink, Counselor?" he asked magnanimously.

"Well, sure, Jack. And how was your day?"

"Pretty damn good until I got in here and heard the vigilantes are back in town. The thought that I might get another crack at your clients is making me giddy as hell. You should be feeling pretty good yourself, Lizzie."

Lizzie swivelled around on the bar stool and

leaned forward. Jack could smell the scotch on her breath, the perfume on her long, elegant throat. A heady combination along with the silky expanse of leg he could see out of the corner of his eye. "You know what I think, Jack? I think you started that rumor. I think it's a smoke screen. You know what else I think? I think I would have beaten you in court. You couldn't find your ass if I handed you a mirror. Nice seeing you again." She turned around to stare into the mirror over the bar.

Jack turned to Harry, who was standing right behind him. He nodded slightly, which meant, *Don't let her get off the bar stool.* Harry returned the nod as he wedged his slim body up against the back of the stool.

"Funny you should say that, Lizzie. I was thinking the same thing about you. Then I asked myself, Why would you do something like that? You know what I came up with? I think Mitch Riley told you to do it. You remember good old Mitch, don't you? That superstud you were screwing around with in law school. That Mitch Riley. What's he got on you, Lizzie? Maybe I can help."

"You! Help me? Pul-eez!"

Jack thought she sounded like she was saying he was the devil with a burning pitchfork ready to spear her. He wiggled his eyebrows and leered at her. Lizzie reared back, uncertain what was coming next. She tried to slide off the bar stool but Harry leaned against it. One look at Harry's bland expression told her it was time to backpedal.

"You want me to scream, Jack?"

"Why, do you want to scream? If so, go for it. What's Riley got on you, Lizzie?"

"Not a damn thing and I haven't seen Mitch Riley in . . . in years!"

"Your nose just grew a whole inch, Lizzie." Jack slapped at his forehead. "Damn, I guess you forgot about that little run around the Tidal Basin. Well, I can certainly understand that. I wouldn't want to be seen running with that crud, either."

Lizzie didn't bother to deny or confirm Jack's words. "Are you having me followed, you son of a bitch?"

Jack held up his empty beer bottle for a refill. "Obviously you have me mixed up with someone who cares what you do. Nope! I do not have a tail on you. Guess somebody does, though. On the other hand, maybe that someone has it out for Riley. You better be careful, Lizzie, or you might get caught in Riley's crosshairs."

"Eat shit, Jack. I don't have to explain myself to you or anyone else. Tell your goon to ease up or I'm going to scream my lungs out. I mean it."

Harry stepped back as Lizzie gathered her dignity and fought her way out of the bar. Harry hopped up on the vacated stool. "What'd we learn, Jack? Other than the fact that the chick has great legs, smells good, can hold her liquor and is smarter than you."

"You gotta be able to read the eyes. She didn't start the rumor. I don't think she believes I did, either. She was just throwing out stuff to see if it would stick. I can see Mitch Riley starting a rumor like that. He'll get a lot of publicity out of it. They'll be interviewing him 24/7 and it will get the Bureau off his back. That short leash he's on just got a lot of slack in it. Up till now he's been chasing his tail. Now all he has to do is sit back and wait to see what happens."

"Don't you think it's a little coincidental that the rumor is floating out there right now, in real time, just when . . . ? You know what I'm saying here?"

"Yeah, I do know. Life is full of coincidences or haven't you realized that yet? I could be off base here thinking it's Riley. It could be Ted or Maggie. She did come to visit me and I made short work of her. Let's face it, this city is alive again." He pointed to the television screen. "They're still talking about it. We'll go to sleep tonight listening to it and wake up to hear it all over again. Wanna bet?"

"Nah, it's a sucker bet. What's your gut telling you?" Harry asked, swigging from his beer bottle.

"My gut is telling me it's a crapshoot. There's no way anyone can know what is about to transpire. So, that has to mean someone else has their own agenda. It makes for fodder for Ted and Maggie. It takes some pressure off Lizzie. As for Riley, it gets him a slight reprieve. Take your pick. Who has the most to gain, to lose?"

Harry looked around nervously. "What about . . . ?"

"No, the judge wouldn't take a chance. She has too much to lose. Old people lose their edge as they age. They coast to retirement. You know that, Harry. I'm 100 percent certain she has nothing to do with the rumor. My money, for what it's worth, is on Maggie Spritzer. Her timing is incredible. Guess that's why she's a reporter."

"What's our next move?" Harry asked.

"I guess we just wait and see what happens."

"It's gonna hit the fan, right?"

"Yep," Jack said as he held up his beer bottle for another refill. "Let's just drown our sorrows and take a cab home, okay?"

"Works for me, buddy."

Chapter 15

Mitchell Riley watched his wife through suspicious, narrowed eyes. Her eyes were wide and guileless. He hated her as much as she hated him, but they'd made a pact to stick together until he was appointed director of the Federal Bureau of Investigation. He'd recognized a long time ago that he'd lost whatever hold he had on her. Now, the best he could hope for was to get to her through their daughter, Sally. Sally, after Alice's mother.

"You look like you have something to say, Mitchell. Why don't you just say it? And then as usual I will take it under advisement and get back to you. Do you think you can fit me into your schedule, say, late next week?"

Mitch's gaze turned to the small television on the kitchen counter. He felt his stomach start to rumble when he heard the morning news anchor's excited voice extolling the latest sighting of the vigilantes. "Now that you've managed to ruin my day, let me warn you one more time, Alice. I don't want to see you at any rallies for those goddamn women. I don't want one report to cross my desk. Are we clear on this?"

All 102 pounds of Alice Riley were behind her hands when she slapped them down on the butcher-block island in the middle of the kitchen. "Your days of telling me what to do and when to do it came to a close the last time you cheated on me. When was that, three years ago? We don't live together as man and wife. We don't share a bed, we don't share dinner together and we don't even have a joint checking account. I support myself and our daughter. I'm the one who opened accounts to save for Sally's college years. If I want to go to a rally, I'll go. If you lay a hand on me, I'll have your ass slammed in jail so quick you won't know what hit you."

Mitch's eyes narrowed again. Alice was like a stick of dynamite, she could be set off at any given moment. He took a second to wonder when he'd come to that realization. "And while you're trying to do that, what do you think I'll be doing? I think maybe you're forgetting who I am and the power I have."

"Oh, I'm not forgetting anything, Mitchell. I think you might be forgetting who I am. I know what a bottom-feeder you are. I've taken . . . measures in case anything happens to me. Chew on that one. I learned a lot from you, but nothing good, that's for sure. You try anything and I will retaliate."

Mitch advanced a step, then backed off when he saw his wife of fifteen years assume a stance he was more than familiar with. He couldn't remember if she had a brown or a black belt in martial arts. What he did know was she could wipe the floor with him if she wanted to. Thanks to that twit Harry Wong.

"You were going to hit me, weren't you? Oh, let me correct that statement, *try* and hit me. Then you remembered what I could do to you. Don't bother to deny it. I'm sick of looking at you, Assistant Director of the FBI. Please leave."

Mitch turned on his heel and stalked out of the kitchen, his back straight, his shoulders squared.

The minute the front door closed behind her husband, Alice Riley's eyes filled with tears. She'd wasted so many years of her life by staying in this marriage. Maybe it was finally time to do something about it. Her daughter would understand if she said she was leaving her father, the father Sally saw for an hour each weekend.

She had to get out of this toxic house, out into the warm sunshine where she could think.

Five minutes later, her jacket, keys and purse in hand, Alice was standing in front of the BMW she'd bought with her profits from the boutique she'd opened in Georgetown four years ago. She remembered how angry Mitch was when she parked it in the driveway next to his Nissan, a nondescript brown car that he was required to drive. He'd told her to take the BMW back and she'd flipped him the bird and kept the car.

Alice looked up and down the street. She'd miss this pretty tree-lined neighborhood if she decided to move. The neighbors were nice, all the kids were friends, and the husbands always helped her because Mitch was never around. And yet, because of Mitch's job, she had no close friends, no confidantes. Sometimes life was a bitch.

Alice opened the car door and slid into the driver's seat. She'd chosen this particular car because she was always transporting Sally and her friends from one place to another, and she was concerned about safety. Mitch had no comeback when she threw that at him.

The motor turned over but Alice didn't shift into reverse. Instead she opened the glove compartment and withdrew a map of the District and a particular route she'd marked two years ago with a red Magic Marker. She studied it carefully until she knew the route by heart. She replaced the map and then called her assistant to ask her to open the boutique in Georgetown.

Did she have the guts to show up at the law office without an appointment? All the office manager could do was turn her away. Maybe if she told her what she knew, assuming the manager knew how to reach Nikki Quinn, someone in the firm would see her.

How well she remembered the consultation she'd had with Nikki Quinn two years ago. The lawyer, who was around her own age, had looked at her with such compassion before she said she would help her. She hadn't been afraid of Mitch Riley and his position at the FBI. She'd appeared fearless. Alice had been really impressed. Then, when the vigilantes were caught and she'd seen Nikki's picture plastered all over the television and newspapers, she understood what the attorney had been trying to tell her without coming right out and saying it.

In the end Alice had walked out of the office saying she would return when the time was just right. Nikki Quinn had smiled, hugged her, told her she understood what she was going through and then handed her a card with a phone number penciled on the back. She'd kept the card, but to this day she didn't know whose number that was. Maybe it was time to call and find out. Or should she go to the firm first?

She'd been in court the day the so-called vigilantes were arraigned. She'd done her best to will Nikki Quinn to look at her and she had. She'd even winked at her. Sort of. Then again she might have been crying, although all the women had been defiant. Alice contributed to a fund for the women, running the check through her business account, but somehow Mitch had found out. There had been hell to pay over that but she didn't care. Neither did her daughter.

Alice got out of the car and popped the trunk. For months now she'd been copying all of Mitch's files that he brought home for safekeeping. She had a plethora of . . . what it was she didn't know. Someone like Nikki Quinn would know, or maybe Jack Emery and Harry Wong. She had to get word to them, too, since Mitch's files on both men were getting thicker by the day.

What to do?

Alice looked down at her prepaid cell phone. She'd long ago given up her regular cell phone because she knew her husband could track her at any given moment. She'd given Sally a prepaid phone, too.

An expletive ripped from her mouth. She couldn't go to Nikki Quinn's old law firm because there was a GPS tracker in her car. Put there by her husband. He didn't know she knew it was there. Her mechanic had found it months ago. He'd showed her how to remove it and how to put it back.

Alice leaned back and closed her eyes. How had she allowed all of this to happen?

If she called the number on the back of Nikki Quinn's business card, who would answer? Was she prepared to open up to a stranger? If it was Nikki's personal phone number, it would have been disconnected. No, Nikki had said something to the effect that, *"If you can't reach me, the person at this number will help you."* Alice was almost certain that's what the young lawyer had said, but almost wasn't quite good enough. She needed to know, and she needed to know *now*, before she started spinning her wheels.

Alice rummaged in her wallet until she found the small, cream-colored wrinkled card. She turned it over and looked at the number. It was a cell phone number, possibly Verizon. Before she could change her mind, she punched in the numbers and hit SEND. Three rings later she almost dropped the phone when a deep, throaty voice on the other end of the phone said, "Liz Fox."

Alice's hands started to shake. Lizzie Fox, the vigilantes' attorney. Lizzie Fox, Mitch's old law school lover. Oh, how he loved to taunt her with that. She broke the connection without saying anything.

Alice climbed out of the car and bent down to remove the GPS tracker from under the left front fender. She tucked it into one of the tulip beds and drove off.

Chapter 16

It was a beautiful bedroom, spacious and comfortable, decorated in earth-toned shades with splashes of bright color on the walls. Sheer curtains billowed inward from the wide-open French doors. The gentle mountain breeze was more than welcome because it carried the scent of all the spring flowers that decorated the Spanish porch, which wrapped around the entire house.

Nikki flexed her arms and did a few stretches to limber up. She looked down at the others, who were sitting Indian-style in the middle of the floor. In the center of the circle was Alexis's Red Bag of Tricks. Inside the red bag was everything a makeup artist would need to turn one person into another. Alexis had the capability to change a person into a glamorous movie star or to take an ordinary person and, with a few deft turns of her wrist, create a monster.

Near the door were seven large boxes that as yet had not been opened. They'd come up earlier on the cable car when the day workers arrived shortly after dawn. The women eyed them curiously.

Myra called for order. The girls fell silent immediately. "This is informal, girls, so let's just talk out our plans. According to Charles, no news came through overnight so things are the same as they were yesterday. We leave tomorrow at dawn for the United States on two separate flights. Annie, Nikki, Kathryn and I will be on the first flight. Judge Easter's housekeeper will pick us up at the airport and take us to Nellie's farm where we will all convene. At this moment, the plan is for Jack Emery to have someone pick up Alexis, Isabelle and Yoko. He will arrange for one of Harry Wong's partners to transport the three of them to the farm, preferably at night. Those are the travel arrangements as of right now, but they could change in a moment. We all have to be ready.

"Alexis is going to explain how she's going to alter our appearances. There will be little sleep for us tonight because it is going to take a very long time for all these changes. Are we ready, girls?"

Eyes bright, smiles on their faces, the women all nodded. How could they not be excited? They were going back to that wonderful place called home.

They squirmed and wiggled until they were closer together to allow Alexis more room to spread out the contents of the magical bag in the center of the group. She explained what each item was and what she planned to do with it.

"Goodness, Alexis, are you saying Annie and I are going to be rotund, bald-headed monks?"

Alexis giggled. "That's what Charles said. These little gizmos inflate to make you, as you said, more round. These skullcaps are a work of art. Whoever made them is a genius. Of course, you will be wearing the hood to your robe so it really won't matter a whole lot. It's just in case the hood slips or something. I'll show you your robes in just a minute. They're wonderful, with all kinds of hidden pockets and little places to hide things. The padre showed me a sample last week."

"What's all that stuff?" Kathryn asked, pointing to an assortment of vials, bottles, tins and a clear bag of white powder.

"I have to take a plaster cast of your feet and hands. Think about it, you're supposed to be male monks. That means your feet and hands have to look like a man's. Monks wear sandals. That's why this is going to take all night."

"My dear, you are so ingenious," Myra said, patting Alexis's hand.

Alexis started to mix her concoction. "It was Charles's idea. He thought of everything, the way he always does. Our safety is his main concern." She continued to talk as she sifted, measured and stirred. "When I'm finished mixing, we have to act quickly as this will harden very fast. Making the molds to slip over your feet and hands is the easy part. While I'm working at this, check out the robes. Isabelle and Yoko can model their outfits for you to get your opinions. The hair has to go, Yoko."

Yoko reared back onto her heels, her hands holding on to the long, silky braid that hung down to her buttocks. "No!"

"Yes," Alexis said firmly, not missing a beat. "If I am going to make you look like a ten-year-old girl, the hair has to go. You will be sporting a Buster Brown hairstyle. A wig won't cut it, Yoko."

"No, I cannot give up my hair. Think of something else, Alexis."

"It wasn't a suggestion, Yoko, it was an order issued by Charles."

Sensing a brewing battle, Kathryn stepped in before it could get out of hand. "Harry will love it, Yoko. The short styles are in this year. I saw that on television last week. Don't you want to be a trend-setter?"

"How do you know Harry will love a short haircut?" Yoko asked suspiciously.

Annie decided too much time had passed since she offered up an opinion on anything. "I saw the same show Alexis saw. They had this panel of men and women and the men were saying they're tired of the girl-next-door look and are looking for style and sophistication this year. Men are such fickle creatures. Next year they might want your grandmother's look. The topknot or the bun in back. You have the perfect face for a Buster Brown bob." She wondered if what she was saying was a lie or if she'd really seen it on TV.

Whatever it was, Yoko agreed. "If Harry doesn't like it, I'll kill all of you," she said sweetly.

"Well, my dear, I don't think such drastic measures will come into play. Men are fickle, as I said," Annie added. "The good thing is your hair will grow back."

"In perhaps twenty years," Yoko mumbled. She swiped at the tears welling in her eyes.

Nikki reached out to Yoko. "I don't think Harry will even notice. He's going to be so happy to see you he won't care if you're bald." Seeing that more tears were about to flow, she said, "Let's check out our duds. We also have to decide what we're going to do with Maggie Spritzer. There's something I'm missing," Nikki muttered, more to herself than to the others. "I really hate it when it's almost there but I can't catch the thought."

"Shift gears," Kathryn said as she slit the top of one of the cartons. "Oh, my God! These robes are heavy. Would you look at the floppy sandals? They're not even new!"

"It fits our MO," Isabelle said as she spread out the robes on the champagne-colored carpet. The girls dived in to explore the hidden pockets, the knotted rope belts and the weighty string of beads to go around their necks. "I never really liked brown as a color," she said. The others agreed.

"Now, what about Maggie Spritzer, everyone?" Nikki said. "Let's decide now so when we're on the plane we can refine our activities."

Kathryn sat down and hugged her knees. "We call her up. She won't recognize any of our voices. Tell her to meet us somewhere and we converge. We make it perfectly clear that she is not to bring Ted Robinson with her. Jack did say she likes to work independently and considers herself superior to Ted. She's a hothead, too. If she thinks she's going to get a scoop, she'll do what we ask. We'll simply pretend one of us saw and recognized the vigilantes. We can work on the dialogue when we're on the plane. It will give us something to do. Damn, I hope I get to see my truck. I really want to see my truck."

"Oh, dear, that would be such a giveaway," Myra said. "I'm sure there is someone watching it night and day. Charles said it is secure, but those . . . those awful people in authority might have found it by now. It is rather hard to hide an eighteen-wheeler."

"I don't care. That truck is my life, and I want to see it. That truck is who I am."

Yoko punched Kathryn's arm. "Isn't that the same thing as telling me I have to cut my hair? For reasons of safety?"

"Okay, okay! No truck," Kathryn agreed and then grinned. "When did you get so smart?"

"You taught me everything I know." Yoko giggled.

"Next!" Alexis called.

As the hours wore on, the girls submitted to being transformed until it was impossible to recognize them.

"Oh, dear, I just thought of something," Annie said. "We'll have to use the men's room at the airport." The others gaped at her.

"Good lord!" Myra exclaimed.

"Oh, for heaven's sake, Myra, get real. I always wanted to see the inside of a men's bathroom. There's never a line, as you know, whereas the ladies' bathroom has a line all the way out the door. Think of it as . . . as an experience. Just don't . . . don't sit on the seat."

"That I can do without," Myra retorted. Annie shrugged.

The hours continued to wear on as the girls submitted their hands and their feet for the latex molds that Alexis crafted. As one, they agreed it was impossible to tell the difference. "Our feet are just bigger and wider," Annie said, holding out one of her feet to inspect it. "Look, we even have fine hairs on the back of our hands. What a true artist you are, my dear!"

Alexis bowed and sighed wearily. "I'm going to try to sleep for a few hours. I'll see you in the States. Good luck." The women hugged one another as they made their way down to the first floor.

Charles gasped, his eyes widening in astonishment. "In a hundred years I would never guess you are anything but what you present to the eye. Magnificent! Coffee, ladies?"

While Charles poured, Myra said, "I wish you were coming with us, Charles."

"I wish so, too, but someone has to be here to coordinate everything. I'm a phone call away. That's how you have to think of it. I hear the cable car. Quickly, ladies. From this minute on, you are on a schedule. Call me the moment you land."

Outside in the cool morning air, Charles felt his heart take on an extra beat. "Good luck," he whispered as the women filed into the cable car and turned it on. He stood on the concrete pad, Murphy and Grady at his side.

"They'll be back before you know it," he told the dogs, giving each one a pat.

On the walk back to the house, Charles called Jack Emery. His message was short and curt. "The cable car just left the mountain. Take care of them, Jack."

Chapter 17

J udge Easter hung her black robe on her grand-
father's antique coatrack. She'd brought it to
these offices years and years ago. With painful,
arthritic hands, she smoothed the folds of the heavy
material that was worn and threadbare in certain
places. It was her only robe, one she took care of,
taking it personally to the dry cleaner's every Friday afternoon and picking it up on Monday morning.

The robe, the coatrack, the books on the shelves,
the green plants . . . all meant a lot to her. No, that
wasn't quite true. Once they had been her very
life, but these days they simply didn't seem as important. They were just things. Things.

Nellie Easter looked up to see her clerk standing in the doorway. No one, not even her trusted
clerk, ever crossed the threshold to her office until
she invited them to join her. "Just put it on the
desk, Jane. Thanks. Go home to your family. I'll be
leaving in a few minutes myself. Have a nice weekend."

"You, too, Judge. Call me if you need me for anything."

Nellie nodded. There had never been a need to call Jane over a weekend during the last twenty-five years and she seriously doubted if the need would ever arise, but she made the same comment she always made: "Thank you, Jane, I will call if I need you."

Nellie sat down and reached for what she always called the perfect cup of coffee, made by Jane with fresh beans and brewed to perfection. Jane said it was the real cream and not the coffee that made all the difference. Nellie didn't care what it was, she just liked it.

Nellie leaned back in the old, comfortable chair that had once been her father's. The leather was cracked, patched with strips of duct tape to protect the stuffing. It was softer than butter and hugged her aching bones. She'd often said she would part with her left foot before she'd give up her father's chair.

She should have retired when her daughter died, but Myra Rutledge and Nikki Quinn had talked her out of it. They said she couldn't wallow, she had to take their advice. Since she loved and respected both women she did her best to get on with her life. Like Myra, who had also lost a pregnant daughter, she went through the motions like a robot. While her days were busy and active, the nights had never gotten any better. In many respects she was still a robot, but that was slowly changing with the recent turn of events.

Nellie looked down at her hands that were holding the cup of coffee. They were trembling. She carefully set the cup on the desk. Maybe she needed to lay off the caffeine. Maybe she needed to back out of the deal she'd made with Myra. She knew she'd never do the latter. Giving up caffeine would be easier.

She thought about everything she knew, all the secrets Myra and Annie, her two best friends in the whole world, had confided in her. She remembered how intently she'd listened to Charles Martin when he'd detailed the operation he headed. How quickly she'd agreed to become a member of the Sisterhood. How quickly she'd agreed to what went on in court that day ten months ago. She hadn't even blinked. Nor had she blinked when the press railed at her day after day. Nor had she caved in when Mitchell Riley came after her like a pit bull. She'd held her ground and thumbed her nose at all of them.

Nellie knew she could walk out of this office right now with her robe, her coatrack and her father's chair and never come back. If she wanted to. Well, she did want to but she was going to toe the line and do what she'd signed on for. Because? Because she was disgruntled with the judicial system, sick and tired of defense lawyers who convinced juries that a triple murderer was an otherwise upstanding citizen, sick to death of seeing prosecutors dropping like flies because of technicalities in the law. Which brought to mind Jack Emery. She squeezed her eyes shut and then laughed out loud. She adored the pugnacious prosecutor and often found it hard to hide her feelings. More often than not she wanted to give him carte blanche in her courtroom and had to physically pinch herself not to do so.

Nellie remembered his sterling performance in

court the day the Sisterhood had been arraigned. It was nice to know that she wasn't the only actor in this particular courthouse on that infamous day.

As Nellie gathered up her purse and briefcase, she wondered if her reputation as a predictable judge was going to be a blessing or a hindrance where Mitchell Riley was concerned.

Nellie juggled her robe, her purse and briefcase along with the special key to her office. Finally she was ready to leave this airless hellhole for the weekend. Albert Fazio, her personal bodyguard, and Joseph, her driver, were waiting for her at the end of the hallway by the elevator. Both were kind men, caring men with families, who protected her with their lives. Both men told her on a daily basis that being a judge these days was a dangerous business. They'd made a believer out of her on two separate occasions that she didn't want to think about.

Ten minutes later she was settled in the back of the specially equipped Crown Victoria. Albert climbed in beside her, and then Joseph expertly guided the car out of the parking garage toward the highway.

The things she'd learned from these two boggled her mind. In particular was the lesson on cell phones. Who knew that when your cell phone was turned on, even though you weren't talking to anyone, towers could track your whereabouts. In a panic that did not go unnoticed by either man, she'd turned off her phone. She'd learned some other things that had given her a raging case of hives that had taken months to control.

Being a bad guy wasn't easy these days.

The conversation on the ride home was mostly about both men's families, the weather, Joseph's dilemma concerning the new car he had to buy for his wife.

"So, what's going on in the world today, gentlemen? Any more sightings of the vigilantes?"

"Four." Albert chuckled. "Dimples," he said, referring to Mitchell Riley, "was ranting on the noon news that he has them in his crosshairs and it's just a matter of time before he hauls them in."

"Really," Nellie drawled. "I thought it was all a ruse on a slow news day. Those women are way too smart to come back to the scene of the crime, so to speak. What are your feelings, Albert?"

"Well, Judge, my wife says those dames are smarter than the entire FBI. She also said if it's true, she pities the person they're after. I tend to agree with her. It's a given they skipped the country, so to take a chance on coming back *into* the country would take some planning and some . . . uh . . . some inside help. That's my personal opinion."

"Mine, too," Joseph said from the driver's seat.

Nellie's heart kicked up a beat. "Are you two just trying to be polite or is there a reason you haven't mentioned Riley's crusade against me?"

"That's all smoke and mirrors, Judge," Joseph said. "He's under the gun with his superiors. Scuttlebutt is he's just days away from having the case ripped out from under him and turned over to the CIA. Something like that hanging over your head could make a person stick his neck out a little too far. My wife thinks he started that rumor himself, just to make himself look good. Since you brought it up, Judge, if Riley can make you look bad, if he can successfully smear you, he gains time."

Nellie's heart kicked up another beat. "I think I can hold my own. My record stands on its own." She thought about the special encrypted cell phone at the farmhouse. Would Riley get a subpoena and search her house if he was serious about framing her?

"With all due respect, Judge, you have been life-long friends with two of those vigilantes. There are those who are saying, and Dimples is one of them, that you should have recused yourself."

"I tried, Albert, as you well know. Miss Fox and Mr. Emery were fine with me presiding. I conducted the arraignment by the book."

Albert, who could have posed as a linebacker, patted the judge's arm. "I got your back, Judge. I don't want to alarm you, but today's rumor is that the vigilantes are after *you*."

Nellie forced a laugh she didn't feel. "That is so absurd I can't even comment on it."

Joseph brought the Crown Victoria to a stop outside Dell Cleaners. He hopped out, opened the back door for Nellie. She was back within five minutes and the drive out to McLean continued.

"There's talk, Judge, about posting a security detail outside your farmhouse," Albert said.

The judge reared up in the backseat. "Absolutely not! I will not live in fear. Who do I need to call to settle that issue immediately?"

"Relax, Judge. I knew you wouldn't go for it. I'm doing double duty. Joseph is going to help. The powers that be agreed. For now."

"It had better be forever," Nellie snapped. "I will not have cops and agents disturbing my weekend with my guests. Religious people do not understand that kind of nonsense. I am hosting this retreat and I don't want anything to tarnish it. Whose brilliant idea was it, anyway?"

"Judge Spano's."

"He's a twit, afraid of his own shadow. He sentenced a man to two years' probation and then had a nervous breakdown. *Probation!*"

"I hear you, Judge."

Oh God, oh God! Nellie squirmed in her seat, fidgeting with her seat belt, wishing she had a cigarette. What the hell, she could do whatever she pleased. She rolled down the window and fired up one of her cigarettes. Neither man said a word as she puffed away.

Twenty minutes later the Crown Victoria sailed through the electronic gates Myra and Charles had installed two days before Nellie took up residence a year ago. She let out a sigh that was so loud, Albert turned to look at her, a frown on his face.

"It's been a hard week, Albert. I'm just glad to be home. My hip is bothering me and I have this retreat to look forward to. Seventy-two hours of trying to be the perfect host is not something I do well. If you hear any other rumors you think I should know about, call the house. Thanks for taking care of me."

Joseph opened the back door and helped the judge step out onto the shale driveway. She waved him away as she walked up to her back door where her cats always waited for her. The two men looked at one another, their eyes full of questions that neither man felt comfortable asking aloud.

Joseph turned the car around and headed back the way he had come. On weekends the judge was on her own, though protected by every security device known to man. He knew for a fact that there were panic buttons in every room of the house. Monitors were attached to the electronic gates and on the corners of the house. The judge was electronically safe.

Inside the house, Nellie dropped her gear on top of the butcher-block table. Her cats scurried around her ankles as they tried to tell her it was dinnertime. She obliged and then poured herself a double scotch on the rocks. Her shoes found their way to the far reaches of the kitchen. The cats would eventually discover them and push and shove them into the living room.

Nellie eased her tired body down into her old chair, lifted the footrest and leaned back. She gulped at the drink in her hand as her other hand rummaged in her knitting bag for the encrypted phone. She would use it when she finished her drink. Or her second drink, or maybe a third. *A special security detail.* "Not in this lifetime," she sputtered.

Chapter 18

Alice Riley was glad it was Friday. On Fridays she allowed her daughter to attend sleep-overs. With her husband in such a foul mood it was better for Sally not to see or hear the verbal confrontations that went on. When Sally returned at noon on Saturday, Alice made sure she had the hours covered with meaningful things to do that interested both of them.

The clock on the kitchen stove made a slight buzzing sound to indicate another hour had passed. Over the years she'd tried to do away with the buzzing, to no avail. Now she just lived with the sound and chalked it up to modern technology. Normally it didn't bother her. With her daughter gone, the house was quiet. She heard the pinging sound from the front door, another modern technology gizmo that irritated her because it meant someone had just opened her front door. At four o'clock in the afternoon! She looked out the kitchen window and stifled a gasp when she saw her husband's car in the driveway. She hoped he was sick. Maybe dying. But she knew she couldn't be that lucky.

Alice turned on the kitchen television just for sound and was startled to hear the Fox News afternoon anchor's excited voice describing a massive accident on the Beltway. She almost fainted when she heard the name Josh Carpenter. Carpenter was the director of the FBI. She pulled on her earlobes to make sure she was hearing clearly. The director, suffering head wounds and internal bleeding, had been taken to Walter Reed Hospital and was at this moment in the operating room. The prognosis probably wouldn't be good.

Alice shivered under her lightweight sweater and hugged her arms to her chest. She whirled around to see her husband watching her from the doorway. She knew she was pushing her luck, and hating herself at the same time, but she did it anyway: "Congratulations, Mitch!"

"Why, thank you, Alice. I'm going to be the best director the nation's capital has ever seen. For starters I'm going to haul in that goddamn Judge Easter to make sure she never sees the light of day again. She was part of that little group you admire so much."

Alice worked her tongue around her teeth as she grappled with what she was hearing. "I thought you said it was your old girlfriend Lizzie Fox who was in on that whole thing."

"Her, too. I'm going to have them both hauled in as soon as I can get things squared away here. They'll be behind bars by morning. That's how long the director is supposed to last."

Squared away here? Alice was surprised at how casual her voice sounded when she asked, "Does that mean Jack Emery is in the clear? I thought you hated him, too. Isn't this all about your own personal vendetta against all the people you think are against you? Didn't you say the three of them made you the laughingstock of the Bureau? Well, I guess this shitful town will have to stand up and then bow down to worship at your feet."

"Any day now. Old Josh isn't going to make it. I have it on very good authority. Like I said, they say he'll be lucky if he makes it through the night. Then it's that big place in the sky for him. No one will miss him. He's a Neanderthal and he's outlived his career. But to answer your question about Jack Emery, he's in this up to his teeth. We've been stringing him along, just waiting for him to step out of line. The whole thing is a goddamn conspiracy."

"Do you want to know what I think? I think your old lover, the judge and Emery bested you and the entire FBI. Now you're trying to save face and you're prepared to do whatever you have to do to ruin all three of them. You can't get the vigilantes so you're going after those three, probably concocting some story that will ruin their lives. That's what you're doing, isn't it? How cruel you are, Mitch."

"I prefer the word *realistic*. What are you doing home, anyway?" Mitch asked, suspicion ringing in his voice.

Alice sighed as she turned around to prepare a pot of coffee. "I take Friday afternoon off because I go back and close the shop at 10:00 PM; Fridays are our late nights. I've been doing it for four years, Mitch. How strange that you finally noticed. Now it's my turn: What are *you* doing home at this hour?

Oh, right, I forgot, this is where you do all your dirty work so no one at the Bureau can point fingers."

Alice's mind raced as she spooned coffee grounds into the filter in front of her. He was going to go into his home office with the special lock on the door. One she'd been able to pick with the aid of a few sharp little tools. She'd then had a key made and every day, after Sally went off to school, she went in there and photocopied everything in sight. Right now, this very minute, she had four huge boxes in the basement labeled KITCHEN FLOOR TILES, each with a different tile glued to the top of the box. She'd stacked them right out in the open. As far as she knew Mitch never went down to the basement and even if he did, the last thing he'd be interested in looking at would be kitchen tile.

Alice's mind continued to race. She had to give him time to do whatever dirty work he was going to do and then she needed to copy it, but she had to get him out of the house quickly. And she needed to get back to her shop. She had two and a half hours to work some magic. She whirled around but her husband was gone.

Every plop of the coffee dripping into the pot sounded like a thunderclap to her ears. Alice sat down on one of the kitchen chairs. She was shaking inwardly and outwardly. She tried taking deep breaths but she was so wired up it wasn't working. She bounced up and then sat back down on her hands. She needed to think. She needed a plan of action. What she had was a pot of dripping coffee, and that was it.

She liked Josh Carpenter, always had. He'd been kind to her the few times they'd met, always asking about Sally, the shop and how she was doing. In his heyday he'd been a fierce man but a fair man, or so the stories went. She knew he didn't like Mitch. Not that he ever said anything but she could tell. There weren't a whole lot of people who did like her husband.

Alice closed her eyes. Maybe now she could finally get away from Mitch. Maybe he'd let her go without any ugliness. Then again, maybe he wouldn't. He might need her image to bolster his own if Josh Carpenter died.

The red button on the coffeemaker blinked. The coffee was ready. So was the brandy bottle in the cabinet. With trembling hands she poured a healthy jolt into the cup and then dumped it down the sink. She couldn't drink if she was going to drive later on. She poured the coffee, added an ice cube and gulped at it. She was on her second cup when a plan began to form in her mind. She closed her eyes and let her thoughts go in all directions.

The crazy clock on the stove buzzed at six o'clock. Alice got up and called her shop to ask her assistant if she would close the store at ten o'clock, citing the accident to the director of the FBI and saying her husband needed her. Like anyone at the shop would believe that little story.

Her shoulders thrown back, her teeth clenched, Alice marched down the hall and knocked at Mitch's private door. He growled something indistinguishable and then opened the door.

"I'm getting ready to leave for the shop. I was thinking about Josh and how much he's done for the Bureau. Since you're a man and men think with their lower extremities, I thought I would pass on a thought. If you want good press, if you want to look like you're ready to step into Josh's shoes, you might want to think about carrying out a personal vigil at his bedside."

"And you're telling me this . . . why?"

Alice sniffed. "Because I don't want to be tarred with the same brush you're going to be tarred with. Make no mistake, I hate your goddamn guts. I'm thinking about myself and our daughter. Never you." Without another word, she turned on her heel and left the house. Mindful of the GPS tracker under her car, she headed for her boutique, parked in the lot, removed the tracker and placed it underneath a weeping willow tree whose fronds covered the tracker completely.

Within minutes she was back on the road and heading for home. She battled with her thoughts: Would Mitch's car be in the driveway or wouldn't it be in the driveway?

Alice turned the corner to her street fifteen minutes later. She felt relieved at the sight of the empty driveway. She took great, gulping breaths as she climbed out of the car that she'd backed up against the garage door. In fifteen minutes she had the four boxes loaded into her trunk. She closed the door, fished for the key to Mitch's secure office and proceeded to systematically go through what he'd been working on. She was so nervous, she didn't bother to look at anything. All she did was study his work area to make sure she put everything back the way she found it. It took her a full thirty-eight minutes to copy everything. When she was finished, she dumped it all in a brown grocery bag. Ten minutes later, a cola in hand, she was back on the road.

* * *

Alice drove until she found a crowded parking lot at a local Burger King. She went through the drive-thru, ordered a Whopper, fries and another Coke that she didn't want, collected her change and then parked at the far end of the lot. Now she could relax. She leaned her head against the headrest and closed her eyes. What had she just done? What was she going to do? She opened her eyes to look down at the untraceable cell phone on the passenger seat.

For the life of her, she couldn't remember if the cell phone was part of Plan A, B or C. Her thoughts whirled. Did she have the guts to do what she was contemplating? Had she lost her mind today? Without further thought, Alice got out of the car, popped the trunk and opened one of the boxes. She lifted out a three-inch-thick printout that she'd copied. The phone numbers and addresses of every politician in Washington, DC, every judge, every law enforcement officer, every lobbyist, every federal employee were on that list. She struggled to carry the heavy block of paper to the passenger side of the car. She slid it onto the seat and then climbed back in the car. Before she could change her mind she riffled through the pages until she found the home phone number of Judge Easter. The contents of the Burger King bag went on the floor. She smoothed out the bag and scribbled the home number as well as the cell and office numbers on the bag. She then repeated the process two more times for Lizzie Fox and Jack Emery.

Alice felt so lightheaded she thought she was going to faint. She tried again to take gulping breaths of the early evening air. Just do it, her mind shrieked.

"All right, all right," she muttered. Who to call first? She wrestled with her thoughts and finally decided to call Jack Emery. Before she could change her mind, she punched in the land line at Jack's Georgetown home. His voice was deep, pleasant sounding. Even friendly. Alice took a deep breath.

"Mr. Emery?"

"Speaking."

"Mr. Emery, for reasons you will soon hear about, I cannot tell you who I am right now. Please listen to me very carefully because I won't answer questions nor will I repeat what I'm about to tell you. I'm sure you've heard that Josh Carpenter had a near-fatal accident today. The assistant director, Mitchell Riley, will be stepping up to the plate and his first order is going to be to arrest Judge Easter, Attorney Liz Fox and you, Mr. Emery. I have four boxes of documents I'm willing to turn over to you about Riley's . . . shall we say, shady comings and goings.

"He's manufactured a case against the three of you. I might be wrong about this but I think the moment Josh Carpenter dies, the three of you will be arrested. I'm giving you a few hours' heads-up. I wish I could do more but I can't. I'm not some quack. If you agree, I will drop off four boxes of photocopied documents for you in Saint Theresa's cemetery. Meet me there at eight o'clock. I'll leave the boxes by the second statue on the way down the gravel road that leads to the main part of the cemetery. The main gates are closed at six o'clock, but there is a small walk-through gate a little to the south of the main gate. It's never locked. Will you pick up the boxes? Just say yes or no."

Stunned at what he'd just heard, Jack asked, "Why are you doing this?"

"I have my reasons. Yes or no, Mr. Emery?"

"Okay. How reliable is your . . . what's in the box? What about the judge and Lizzie Fox?"

"You can take it to the bank, Mr. Emery. Will you call the judge and Ms. Fox to alert them?"

Jack struggled with his thoughts. All he could think about was Nikki—and her arrival within hours. Her destination was the judge's farm in McLean. He felt sick to his stomach. "I would but I don't have the judge's phone number. I don't think I have Lizzie's, either."

"Do you have a pencil?"

"You have the judge's private, unlisted number?" Jack asked in awe.

"And her cell phone number. I have Ms. Fox's numbers, too. Are you ready to copy the numbers down?"

"I'm ready."

Alice rattled off the numbers. "Mr. Emery, if you don't pick up these boxes, this town could implode. I want your word as an officer of the court that you will pick up these boxes. I'm putting myself in great danger by doing this and I want your assurance that this isn't going to explode in my face."

"I'll do what you want. How do I get in touch with you if I need . . . if I have to talk to you?"

"This is a one-shot deal, Mr. Emery. I won't be calling you again. Do what you have to do. I'm going to hang up now. Call those women before you leave. Alert them before it's too late."

Alice scrambled out of the car, ran over to the darkest part of the lot and retched. All the coffee she'd consumed back at the house spewed forth.

Back on the road, she did her best to compute the driving time for Emery from Georgetown to Saint Theresa's. The best she could come up with was that she would have about a twenty-minute window of time to unload the boxes, stash her car, and find someplace to hide so she could make sure the boxes were picked up. Only then would she feel comfortable enough to have a nervous break-down.

Forty-five minutes later, Alice stashed the last box behind the huge statue. It was almost dark now. Exhausted, she parked her car farther down the road and then made her way back to the cemetery where she hid behind a headstone with a giant angel on top. She slid down against the back of the stone, willing herself to be calm. For one wild moment, she thought she was going to black out after she saw a pair of headlights approaching the walk-through gate. She waited, hardly daring to breathe, until she spotted Jack Emery. Then she relaxed and started to cry softly into the sleeve of her shirt.

It was out of her hands now. She hoped Jack Emery would know what to do with what she'd just given him.

Alice waited for a full fifteen minutes before she left the cemetery. She was still crying when she turned the key in the ignition. She cried all the way home.

Chapter 19

It wasn't until Jack had called the judge and Lizzie, and was back on the road, that he realized he couldn't return to Nikki's house in Georgetown. Parking on the street was his only option, and he was under constant surveillance. He couldn't take a chance of anyone seeing him carrying the boxes into the house.

Where should he go? He took his eyes off the road for a nanosecond to check the time on the dashboard clock. Nikki and the others would be landing soon at Reagan Airport. The pickup wasn't going to be a problem, but where to stash the women was now a monumental problem. His guts churned with fear as he fumbled with the special cell phone. Charles's voice was crystal clear on the other end. Jack never babbled; he babbled now. When he finally wound down and took a deep breath, Charles's questions came faster than bullets.

"I don't know who she is . . . was," Jack told him. "All I know is I have the files in the SUV and I'm driving around the District like some crazy fool. I can't go home. If Riley is the Second Coming of

J. Edgar, we're all in deep shit. Tell me you have a Plan B, Charles."

"I don't have a Plan B, Jack. This was foolproof. There was no way to anticipate Mr. Carpenter's accident. Are you sure Nellie can make it safely to the tunnels under Myra's house?"

"She said she could. She's taking all four cats. She's pissed, Charles. Did you ever talk to her when she was pissed? It's not pretty. I learned a whole new language. How long can she stay there?"

"As long as she has to stay. She knows the score. What about Miss Fox?"

"She didn't take it too well. She promised to vacate the premises immediately and said she would call me as soon as she was safe. She's got a story to tell, too. I had to admit I was one of you. It was the only way she would agree to cooperate. I am not worried about them, I'm worried about Nik and the others."

"Will you feel any better if I tell you I'm worried myself? I'm going to hang up now and get to work. Keep driving around until I call you back. Has there been an update on the director's condition?"

"He's on life support. Riley is at his bedside. I just heard that ten minutes ago."

"Stay alert, Jack."

"Yeah, right," Jack snorted as he snapped the cell phone shut. He tossed it on the passenger seat. He reached inside his jacket pocket for his regular cell phone to call Harry Wong. He didn't bother with a greeting. "Your guys at the airport, Harry?"

"Yeah. What's going on, Jack?"

Jack told Harry about the unidentified caller and the trip to the cemetery.

"I called Charles and he said I was to keep driving

around. Do I have to tell you how nervous I am? Hell, I don't even know if I was followed to the cemetery. I did everything I could to make sure I didn't have a tail but those Gold Shields are pretty good at this kind of shit. Your guys are going to have to drive the women around until Charles gets back to me. I'm thinking maybe he's going to tell us to go to Marie Lewellen's old house. You know that place. Myra owns it now and it's always ready for emergency use. I don't think the Feds know about it. Give your guys the address so if Charles okays it, they can head straight there. I don't like the idea that they're going to be out in the open. Some damn crazy dude can queer this up without even trying. They need to be out of sight. In case you haven't heard, Carpenter is on life support. Riley is standing vigil."

Harry's voice turned jittery. "Are we going to be able to keep the girls safe? This wasn't supposed to happen. The Brit said it was a piece of cake."

"Yeah, well, he was wrong. He admitted he doesn't have a Plan B. I guess it's up to you and me. Call me the minute the girls are in the van and on the road."

"You got it."

Jack's cell phone rang again when he pulled to a stop at a red light. Lizzie Fox. "Are you safe somewhere?" he asked.

"Yes, I am. No names, okay? If you're as smart as I think you are, sweetie, I'm going to give you a clue. You want to swing by and give a girl a lift?"

Jack bit down on his lower lip. "Yeah, sure."

"You know how I hate to exercise, right?"

"Yeah."

"Take your pick, there are two of them."

Jack's mind raced. "People or houses?"

"Now what do you think? Don't make me wait all night. I'm cranky and I don't do well when I get cranky. If you have what you say you have, it's a walk in the park for you. Any news?"

"The director is on life support. Riley is standing vigil. Just heard it on the radio. By the way, I'm driving an SUV. I'll slow down but won't come to a complete stop. Make a run for it." Jack broke the connection. He was surprised at how light the traffic was as he cruised down 14th Street. God, how he hated neon lighting.

Jack waited for a break in the traffic and made an illegal U-turn. It was probably one of the stupidest things he'd ever done, considering what he was carrying in his truck. Later he would think about his stupidity. Now he had to figure out where the hell Lizzie Fox was. Outside Mitch Riley's house? Hiding in the bushes? Inside Maggie Spritzer's apartment? Hiding in the entryway? What little he knew about Lizzie told him she'd go to Riley's house. She'd see something poetic in being right under his nose, plus he lived near her house . . . no need to exercise.

The encrypted cell phone rang. "Marie Lewellen's house."

Before Jack could blink the connection was broken. "I'm one step ahead of you, Charles," Jack said to himself.

Jack called Harry. "I was right, buddy, it's Marie Lewellen's. Get your ass over there right now so you can be a welcoming committee of one. I'm picking up our lawyer friend as soon as I can find her. I'll bring her to the house. Listen, I need to hang up because I have to pay attention to the street signs.

Call Charles and find out if there's anything we can do to spring our other friend. Both of those farms are going to be crawling with Feds come morning. Who's picking up Nik?"

"Will do. I dispatched two of my guys to pick them up. Guess this kind of explains why he wanted us back here, huh?"

Jack shuddered. "Yeah, I guess it does. I don't even want to think about what would have happened if we weren't on the scene. I sure would like to know who our benefactor is." Jack realized he was again talking to himself when Harry didn't offer up a response.

Jack exited Rock Creek Park and headed for the development where the assistant director of the FBI lived. He was right—all the houses were landscaped with old shrubbery, excellent for hiding. Not too many people burned their outside lights, he noticed when he turned the corner that led to Riley's house. It was totally dark. He slowed to a crawl, reaching over to unlock the passenger side door. He dimmed his lights.

She was in the SUV before he could blink, and was buckling her seat belt. "I do like a man who is punctual. Nice going, Emery. I wasn't sure if you got it or not. You prosecutors aren't as smart as us defense lawyers."

Jack took his eyes off the road for a second. "Stuff it, Lizzie. Who's on the run and who's driving this fine vehicle? I rest my case, Counselor."

"You know what, Jack? I'm never wrong."

"You know what, Lizzie? I'm never wrong, either. So, stick it in your ear and shut up. I need to think."

Lizzie ignored him. "What about the judge? Are

you just going to hang her out to dry? If you're afraid to go get her, tell me exactly where she is and I'll go."

Jack swerved to avoid a white van turning the corner without its signal lights flashing. "I thought I told you to shut up?"

"Do you see how I'm listening to you? Where are we going?"

Jack pulled up to a stop sign. "To a safe house. Look, I want to get the judge, too. She's a federal judge, Lizzie, she's got security. Both of those farmhouses are under surveillance and you damn well know it. She can hole up at Myra's for years and no one will know. Not an ideal situation but it's what we're dealing with. For now."

"The clock's ticking. How much time do we have until . . . ?"

"I don't know. Morning would be my best guess. Did you ever hear that sick people usually die in the early hours of the morning?"

"Yes, I've heard that. Josh Carpenter was a good man. I know him well. A real family man, dedicated to the Bureau, and he was fair. He always looked at both sides of everything. Old school. I hate to think what Riley will do to his beloved Bureau if he gets in."

"I never heard a bad word about Carpenter. We're almost there. Keep a sharp eye, Lizzie. I don't think I picked up any tails along the way but you never know. I need to stash this truck and use the one in the garage from here on in."

"Jack, look at me, read my lips. I don't give a hoot about your car, your truck or any of that other crap. I want to get the judge. *WE* need to get the judge."

"Okay, okay. I'll run it by the others. Will you shut up now so I can think?"

"You want me to be quiet? I can't be quiet. What kind of neighborhood is this? It looks familiar. I've seen these houses on television. I know I have. I have a photographic memory. Where the hell are we, Jack?"

"One more word and I'm going to kill you. K-I-L-L you!"

Lizzie clamped her lips together and turned to look out the window. She wasn't sure but she rather thought the man she was driving with meant every word he said.

Ten minutes later, Jack pressed the button to raise the windows. He slowed and then turned right into the driveway of Marie Lewellen's house. To him it would always be Marie's house. The garage door slid open. In the headlights, he could see Harry guiding him into the garage. The door closed just as he turned off the engine.

"I know whose house this is," Lizzie said. "That woman who shot the guy on the courthouse steps. Myra Rutledge paid her bail and she skipped out with her family. You blew that one, Jack. So is she a member of the Sisterhood?"

Jack didn't answer. He turned to Harry, who was standing next to his car window. "You hear anything?"

"They landed safe and sound. They're on the way. With no baggage to claim they should be here in forty minutes. I made coffee."

"Coffee?" Lizzie shrilled. "I need something stronger than coffee."

"Well, Counselor, we have that, too."

Lizzie hauled a backpack out of the SUV that looked like it weighed a hundred pounds while Harry backed a Dodge Dakota out of the opposite side of the garage. The SUV from Montana was now secure and out of sight.

In the neat tile kitchen, Lizzie headed straight for the coffeepot. She looked around to see where the liquor was. She opened one cabinet after another, marveling at the canned and boxed food lining the shelves. When she found a bottle of Old Grand-Dad she opened it and swigged straight from the bottle. Eyes watering, she swallowed the hot coffee. Tears rolled down her cheeks.

"Okay, I'm ready. Let's go, Jack."

Jack whirled around to see Lizzie Fox pointing a gun at his midsection. "What the hell are you doing?"

"I'm going to kill you if you don't move your ass. We're going to get the judge. Don't even think about it, Harry. Now move!"

"Lizzie . . . this is not . . ."

Lizzie slid back the hammer. The sound was so loud, Jack flinched. "I thought I told you to move. Back away, Harry. I'll shoot you right in the balls if you even breathe.

Hustle, honey, I'm not known for my patience."

Jack hustled.

Chapter 20

The 747 landed smoothly with hardly a jolt to the passengers on board. They clapped loudly to show their approval of the smooth landing after the long overseas flight.

The four hooded figures sitting in the back of the plane looked at one another. No one had to say a word. They were *home*. On American soil once again.

"Showtime!" Kathryn hissed between clenched teeth.

"We wait and are the last to disembark," Myra whispered. "Heads down, hands inside our robe sleeves. Someone will be waiting for us once we go through customs."

Nikki tightened the corded belt around her waist just to have something to do. All she could think about was seeing Jack. Would the meeting take place within the hour or would it be many hours? She could barely wait for him to wrap her in his arms and whisper all the words she had hungered to hear these last long months.

Annie was the first to stand up and adjust the

heavy robe. "It's midnight, you know. The witching hour. This is so exciting. Hurry, girls, there are people waiting to whisk us off to our next . . . gig. All right, Myra, our next assignment," she said, seeing the scowl on her lifelong friend's face.

Twenty minutes later the women shuffled down the aisle and were on their way out to the terminal.

Nikki led the way to customs, the others behind her. It was suddenly hard to breathe. Her gaze traveled everywhere, or as much as the hood to her robe would allow. No one said a word and it didn't look like her little group was drawing much attention. *Oh, Jack, where are you? I wish you were meeting us.*

Nikki stepped aside to allow Myra to be first in the customs line, passport in hand. Since they had nothing to declare, she hoped things would go fast and smoothly. The questions were simple, non-threatening, and then their passports were stamped and they were in the open. Waiting for them were two men from Harry Wong's dojo. No words were spoken. They simply followed the men who were holding a placard that said PADRE MESSINA.

The encrypted phone vibrated in one of the many pockets of Myra's robe. She looked around to see if anyone was watching her before she clicked it on, even though a monk with a cell phone was not an unusual sight. How strange, she thought. She mumbled a greeting, then she listened intently to the voice on the other end of the line. When she clicked the phone shut she started to shake. Kathryn reached for one of her arms, Nikki took the other.

"What's wrong?" Kathryn grumbled.

"A big problem."

"How big is big?" Annie chirped from under her hood.

"Jack has to find a way to snatch Nellie and her four cats who are at this moment hiding in the tunnels at my farm. It seems Mitchell Riley does indeed have a plan to frame Nellie and Lizzie Fox. Lizzie is with Jack at Marie Lewellen's house, which, by the way, is our final destination. We can't go to Nellie's now. In addition to that, the Fibbie director, Josh Carpenter, was involved in a near-fatal accident. He's on life support and not expected to last till morning. But, that isn't all. An anonymous woman called Jack and met him at Saint Theresa's cemetery earlier this evening and left four huge boxes of Mitchell Riley's files. Think shades of J. Edgar Hoover."

"The cemetery! Lordy, Lordy, this is just like in the movies," Annie said as she climbed into a battered burgundy-colored van. "What's our next move? Who is Marie Lewellen and why are we going to her house? Why am I out of the loop on these details? Shouldn't someone have told me about this person, whoever she is?"

"She shot and killed a man who killed her daughter. She did it right on the courthouse steps," Kathryn said with an edge to her voice.

"Well, I would have killed the son of a bitch myself. Is her house safe these days? Charles is big on safe houses. They always have safe houses in movies. That way everyone stays safe. Going right to the scene of a crime. How original."

Myra adjusted her hood as she looked at her friend. "I've decided that I really am going to kill you. Do not say another word, Annie. Not one word."

Nikki struggled to make sense of what she'd just heard. Something teased at her memory, but she couldn't bring it to the surface. "Did Charles say what was in the boxes?"

"No, he just said Jack had them," Myra said. "But I'll bet they are incriminating files about everyone in Washington. I'm sure there are extensive files on all of us. Who could hate the man enough to copy his files? Then you have to ask yourself how close that person is to Mr. Riley to even have access to those files. Charles seems to think Mr. Riley gets a seed of information and then creates a dastardly profile on the person he's interested in keeping for his files. In other words, a recipe for blackmail. Remember those infamous files J. Edgar held over everyone's head. People in this town were petrified of Hoover and his power. Charles is very concerned about what Riley may have on Nellie. Someone must have a very big hate on for that man. I wonder who it is," Myra whispered.

"It could be anyone close to him. Maybe a trusted agent who works under him. Since the files are in our possession I bet we could sell them to the highest bidder and make millions," Kathryn said.

"It has to be someone he trusts. Someone who is playing a devious game," Nikki said. "I've heard he's a womanizer. He had a fling . . ." Whatever else she was about to say came to a grinding halt when the driver of the van started to jabber in a foreign language into a cell phone. The passengers of the van turned mute as they huddled together.

The driver's companion turned toward the women and said, in accented but perfect English, "We will arrive at our destination in exactly one minute. This van will be backed into the garage and you will get out. We will then leave. You must be very quick. Do you understand?"

"Of course we understand, young man, we're not idiots. We're very agile for our age, aren't we?" Annie asked.

In another minute, Nikki was going to see Jack. She sucked in her breath in anticipation.

Their arrival went like clockwork. Annie leaped down from the truck like a gymnast, Myra right behind her. Kathryn went next, with Nikki being the last one out of the van. They were in the kitchen just as the door to the garage slammed downward.

Nikki and Jack looked at one another, neither moving, nor saying a word. Then the world tilted and they were in each other's arms in the suddenly empty kitchen. The kiss was soul burning.

When they finally drew apart, Nikki gasped. "Oh, Jack, I missed you so much. God, how I love you!"

Jack drew her to him again, too choked up to speak. She smelled like spring rain and summer sunshine even though she was disguised as a fat monk. He loved her more than life itself. He finally found his tongue to tell her so. "I can't let you go again, Nik. I just can't."

"I know, I know," Nikki whispered. "It's a good thing you're here. We would have walked right into a trap. What's going on? Has anything new happened? Who is picking up the others? There's something I'm missing in all of this, something I can't remember. I don't know. It's bothering me."

"Don't dwell on it and it will come to you. Some little thing will trigger it," was Jack's advice. "Look, don't be surprised when you see Lizzie Fox in the living room. She's got a story but I'll be damned if I know what it is. She's as ornery as ever." Linking their arms, they waltzed into the living room where the others were waiting for them.

The four huge cartons containing Mitchell Riley's files were piled up in the center of the living room. They looked intimidating to the four women staring at them.

Lizzie Fox waved airily from a chair by the fireplace. A clear indication that she wasn't *really* a part of the group.

Harry Wong looked Myra in the eye. "What about Yoko and the others?" His voice and demeanor were every bit as intimidating as the four boxes in the center of the room.

"Charles didn't say anything to me so I assume everything is all right," Myra said in her best motherly voice. "If changes have been made since we arrived, he hasn't told me. I'm thinking they will be joining us right here in Marie's house. Yoko will be fine, Harry."

Harry wasn't buying it. "She better be."

Myra did her best to hold Harry's bitter gaze. In the end she had to look away.

"That's what I thought. This is all screwed up," he said.

Jack finally released Nikki's arm and moved toward the martial arts expert. "Ease up, Harry. We're going to make this work. Right now you and I have to go get the judge." He looked over at Lizzie and mentally apologized for karate chopping her.

"I say we park out on the main road, hike in and

go in like we belong. I'm clean and so are you, Harry. We can say we're there to retrieve something or other. A letter, backdated by Myra, should cover our asses. I can get us in and out, Harry. I spent weeks up in a tree in the dead of winter with nothing to do but look around and watch."

Myra dithered as she tried to figure out what she could *give* Jack. "My Mercedes. The keys are in the kitchen drawer. The title to the car is in the top drawer of my little desk in the den. You can say I wanted you to have the car and now you need it because your car was stolen. Will that work for you, Jack?"

"It will have to work. Why am I picking the car up in the middle of the night?" Jack asked.

Myra pondered the question. "To avoid anyone seeing you and thinking you're tied into the vigilantes. I don't know for certain they aren't monitoring my farm but if they are, they're probably doing it from a distance, unlike the surveillance on Nellie's house. There's a lot to be said for being bold and brazen."

"Then when you leave the premises, burn rubber," Annie said.

"It's a dark night so that will work to your advantage," Myra told him. "The weatherman said it's supposed to rain before dawn. We heard that on the radio on the drive out here. The rain will be good cover. Hurry, Jack, Nellie is probably frightened out of her wits. We'll peruse these boxes while you're gone. Wait, wait. I have to do the letter." From the desk in the corner of the living room, Myra found paper and pen, scrawled a short note and dated it twelve months earlier.

Harry followed Jack, but reluctantly. He looked ferocious. In Kathryn's opinion, Jack looked even more ferocious.

"I'm hungry," Kathryn said once the men were out the door. "The food on the flight sucked."

"Fix us something, dear, if you don't mind," Myra said. "Be sure the coffee is strong. I'm going to call Charles. I hope we can discard these disguises. I'm very uncomfortable."

Nikki and Annie sat down cross-legged in the middle of the floor. Myra paced the living room as she spoke with Charles. When she finally clicked off the connection, the others looked at her expectantly.

"The girls will take a taxi here. That will appear normal. People do take taxis at the airport. This house has gone through the real estate market three different times. The current owner of record is a woman named Carmen Matis, who travels more than she's home. What that means is we're safe here. There's clothing upstairs in the closets. The pantry and the freezer, as well as the refrigerator, are stocked. The worst thing that can happen is we might have to sleep in shifts. Charles said Alexis's red bag is on the way and should arrive early tomorrow. He waived the signature on delivery so the driver will leave the package by the front door. That means we can discard our disguises as of right now."

"That makes me feel better," Annie said as she patted a cushion next to her for Myra. She started to tug on the latex molds on her feet and hands.

Kathryn came out from the kitchen with a platter of sandwiches and coffee and set it on the coffee table before she turned on the television set to

CNN. The women munched and sipped as they waited for word on the FBI director's medical condition. A clip of Mitchell Riley standing outside the ICU with his hands pressed against the glass was probably heart tugging to some but not to the four vigilantes.

"He's good-looking," Kathryn said, biting into her third sandwich.

"He's power hungry," Myra said.

"He's an asshole," Lizzie Fox said quietly from her chair next to the fireplace.

"He looks like he's crying but I think he's acting. He's probably praying for Mr. Carpenter to die so he can take over," Annie said.

The four women looked at Nikki to see what her opinion was. She frowned as she poked around inside one of the boxes. "It's not just Riley. There's something I can't quite put my finger on. I agree he looks like he's about to lose his best friend. I think these boxes hold the key to who he is and what he's all about. Who hates the AD enough to give Jack all this stuff? Who? And why Jack? What does that person stand to gain by whatever is in these boxes going public? If we can figure that out, we might get a bead on what's going on. It can't just be capturing us, though that would definitely give Riley a gold star. He'd be the Bureau's golden boy if he could haul us in. Lizzie, look alive here! Do you have any thoughts on the matter? Now's the time to share them."

Lizzie looked from one to the other. "Well . . ."

Annie can start copying them as soon as we finish a file. When we're finished, we'll have to find a way to get these files to Charles as soon as possible. If we have to charter a plane, then that's what we'll do."

Annie turned on the television, the sound level low. "In case there's a report on the director's condition," she said.

The time was 2:10 AM.

A light drizzle was falling when Jack parked the vehicle he'd driven from Marie Lewellen's house deep in the roadside shrubbery. "We hoof the rest of the way," he said, locking the car door. He tossed the keys to Harry. "Follow me and don't talk."

Harry nodded as he swatted at branches and brambles. The drizzle escalated to a steady, chilling, soaking rain. He cursed in three languages under his breath. Jack grinned as he yanked at the collar of his windbreaker.

Thirty minutes later, Jack held up his hand. "Okay, see that orange strip of plastic on that pine tree? That means we're on Pinewood property now. Who the hell knows if the Fibbies have any surveillance out here, so stay alert. That dumb bastard Riley wouldn't think twice about spending taxpayers' money to keep watch on this place even though he knows in his gut the vigilantes are long gone."

The two men walked for another ten minutes, their sneakers making squishing sounds on the pine-needle floor of the forest. "See that tree? I spent weeks up in that goddamn tree with binoculars, watching the comings and goings of those women. I had shifts of guys doing the same thing. I used up all my personal savings paying them, in the hopes of catching those women in the act. Nothing worked. Now, we climb the tree and then leap over the fence. Yeah, yeah, I know it's got the razor wire on it and it's electrified, so unless you want to fry your ass, jump high and wide. The branch is strong so it will hold your weight. You can do it, right, Harry?"

Harry growled something that sounded like, "Yeah, I can do it. The big question is, Can *you* do it?"

Jack shook his head to clear off the rain from his already-soaked head. He wished he'd worn a cap of some kind. "Guess you didn't hear me, Harry. I lived out here. I know these grounds like the back of my hand. I will say one thing: the minute I activate the electronic gates to drive Myra's Mercedes through, an alarm of some kind is going to go off and Riley will know within minutes so, like Annie said, we burn rubber once we leave here. I'm not going to be able to slow down so you head for the bushes and run to the car we came in and drive it out of here. You'll be in the clear. About five miles down the road there's an auto body shop. Pull in there and we'll mud up the license plates or switch them up. Whatever it takes to get clear of this place. Ready!"

Harry was already out on the limb and testing its weight.

"Drop, tuck in your legs and roll. Go!"

Harry was gone in the blink of an eye. Jack followed just as quickly. Together they raced across the compound to the kitchen door of Myra's house. It took only seconds to unlock the door and deactivate the alarm system.

With only a low-beam flashlight, Jack headed to the secret panel, opened it and together the two men ran down the ancient, moss-covered steps. Jack rang the bells at each intersection as he did his best to remember Myra and Nikki's instructions. At one point, he shouted out, "Judge Easter! Judge Easter! It's Jack Emery. Myra sent me to get you. Come out. We're by the cells. Hurry, Judge, we don't have much time."

A thin, reedy voice could be heard from far off. "Jack, is it really you?"

"It's me, Judge. C'mon, c'mon, hurry up."

"The cats are slowing me down," came the response. "They're heavy."

Jack shoved his finger under Harry's nose. "Go!"

Harry escorted her to Jack through one of the tunnels and she fell into Jack's arms. "What happened?" she gasped.

"There's no time to explain now. We have to get out of here, Judge. Are you okay?"

"I'm okay."

Harry hefted the two carriers, each with a pair of hissing, snarling cats, as the little parade made their way to the first floor of Pinewood.

There was a moment of indecision on Jack's part when he looked at the control panel that activated the security system. Arm it or not arm it? Did Riley have a line into the alarm company? Probably. He ignored it, opened the kitchen door and then locked it.

Outside in the hard, driving rain, Jack picked up the judge before she could say a word. Together they sprinted through the rain to the barn where the Mercedes was parked. Jack prayed the high-priced car's engine would turn over after being stored so long.

It did, without a squeal or a grind. Harry locked

the barn, stashed the cat carriers on the backseat and ran to hop in the car that was already moving. Jack pressed the code to the gates on the control panel. They swung open and he sailed through at ninety miles an hour. The gates closed just as Harry tumbled out of the car. The judge struggled to close the door as Jack sped down the road and out to the highway.

"What in the name of God is going on, Jack?" As Nellie talked, she tried to calm the cats who were meowing and fighting with each other in the plastic carriers.

"Not yet, Judge. I have to pay attention to the road. We're going to meet up with Harry shortly. This car is probably on someone's radar screen as I speak. I will tell you this: Myra, Annie, Nikki and Kathryn, along with Lizzie Fox, are at a safe house. That's where we're going. Alexis, Isabelle and Yoko should be arriving around dawn if their flight is on time."

"Is there any news on the director? He's a good man, Jack. I've had dinner with him many times. Mitchell Riley is a rogue agent. I can't believe no one has reeled him in. Now, it's too late."

"It's never too late, Judge." Jack slowed the car as he swerved to the right into the auto body shop. "Don't move, Judge. I'll be right back." He doused the headlights and ran to the rear of the car. Within two minutes, Jack had the license plate on the Mercedes off. Then he headed to the back apron where several battered cars waited to be restored. He worked quickly in the driving rain to remove the plate from one of the cars. He heard Harry before he saw him. The minute that license plate was attached to the Mercedes, Harry and Jack both proceeded to dirty up the pricey car with mud and debris they found at the end of the lot.

"Looks like a bubba set of wheels now. Yank off the hood ornament and we're in business." Jack obliged by tossing the hood ornament into the bushes alongside a broken-down fence. Five minutes later they were back on the road driving at a sedate sixty-five miles an hour, ten miles under the speed limit.

The clock on the console said it was 4:20 A.M. "Now we can talk, Judge."

Nikki closed the last box and shivered. "This is all so incredible. What are we going to do? Our cover as monks is blown, we have no plan of action, and to my way of thinking, we're sitting ducks. It's another way of saying we're back to square one. Safe house or not, I'm not feeling particularly safe right this minute. We need a plan of action here as our clocks are ticking. Loudly. C'mon girls, I need some input here."

Kathryn picked at some stray crumbs on the cake plate. "Plan? I think we need to kick some serious ass. The original mission was to come here and take out the assistant director of the FBI. The plan is still the same, isn't it? The man is framing the judge for his own personal gain. We came here to stop it. In that sense, nothing has changed. As sad as it is to say, the current director's terrible accident is a road bump in our plan. Or am I wrong?"

Lizzie Fox looked around at the group. "If my opinion counts, you're right, Kathryn. The only problem is this: the minute the Director was taken to the hospital, Riley stepped up and has so much security he can hardly draw a breath. If you have a plan to get through that cordon of agents I'd like to hear it."

Annie wiggled her rump on the floor, her eyes sparkling. "How about this idea? We photocopy a few of these files and messenger them to Mr. Riley along with a note signed by the vigilantes. You know, a Zorro-type letter, that kind of thing. Even the lowest of underlings will understand what he has in hand and make sure Riley gets it."

Kathryn tilted her head to the side as she stared at Annie. "Now that's a thought. One of us can go to a messenger service or one of the guys can do it. Great idea, Annie."

The others agreed, even Myra. Annie preened.

Lizzie Fox threw her head back and laughed. "Mitch will go nuts trying to figure out who the mole is. Unless, of course, it's someone he knows, and then it's not going to be pretty."

"Like who?" Myra asked. "Would it be someone who loves him or hates him?"

"Either or," Lizzie said smartly. "He not only tried to intimidate me, he outright threatened me. He said he would ruin me professionally, smear my reputation, make sure I'd be disbarred if I didn't help him frame the judge. He didn't use the word 'frame' but I got his message. You girls really have to get that bastard."

Nikki massaged her temples. "What's with that 'you girls' stuff? You're one of us now, Lizzie. There's something clicking around inside my head in regard to Riley, but I can't put my finger on it. It's making me crazy because I know it's important. Don't ask me how I know this, I just do."

"Always pay attention to your instincts, dear. Al-

ways. Isn't that right, Myra?" Annie asked cheerfully.
"Maybe we should think about Mr. Riley's wife.
Sometimes husbands and wives hate each other.
You did say Mr. Riley cheats on his wife. Being in
her position, I would think she might be afraid to
leave or to make waves with such a powerful man if
that is indeed the case."

Nikki's jaw dropped. For one wild, crazy moment, she thought she was going to black out.

"What? What's wrong?" Kathryn shouted.

Nikki blinked and then blinked again. She licked
at her dry lips. "That's it! That's what I couldn't remember. Annie, you are the marvel in 'marvelous.'"

If Annie had been a bird she would have flapped
her wings at Nikki's praise. Even Myra and the others looked impressed.

"Take a deep breath, dear," Myra said, patting
Nikki on the arm. "Tell us what it is you remember."

Nikki took a great, heaving breath. "Mrs. Riley
came to see me . . . I want to say at least two years
ago. She wanted a divorce but was scared out of
her wits. I think her name was Alice. Yes, yes, it was
Alice. I gave her my home phone number and told
her if for some reason she couldn't reach me, to
call you, Lizzie. I wrote your number on the back
of my business card along with my home phone
number. I never do that, give out my home number, but she was so agitated. She was afraid to make
a decision. I told her to go home, to think about it.
I told her what I thought she could expect in the
way of retaliation. Now that I think about it, I probably frightened her even more because she never
came back. She never called, either. I did see her
the day we were arraigned. It could be her."

"How strange," Lizzie said thoughtfully, a frown building on her face. "I had a phone call on my court-issued cell phone. I could hear breathing but no one said anything. I never get strange calls on the court cell. I don't know why but I had a bad feeling when that call came in. Knowing that bastard Riley like I do, you better find a way to get her someplace safe before you go after him. The man can cover up anything. Remember, he was willing to frame a federal judge to get his way."

Annie looked at Myra, her eyes wide.

Kathryn stood up. She smacked her clenched fist into her open palm. "Why don't we call her when Jack gets here so he can listen to her voice. If she's the one who delivered these boxes to the cemetery, we have to help her. People, are we out of our league here?"

"Momentarily, Kathryn," Myra said quietly. "I'm going to call Charles to see if he can make some . . . uh, arrangements in case Mrs. Riley turns out to be our informant. Does anyone know if there are children involved?"

"One daughter," Nikki said. "She was very concerned that he would find a way to take her child away from her."

Suddenly, a muted, alien sound could be heard. In a nanosecond Kathryn and Nikki had their Glocks in hand, the hammers pulled back. Both motioned for Annie, Lizzie and Myra to lie flat on their backs as they scrambled on their knees to the doorway leading to the kitchen. Nikki mouthed the words, *"On the count of three, I'll kick the door open. One, two, three!"* The door swung open as both Kathryn and Nikki hit their stance, their guns at navel level.

"Jack!"

"Judge!"

Nellie's hands went to her chest. "Dear God, I am too old for this! Girls, put those guns away!"

"Why didn't you call me?" Nikki shrilled. "We could have killed you! Do you hear me, Jack? We were going to fire first and ask questions later."

"Shhh, it's okay," Jack said, taking Nikki into his arms. He led her into the kitchen. He gently pried the gun out of her hand and laid it on the kitchen counter.

Nikki calmed down immediately. "We came up with something, Jack." She kissed him quickly and knew it was a mistake. She didn't want to move. What she wanted more than anything in the world was to drag him upstairs and into bed. She drew a deep breath, grinned and said, "Later."

"Promises, promises. Listen, Harry and I have to get out of these wet clothes. Tell me there's stuff upstairs. Please tell me that."

This was the Jack she loved, chattering teeth and all. "There's clothing upstairs. I'll send Harry up right away. Hurry, Jack, this is important."

"Any news on the director's condition?" Jack asked, looking down at his watch.

Nikki shook her head from side to side. She pushed open the swinging door that led to the living room and motioned for Harry to go upstairs.

Myra was still on the phone with Charles while the others whispered among themselves.

Nikki could feel her stomach muscles tighten up. It always happened like this right before they hit the streets for a mission. She jammed her hands into the pockets of her sweatpants and crossed her fingers the way she did when she was a kid.

Outside, a lightning bolt ripped across the sky, followed by an ominous roll of thunder. Nikki shivered as she sat down on the floor to hug her knees to her chest.

It was an omen, she was certain of it.

Chapter 22

The women sitting in the circle on the floor squirmed to make room for Jack and Harry when they thundered into the room. They quickly brought them up to date.

Jack's jaw dropped. "The wife! If you're right, the lady must have one kick-ass, hard-on hate for her husband. If it's true, we're going to be trampling in some heavy-duty crap here, ladies. If Mrs. Riley is the person who called and delivered these boxes, she's taking one hell of a chance. If she is the one, that has to mean Riley has a home office and keeps his files there. It makes sense. It also means there will be some kind of hidden, top-of-the-line security. If the plan is to go there, think again. You have to get the wife and kid out of there as quickly as possible. Start thinking!" Jack ordered.

"It's all we've been doing, Jack. We're coming up dry. It's almost five o'clock. Mrs. Riley will probably still be sleeping." Nikki looked at Jack and said, "Do you think there is a tap on their home phone number?"

"You can count on it."

"Then I have to call Maddie and have her go to my office to get Mrs. Riley's cell phone number. When she came to see me two years ago, she told me if I wanted to get in touch with her I was to call only that number. I think it's one of those track phones where you buy cards that are untraceable. I think. I'm not sure, Jack."

"If you're right, it makes sense that she would be cautious. You realize, of course, that the phones at your old firm and probably your office manager's home numbers are monitored. Riley wouldn't miss something like that. How do you propose getting to Maddie?"

"When Alexis and the others get here, we'll have her work some magic and we'll brazen it out. The red bag is due at first light, thanks to Charles. Unless you can think of something else. It's the weekend, Jack. Mrs. Riley may or may not be going to her shop. I have no idea what Maddie does on the weekends. We just might need these two days to come up with a workable plan."

"Will Mrs. Riley be safe?" Myra asked. "I worry about her daughter."

"As long as we don't go public, she'll be okay," Jack said. "Providing Mrs. Riley hasn't tipped her hand in some way to her scumbag husband. We have to snatch her and the kid and get them some-place safe before we go after Riley. Has there been an update on the director's condition?"

"They give updates at the top of the hour. The last one said Riley was keeping his vigil outside the ICU but the director's vital signs weren't good," Kathryn volunteered.

"Do you think we could get something to eat?" Harry asked as he paced the confines of the room.

"I'll make some more sandwiches. The girls should be here in about twenty minutes. They'll probably be hungry, too," Kathryn said. She turned in the doorway and called over her shoulder. "What about those two reporters? Let's figure out a way to use them before we squash them like bugs once and for all. Let's give some thought to making them work for us. For a change."

Myra reached over to pat Jack's hand. "You look worried. Do you know something you aren't telling us?"

Jack forgot all about being respectful of his elders. "Well, hell, yes, Myra, I'm worried. We're diddling with the goddamn FBI here." He looked over at Judge Easter, who was trying to comfort two of her cats. "Tell them, Judge, what happens when you mess with those guys."

"You don't want to know, Myra. Trust me. I cannot believe that man is trying to frame me. I hate to use a cliché but I wouldn't have a snowball's chance in hell of coming out whole if he presents what is in those boxes. No one will want to hear what I say, nor will anyone believe me. I could have Clarence Darrow representing me and I'd still go to prison. You can't win against people like that bottom-feeder Riley. I know what I'm talking about. I've seen fair, honest people fall under his sword, their lives and their families' lives in ruins."

Annie leaned over to put her arm around the judge's shoulder. "Well, guess what, Nellie, those people don't know *us*. We number ten now, with brain power to match. Kathryn was just saying we need to make those reporters work for us. I think we should let them do a full-court press while we stand back and watch. I believe it's called stirring the pot."

"That's a splendid idea, Annie, really splendid," Myra said. "I think that just might work."

Suddenly the air stirred. The women moved as one. Harry was out of the door so fast, they could only gasp.

"I think the rest of your little group is here," Jack said as he sprang up, gun drawn. He sprinted past the women who were hot on his heels.

The garage door slid up and then down as Alexis, Isabelle and Yoko hopped out of the battered van. Harry swung his love high in the air while the others smiled and Yoko squealed her delight.

Isabelle tripped over a bale of pink insulation but righted herself at the last moment. Nikki hugged both her and Alexis. "Things are moving fast," she whispered. "You guys must be tired. Go on upstairs and get into some comfortable clothes. Kathryn's fixing some sandwiches. We have all the time in the world right now. A few hours from now is up for grabs."

Thirty minutes later, the circle in the middle of the Lewellen house—and as Myra explained it, it would always be Marie Lewellen's house—widened considerably. Two of Nellie's cats curled into balls and were sleeping peacefully in the center of the circle. Myra held one of the other cats while the smallest one nestled in Nellie's lap.

The newest additions to the circle were quickly brought up to date.

"That's our situation now," Myra said briskly. "If any of you have anything to add, I'd like to hear what it is."

Alexis, Isabelle and Yoko simply shook their heads.

A moment later a bulletin flashed across the wide-screen television set. The group grew quiet as the early-morning anchor, in solemn tones, announced the death of Josh Carpenter, director of the FBI. A picture of Mitchell Riley, tears puddling in his eyes, his shoulders drooping, appeared on the screen. He waved away reporters who were intent on shoving a microphone into his face. His other hand swiped at tears in his eyes.

"God rest the man's soul," Nellie said, blessing herself. "This town won't realize what they had until Mitchell Riley tries stepping into Josh's shoes."

"He's heading home to shower and shave," Kathryn said. "My best guess is he will be back at the Bureau within ninety minutes, holding court. First, though, he'll go to his office to make it look good. Two hours tops. After that, the wife is fair game. In my opinion."

"Myra, call Charles again to find out where Mrs. Riley and her daughter can be taken so they're safe," Jack ordered. "We're going to have to move fast. If Riley assumes Mr. Carpenter's duties, Security will be on him and his family like white on rice. Things will be jumbled for the first couple of hours while everyone scurries around trying to figure out what to do. I'm thinking we have three to four hours to get them to safety. What do you think, Judge?"

Nellie looked grim. "What I think is Mrs. Riley and her daughter will be an afterthought. I'm sad to say, Mr. Riley will be so intent on his own PR and making nice for the cameras he won't even give his family a second thought. Someone, sooner or later, will ask him what he wants done in regard to his family. Mid- to late morning would be my guess," Nellie said.

"Crunch time, people," Annie said. "Everyone, move in closer."

The doors to Nikki Quinn's old law firm opened promptly at eight o'clock. Outside the main office door a tall, gum-chewing, wig-clad streetwalker, sporting a belly button ring and carrying her life in an oversize bag on her shoulder, paced up and down in stiletto heels. She looked like illegitimate sin packaged in a miniskirt and fishnet stockings. The belly button ring tinkled as she paced.

Madeline Barrows, Nikki's longtime office manager, keys in hand, stopped dead in her tracks to gawk at the gum-chewing mannequin wearing ten pounds of pancake makeup and another twenty pounds of costume jewelry. "Are . . . are you . . . uh . . . looking for someone?" Maddie asked carefully.

Kathryn looked around, wondering if her face would crack wide-open. "Nikki sent me. She needs some information. Quick, get me inside."

Maddie's plump hands fiddled with the keys in the lock. "Okay, okay, what does she need? Look, be careful what you say inside. I'm sure this place is bugged. Better yet, write it down. You look . . . like . . . uh . . ."

"A slut. I'm going to take that as a compliment," Kathryn said.

Upstairs, Maddie ushered Kathryn into her private office. Kathryn raised more than one set of eyebrows along the way. "Write, write," the plump

Maddie said. Kathryn scribbled furiously. Maddie read the note and immediately slid it into the shredder. She held up her hand to signal that Kathryn should wait while she got the information Nikki wanted. When she returned with a tiny scrap of paper, Kathryn stuffed it into her push-up bra that was all push-up with little content.

More scribbled notes followed.

Is Nikki okay?

Yes. She told me to hug you and to thank you and to tell you she thinks about you every day.

Give her my love and tell her the firm is making money hand over fist.

I'll tell her.

Does this have anything to do with what I heard on . . . Never mind, I don't want to know. I remember the day the lady in question came in here. She was white as a sheet. Scared out of her wits. Nikki calmed her down. She never came back. By the way, that's some outfit you're wearing. Bet you could cause a three-car traffic jam all on your own. Hurry, I don't want anyone asking any questions. Be careful.

You got it.

Kathryn looked around before she sashayed across the office and out the door to the steps. Maddie walked her down to the door and opened it for her. A battered van swerved into the lot. Kathryn waved and ran as fast as the stilettos would allow. She fell across the seat as the van careened out of the parking lot onto the main road. Her wig askew, Kathryn started to laugh and couldn't stop. "Guess my work here is done, gentlemen!"

The two men from Harry's dojo looked at one another as if to say, *"Crazy Americans, what do you expect?"*

In the process, they did ogle her and it did not go unnoticed by Kathryn, who just continued to laugh. A minute later, she whipped the encrypted phone out of the satchel on her shoulder. She rattled off the number of Alice Riley's track phone. Now, her work was really done. She leaned back and watched the scenery, drinking it up to store as a memory so when she returned to the mountaintop in Spain, she could pull it up and smile.

Back at the house on Orchard Drive, the women watched the news, hardly daring to breathe. And then Mitch Riley appeared on the wide screen as he was entering the hallowed doors of the Federal Bureau of Investigation.

"Okay, it's safe to call Alice Riley," Nikki said.

"Jack, you make the call and listen to her voice," Myra said. "If it's the same person who called you last night, we'll proceed from there."

Jack sucked in his breath and waited, his fingers drumming on top of one of the boxes. He listened intently to the soft voice on the other end of the line. "This is Alice Riley. Can I help you?" Jack closed his eyes, rolling the words around inside his head. He nodded. Nikki grabbed the phone and spoke rapidly.

"Mrs. Riley, this is Nikki Quinn. Please listen to me very carefully and I want you to trust me. Mrs. Riley, are you there?"

"Yes. Yes, I'm here. What's wrong? Why are you calling me? Did something happen to my daughter?

Please tell me that's not why you're calling," Alice Riley said, her voice rising shrilly.

"There's nothing wrong with your daughter. As far as I know she's safe. As to why I'm calling, I think you know why, Mrs. Riley. You called Jack Emery last night and delivered boxes of your husband's files to Saint Theresa's cemetery. With the director's passing, your husband is going to be stepping into his shoes. I don't know if that will be permanent or not but let's assume it is. Those files are . . . explosive and can ruin many lives. We have to make them known and that puts you in grave danger. We have to assume that's why you turned them over to Mr. Emery. I feel confident in saying your husband would not let another soul know he was collecting files like those in the boxes you turned over, and manufacturing evidence to hurt other people. I assume you knew all this when you decided to give up the files. Did you think beyond that, Mrs. Riley?"

"I didn't know what to do. He's a horrible man. When I realized he was going to ruin Judge Easter I knew I had to do something. I'm locked into this marriage and I'm afraid of my husband and what he can do to me. How did you know it was me, Miss Quinn?"

Nikki drew in her breath and let it out slowly. "I remembered the day you came to my office and how frightened and upset you were. When I heard about the files, I knew it had to be someone who really hated Riley. Your name popped into my mind. You gave me your track phone number and I put it in your file. In other words, dumb luck. Are you going into your shop today?"

"Yes," came the whispered reply.

"What about your daughter?"

"She's at a sleepover. My husband knows about it. Normally, I leave the store and pick her up around noon. She loves helping out in the storeroom."

"You're going to change your routine a little. Not enough to raise eyebrows, however. I want you to pick up your daughter and take her to work with you right now. We'll take it from there."

"When you say we'll take it from there, do you mean . . . *the vigilantes?*"

"Yes, Mrs. Riley, that's what I mean. I'm trusting you to do exactly what I'm telling you to do. Can I trust you?"

"Yes, you can trust me. How can I get in touch with you?"

"You can't. We'll be in touch with you. Hurry and do what I asked. I'll call you again midmorning."

"Just so you know, there's a GPS tracker on my car. My mechanic found it. When I want to go somewhere and not be followed, I take it off. You're scaring me, Miss Quinn."

"I'm sorry about that but you have reason to be scared. We'll take care of you if you do exactly what we tell you to do. Right now our primary goal is to get you and your daughter away safely. You are okay with that, aren't you?"

"Oh, yes. This is no way to live. It's been hard for all of us to live this pretend life. I'll open the shop early as soon as I pick up my daughter. I'll wait for your call."

"Be careful, Mrs. Riley," Nikki said before she broke the connection.

Nikki turned to the others. "Mrs. Riley is on-board. What's our next step?"

Chapter 23

Maggie Spritzer slipped on her backpack. Her destination on this fine Saturday morning was the Federal Bureau of Investigation. Her journalism antennae were vibrating, working at full frequency as she opened the door of the apartment, but her cell phone rang before she could close the door. She muttered a few choice words under her breath when she heard Ted's cell phone ring at the same time in the kitchen. If she answered her own phone, she wouldn't be able to hear what Ted was saying. Still, she didn't want to miss whoever was calling her. She flipped open the phone and said, "Spritzer." She tried to hear what Ted was saying as she listened to the voice in her ear. Stunned at what she was hearing and baffled at the strange tone she was hearing in Ted's voice, she started to shake. "How do I know this isn't some kind of trick?" she sputtered. One of the vigilantes calling *her* on a Saturday morning! *Unbelievable!*

"I don't have time for you to arrange for a voice analysis, Ms. Spritzer. This is Isabelle Flanders and I'm closer to you than you know. I want to talk to you. In person. If you call anyone or tell anyone I've called you, you don't get our story. What's it going to be?"

"Where? When?" Maggie strained to hear what Ted was saying. It seemed to her that he was parroting her exact words. A cold chill ran down her spine.

"I'll get back to you sometime late this morning. Just make sure you're available. There won't be a second opportunity. Are we clear on this?"

"Crystal, Ms. Flanders." Maggie flipped her cell shut, all the while trying her best to hear Ted's conversation. In an attempt to appear nonchalant, she dropped her backpack on the floor and started to rummage inside. Ted came out of the kitchen and looked at her with a blank expression. Maggie knew that look. He was onto something he didn't want her to know about, just as she didn't want him to know about the phone call she had just received.

"So, where are you going? I thought we agreed to picnic in the park today," Ted said, suspicion ringing in his voice.

Maggie zipped up her backpack and got to her feet. "That was before Josh Carpenter died. I'm going down to the Bureau to see if I can get some human interest interviews and some quotes on Riley, since he'll be the interim director. We can do a late-afternoon picnic, say around four or five. We can make it dinner with fried chicken. I'll call you. Where are you going?"

"You know I always check in with my snitches on Saturdays. I'll bum around for a while. Don't worry, I'll call you."

"You know what, Ted, you're so full of the dark stuff, your eyes are turning brown. Since when do you check in with your snitches on Saturdays? Since when, Ted? Never, that's when. Who just called you?" She jabbed at Ted's chest with a stubby finger whose nails were chewed to the quick. Ted stumbled backward.

"None of your business. Who just called *you?*"

"The other guy I'm going to be sleeping with if you don't tell me who just called *you.* That look on your face tells me you have a hot lead on something. Does it concern the vigilantes or the FBI? C'mon, Teddy, tell Maggie. Who called you?" she wheedled.

Ted flipped his roommate the bird as he bounded out of the apartment, Maggie hot on his heels. She longed to tag along behind Ted but she couldn't take the chance of missing Isabelle Flanders's phone call. Maybe she was finally going to get her Pulitzer.

So the vigilantes really were here in DC, if it wasn't some jokester pulling her journalistic leg. How weird was that? With the whole world watching them, how could those women possibly hope to go undetected? How did they get back into the country, assuming they were out of the country to begin with? And why did they call *her?* Her, of all people? For her fine journalistic mind? Pure bullshit! It had to be a trap of some kind. Did they think she was some rookie reporter? A black thought hit her full in the face. What if one of the other vigilantes was calling Ted at the same time? To what end? To pit them against each other? If not, then what?

On the boulevard, Maggie stepped off the curb, hailed a cab and gave the address of the Hoover Building. She leaned back and closed her eyes as she tried to figure out what her next move should be. Within minutes, she knew she'd goofed. She should have followed Ted. She wished now that she hadn't spilled her guts to Ted during their wild sex romp.

Mitchell Riley. Lizzie Fox. Judge Easter. The vigilantes. Ted's reluctance to tell her about his phone call. Jack Emery. Where the hell was Jack Emery, anyway? With his lady love, that's where—which meant here. Maggie felt proud of her insight, for all the good it was going to do her.

Maggie's down-and-dirty instincts kicked in full bore. She tapped the cab driver on the shoulder and said, "I changed my mind. Take me to Kalorama. I'll give you the address in a minute." The driver waited for a break in traffic and made an illegal U-turn just as Maggie rattled off Lizzie Fox's address.

Lizzie Fox was a place to start. The likelihood of Lizzie cooperating with her was so far-fetched she didn't even know why she was going to all this trouble, but in the past some very unlikely sources had come through when she least expected it. Always go with your gut, she told herself.

Lizzie Fox loved notoriety and getting her picture in the paper. No point in even trying to get close to Judge Easter or Mitch Riley. But, that didn't rule out Mitch Riley's wife. "So, Lizzie, I've got you in my sights. Let's see what you cough up for the cause," Maggie muttered under her breath.

As the taxi driver tooled along, Maggie perused the papers in her backpack, hoping there was something she'd overlooked that she could use to scare the lawyer. Zip. Nada. Diddly-squat.

Ten minutes later, the taxi pulled into a neatly

tended driveway. "I need you to wait for me," Maggie said. "I know the meter is running. Just wait for me."

Maggie looked at the small meadow of green in front of the house, the weed-free flowerbeds, the colorful pots of spring flowers on the porch. The hanging ferns looked full and green. Maggie took a moment to wonder if the Silver Fox had a gardener or a green thumb. She guffawed at the thought. She jabbed at the doorbell at the side of the door. Inside she could hear a musical chime. She rang the bell three more times before she headed for the back of the house. She waved to the taxi driver to indicate he should continue to wait.

The backyard had an intricate wooden fence for privacy and was just as neat and tidy as the front of the house. Bright and colorful furniture along with a very fancy grill sat on the patio. A huge matching umbrella shaded the entire area. Everything looked new and unused.

Maggie marched right up to the kitchen door and rang the bell as she peered into the kitchen. Neat and tidy. Early American décor. Shiny appliances. Ceramic-tile floor. Braided rug by the sink. It was obvious no one was home, but Maggie kept ringing the bell. Behind her she could hear tinkling sounds—wind chimes hanging from the shade trees that bordered the entire yard.

Was Lizzie Fox a homebody when she shed her legal persona at the end of the day? Maggie wondered if she would ever find out. At the last minute she stuck her card between the storm door and the main door. Like Lizzie Fox was really going to call her.

Back in the taxi, Maggie rummaged through her

papers again as she searched for Mitchell Riley's home address. She knew the place was close by. It was five minutes to ten when Maggie rattled off the address to the driver.

The members of the Sisterhood sat around the kitchen table, their eyes on the kitchen clock that hung over the doorway to the dining room. The huge red leather bag stood open in the middle of the floor. Propped up in the middle of the table was a picture of Alice Riley that had appeared in the Sunday Style section of the *Post* a year ago.

"I don't like this," Jack growled. He then addressed himself to Alexis. "You can't possibly make Nikki look like Alice Riley. No way, no how."

"Watch me," Alexis said. Jack watched as Alexis worked her magic on his beloved.

"Jack, dear, listen to me," Myra said. "Nikki will look enough like Mrs. Riley when Alexis is finished to pass muster. Yoko will be able to pass for her daughter. Please, you have to trust us. We know what we're doing."

"What if some of Riley's men show up to take the wife and kid someplace else? It is a possibility we can't overlook. You keep cutting things way too close to the wire to make me feel comfortable. I hate to remind you, Myra, but if you get caught this time there will not be anyone who can help you like the last time."

"We know that, Jack. We need to incapacitate Mr. Riley. Our window of time is very small. Try and relax."

Jack nodded, his eyes glued to the clock on the

wall. He didn't like any of this. Right now, right this very minute, Harry's men were driving Mrs. Riley and her daughter to a safe spot where Charles's people would take over. Just minutes ago a messenger had delivered a small packet containing the code to Mitchell Riley's alarm system, the special key to his home office door and the key to the front door of his house. Another of Harry's men in the guise of a mechanic was scheduled to drive Mrs. Riley's car to her home. Another car would be right behind to whisk both men back to Harry's dojo the moment they parked the car in the Riley driveway. They had all the bases covered, but if one of those bases imploded, the game was over. Jack knew it and the women knew it. And for all that, they were still confident.

It was 10:15 when Alexis stood back to view her handiwork. Jack felt his jaw drop. His eyebrows shot upward before his gaze went from Nikki and Yoko to the picture on the kitchen table. He had to admit he was hard-pressed to tell the difference.

"Time to go, girls," Kathryn said as she handed Nikki two huge, colorful shopping bags. Yoko carried a smaller bag.

"What's in the bag?" Jack asked.

"You don't want to know, dear," Annie said, patting him on the back. "Go, girls. Call if there's a problem. Harry is standing by. Remember now, quick and fast."

In the blink of an eye, Nikki and Yoko were gone. They piled into the car Jack had moved to the driveway on his arrival the night before. Within minutes they were on the way, Yoko strapped in and settled in the back, Nikki driving.

They drove in silence. Both women eyed the streets, the parked cars, looking for anything that might cause alarm.

It was 10:35 when Nikki did the first drive-by, circled the block, then pulled up behind Alice Riley's BMW. Armed with the key to the Rileys' front door, Nikki and Yoko walked up the steps as if they lived in the house. "I hope the people next door aren't the type who like to look out their windows to spy on their neighbors."

Inside the house, the two women went to work. They ran up the steps to the second floor, the huge shopping bags in their hands. Wearing skintight rubber gloves, they started pulling strips of pink fiberglass insulation out of the bags. They worked carefully, rubbing the fiberglass over every inch of Mitchell Riley's underwear, his socks, his dress shirts, his suits, his jogging clothes. When they finished with the clothing they headed for Riley's bathroom and proceeded to rub the fiberglass over the man's hairbrush, his toothbrush, and every towel and washcloth in the linen closet.

"How long will it take a surgeon to pick the fiberglass out of his body?" Yoko asked.

"Years!" Nikki giggled. "If the surgeons can figure out what it is. He'll be treated for every rash known to man before they figure it out. You did get his jockey shorts real good in the front, didn't you?" Yoko giggled and nodded. "It's going to be a very long time before Mr. Riley stands in front of a camera."

Downstairs, the women looked around. They froze in their tracks when the doorbell rang. Yoko ran to the window and peered through the miniblinds. "There's a taxi in front and Maggie Spritzer is standing at the door. What should we do?"

"Nothing. Head for the stairs. We need to get into Mitchell Riley's secret room. Don't make a sound," Nikki whispered.

Together, both women tiptoed through the house to a small hallway off the kitchen where a stairway led to Mitchell Riley's secret room. Nikki opened the door, still wearing the skintight rubber gloves. "Quick, Yoko, dismantle the computer, take the hard drive. It goes in this gym bag. I'll carry it. I can't think. What else are we supposed to take?"

"Nothing. Charles said it was up to us if we wanted to leave a 'gotcha' note. Your call, Nikki."

Nikki was already scribbling on an official-looking FBI notepad on the desk. She drew seven stick figures with their names underneath, then wrote carefully in block letters: WE HAVE ALL YOUR FILES. She signed the note with two words: The Vigilantes.

"What time is it, Nikki? The back doorbell is ringing."

"We're running overtime. Damn, the phone is ringing. If Spritzer's ringing the back doorbell we might be able to make it to the car if we run out the front door."

"It is not a good idea, Nikki. What if it is Mr. Riley on the phone? The GPS tracker on Mrs. Riley's car will show she's home. Why isn't she answering the phone? We can wait five minutes. Call Myra or Jack and tell them what's happening. Where is Harry? He should be doing something if he has us in his sights."

Both women rushed back up the stairs when they heard a commotion outside. Peeping through the miniblinds they could see the taxi driver going at it with a burly man in the middle of the road. They watched as Maggie Spritzer ran out to the road, her arms flailing in all directions.

Nikki looked down at her watch and then at Yoko. Yoko met her worried gaze. "We have to get out of here," she whispered.

"I know. We can exit through the back door and stand off to the side until we have a clear path to the car. The phone is ringing again. Quick, Nikki."

They left the house by the laundry room door and waited, squeezed between two evergreen shrubs that were in the shadows. They stood quietly, hardly daring to breathe. They could hear the phone start to ring again.

"I forgot to turn on the alarm," Yoko said. "We don't have time to go back in and arm it."

Nikki shrugged. She didn't know how she knew, but she knew the phone wouldn't ring again. Someone would be arriving at the house within minutes. "We can't wait. We have to make a run for it. Bail into the backseat and I'll get us out of here as fast as I can. I might be wrong about this but I think the big guy belongs to Harry, but just in case he's not— if Maggie or he look like they're coming our way— put your head down and whatever you do, don't open your mouth."

"Okay, go now, quick, Yoko!"

Chapter 24

Nikki and Yoko ran to the side of the house where a thick row of privet lined the walkway leading to the back door. They stepped as deep into the shrubbery as the branches would allow and still give them a view of what was taking place in the middle of the road. The sumo-like person was berating the angry cab driver, and Maggie Spritzer was still flailing her arms.

"We have to get out of here," Nikki said, her brow puckered in worry. "I really do hope that big guy is one of Harry's men."

"I think so. Harry has many such looking men working at his dojo."

Nikki poked her head out of the bushes. She did a halfhearted wave, hoping the big guy in the middle of the road would see her predicament and move things along. Within seconds he moved sideways, his huge body dwarfing Maggie Spritzer. The women made a run for it, barreling inside the SUV and locking the doors. In the time it took her heart to beat five times, Nikki had the ignition turned on and was racing down the driveway.

"Hey! Hey! That's Mrs. Riley! That's who I came to see! Get away from me, you big oaf. Hey, Mrs. Riley!" It was Maggie Spritzer's voice.

"Hold on, Yoko!" Nikki rounded the corner on two wheels. She slowed when she saw a car approaching at the far end of the street. She risked a glance in her rearview mirror to see the white and green taxi gaining on her. A sick feeling settled in the pit of her stomach. And then the heavens opened up and rain poured from the sky.

"Can I get off the floor now?" Yoko asked.

"No, not yet. Toss me that hat on the backseat." The minute it was in her hand, Nikki crunched it on her head. As a disguise it was worthless, as were the sunglasses she struggled to put on. Who wore sunglasses in the rain? She took them off and tossed them on the passenger seat just as a brown sedan passed her. Mitchell Riley! "Mitchell Riley just passed us, Yoko. You can get up now. Call Myra and tell her what happened."

Nikki's foot hit the pedal as she raced down one street after another. Fifteen minutes later, she was convinced she'd lost Maggie Spritzer. The rain continued to pour down so fast the streets were starting to flood.

"I have to pull over somewhere and take the license plate off this car. I'm sure Maggie copied down the number. I wouldn't put it past her to call the cops to run the plate. No one told us whose car this is. Any ideas, Yoko?"

"Tell me where we are. I will call Harry to bring a new plate. It is dangerous to drive in these weather conditions, Nikki."

Ahead, Nikki could barely make out a flashing neon sign: Spangle's Hot Dogs. She slowed to a crawl and turned into the parking lot. She was trembling from head to foot.

"Harry wants to know where we are. He will come immediately."

"Spangle's Hot Dogs. It's a chain, so there's more than one in the District, but I can't see any street signs. Tell him there's a carpet store on the right and it looks like a junk discount store is on the left. That might help him pinpoint it. Ask him how long it will take."

"Ten minutes. Everything with Harry is ten minutes. It could be thirty or forty or it could be five minutes. It is the best I can do, Nikki. Go through the drive-thru and get me a hot dog and an Orange Crush."

"How can you eat at a time like this? Do you have any idea what they put in hot dogs?"

"No and I do not want to know. Harry loves hot dogs."

"Say no more," Nikki said as she steered the big SUV through the narrow drive-thru.

"We got away. We lost Maggie Spritzer. This is a good thing, isn't it, Nikki?"

"For the moment. I sure would like to know what tipped off Mitchell Riley. I can't believe how close we cut it." Nikki accepted her change and the bag containing the hot dogs and the two Orange Crushes. She handed one to Yoko and bit into her own hot dog. It was good. "Jack loves hot dogs, too," she said, just to have something to say.

"Perhaps a second car in the Mitchell driveway alerted the authorities," Yoko said. "It is Saturday and Mrs. Riley works in her shop on Saturdays. We show up and the routine the neighbors are used to is challenged. Maggie, the cab driver and Harry's person were fighting in the middle of the road, directly in front of the Riley house. Those same neighbors might also consider that suspicious."

A moment later, Nikki's cell phone rang. Her mouth full of the hot dog, she mumbled something that passed for "hello." She listened and then said, "Okay."

"What? Something is wrong. What is it, Nikki?"

"There's been a change in plans. Since we're already in costume, so to speak, you and I are the ones who will meet up with Maggie Spritzer. If Harry shows up, we take him with us. Isabelle will be calling Maggie Spritzer to set up the meeting and then call us back."

"Did something happen?" Yoko asked.

"Guess so. You know how it is. Sometimes the less you know the better off you are. Damn, this is a good hot dog."

Nikki almost jumped out of her skin a minute later when she heard a knock on the car window.

"Harry!" Yoko called happily from the backseat. Now everything would be all right.

Across town at the Hoover Building, Mitchell Riley stormed into his office. He was like a wet cat whose tail had gotten caught in a live light socket. He cursed ripely as he slammed the door so hard the pencils danced across his desk. He'd given his beloved Bureau twenty-five years of his life but that wasn't good enough. Did they want his fucking blood? He flopped down on the special chair he'd purchased with his own money. To save the Bureau money. It was a damn good thing he happened to be in the men's room stall during a crucial whispered conversation at the urinals—he heard two hissing voices saying his days at the Bureau were numbered, that old Josh had named a successor and it wasn't him. Elias Cummings. Who the fuck was Elias Cummings? Not anyone in the Bureau. A goddamn outsider who undoubtedly didn't know his ass from his elbow.

Riley bounded upright and kicked the desk. He was pleased to see the dent in the bottom drawer of the ancient metal desk. "We'll see about that!" he snarled. His key ring found its way to his hand. He unlocked the top drawer and stared down at the contents. His eyes narrowed to slits when he bellowed at the top of his lungs. "Massey! Dennis! Lupinski! In my office! Now!"

The door blew open but the three agents remained outside. Everyone knew you didn't enter Riley's office unless you were invited. They waited but they didn't cross the threshold. Riley advanced on them, three stacks of papers in his hands. "Massey, pick Cornelia Easter up and don't let a lawyer get near her. I don't want to hear any shit about her being a judge. Your orders are to pick her up and hold her. Dennis, you get the sex queen. Pick up Lizzie Fox and hold her. No lawyer for her, either. Lupinski, partner up with Frank Peeps and bring in those two reporters from the *Post*. Everyone, listen up. Confiscate their cell phones. You're still standing here! Why is that, Dennis?"

"I'm on it, boss," the agent said, backing away from the open doorway. "Guess he heard the rumor," he muttered to no one in particular.

Riley barked again. "Tomaso, get your ass in here right now!"

A short, squat man with a receding hairline and

tortoise-shell-rimmed glasses appeared in the doorway. "Yeah, boss."

Riley scribbled his name on the papers in his hand, added the date and handed the sheaf of papers over to his agent. "Pick up Jack Emery and that squinty-eyed foreigner Harry Wong. Bring them in and don't let them near a lawyer. Confiscate their cell phones. Are you listening to me, Tomaso?"

"Yeah, boss, I hear you."

"Then get the hell out of here. Report in the moment you pick up those guys."

Riley marched over to the door and shouted to his secretary. His voice softened a little when he said, "Get the task force in here right now. I don't care what they're doing or where they are. Now means *NOW!*"

His secretary nodded. "You have a call on line 2. The agent said it was urgent."

"Now what?" Riley stormed as he stomped his way back to the desk. He pressed a button and picked up the phone. "This goddamn well better be urgent," he said by way of greeting. As he rummaged in his desk he listened with half an ear to the agent in charge of his family's security. Suddenly his head jerked upright. "What the hell are you telling me, Nolan? You lost my family? That better not be what you just told me."

Riley's face went from white to red to purple. "Listen to me, you asshole, if you can't keep track of one little one-hundred-pound woman and one little girl, then you don't belong working for the FBI. No, I cannot go out to the house. That's what you're there for. I have to run this Bureau. In case no one told you, Josh Carpenter died this morning. I have things to do.

"*What* strange car? *What* reporter are you talking about? *What* sumo wrestler? For Christ's sake, Nolan, I don't need this. If her car is still in the driveway then she's somewhere in the house. First you're telling me she went to the shop, then you're telling me she went to pick up my daughter, and now you tell me she drove off by herself in a strange car. You repeatedly called the house and no one answered the phone. Did I miss anything?"

"No, sir. That's it. There's no one in the house. Someone named Julia is running the store. Mrs. Riley's car with the GPS tracker is still in the driveway. What do you want me to do, sir?"

"Where are you right now, Nolan?" Riley had a splitting headache. He always got headaches when it rained. Of late he'd been getting headaches every damn day. He popped four aspirin and chewed them up, washing them down with yesterday's cold coffee that was still on his desk.

"Sitting on your front porch, sir. I didn't think it was right to stay in the house. I did search it and there's no one here. Nothing appears to be missing. There are no locked doors anywhere in the house."

Riley didn't want to ask the question but he asked it anyway. "Did you look in the basement?"

"I did, sir, and the utility room is neat and tidy. Your office seems okay, too. I didn't go in even though the door was open. Tell me what you want me to do, sir."

Riley thought he was going to barf. The aspirin spiraled upward and burned his throat. "I'll be right there."

"Sir! Sir, wait."

"What now, Nolan?" Riley snarled.

"I just want to give you a heads-up. Some garden center just delivered a load of manure and dumped it in your driveway. I checked the guy out and your wife ordered it yesterday along with all kinds of flowers. You'll have to park in the street."

"Yeah, yeah, yeah. I'll be there in thirty minutes."

His stomach churning, his head pounding, Mitchell Riley moved like a deadly tornado in his quest to get to the parking lot and his car. The door to his office couldn't be open. He had the only Medeco key. No one could make a copy. No one. How in hell had that happened?

Twenty-three minutes later, Riley screeched to a stop in front of his home. He looked at the pile of manure, at the mounds of flowers that were drooping in the heavy downpour. He wanted to run but he cautioned himself not to show his anxiety. He picked his way gingerly, his Brooks Brothers loafers slipping and sliding on the slick surface.

One minute he was upright, the next minute he was lying facedown in the pile of wet manure. "Fuck!" he cursed. Now he was going to have to take a shower. What the hell else could go wrong today?

Nolan reached out his hand, getting drenched in the bargain, to help his boss to his feet. He tugged a little too hard and the assistant director of the FBI went down again. This time, his face hit the smelly mound dead center. Nolan backed off when it looked like Riley was going to swing at him.

"Get the hell out of here, Nolan. I'll handle this."

The agent didn't need a second order. He ran to his car parked on the street and climbed in. He couldn't wait to get out of here. He hated this god-damn job. He had loved it before Riley took over, but he sure hated it now.

In spite of himself, Agent Nolan couldn't resist calling his fellow agents to regale them with the story of Riley's header into the manure pile. The final consensus among the agents: shit goes to shit.

Chapter 25

Mark Lane, former FBI agent, former FBI computer programmer and current private dick, stared out his window, wondering if the news he was hearing from a well-respected FBI agent would help or harm his friend Jack Emery. Mark had left the FBI several years ago because of his deep hatred for Mitchell Riley and what he was doing to the FBI to further his own agenda. From time to time the Bureau would still call on Mark when something went awry with one of the intricate computer programs he'd installed. It was his way of staying involved in Bureau business. He drew great pleasure in sending off astronomical bills that demanded payment within ten days. He still had friends in the Hoover Building, good friends to have dinner with or the occasional beer after work—sometimes in the middle of the night, since agents didn't work nine to five. Because they were good friends they kept Mark up to speed on Riley's latest doings.

Mark was bug-eyed as he broke the connection

on his cell phone. Jack was going to spin out of orbit! He hit SPEED DIAL and within seconds Jack Emery was on the line. "I got news, big guy. Where the hell are you? Wherever it is, Riley's agents are on the way to pick you up. Get out of your Dodge, buddy, and head for high ground."

"I'm safe, Mark. Wassup?"

"I just got a call from Linda Parker, one of the best agents at the Bureau. Riley sent agents out to pick up Judge Easter, Lizzie Fox, Spritzer, Robinson, you and Harry Wong. Is there any way you can warn them?"

"We're all in the same location, with the exception of Spritzer and Robinson, and I owe them squat. If you recall," Jack said, trying to give Mark a hint as to where he was, "you and I spent some time here when we had the flu. Let Riley have a go at those reporters. It's all bullshit, Mark. All that bastard's so-called evidence is manufactured. J. Edgar had nothing on this guy. He has reams of files that are now in our hands. You got anything else?"

"Well, hell, yes, Jack, I have more. Don't I always save the best for last? Seems there was a ton of manure dumped in Riley's driveway and he fell smack-dab into the middle of it, and it was raining. Do you have a visual on this one?"

In spite of himself, Jack burst out laughing. "Yep, that one is definitely going to be a keeper in my memory bank. You gearing up for Carpenter's funeral?"

"I'm going to pay my respects today. Josh Carpenter was one of the good guys. Hey, there's a rumor going around that someone named Elias Cummings is going to be taking over the Bureau and Riley is going to be out in the cold. I'll do a Google search on Cummings when I get off the phone. If the rumor is true, that might explain Riley's haste to bring in all you guys, make his case that all of you aided and abetted the vigilantes. Think about it, Jack."

"I have thought about it. Why else do you think I'm sitting where I'm sitting right now? We were one heartbeat ahead of him."

"Do you need any help, Jack?"

"See what you can find out about Spritzer and Robinson. Maggie's on the case big time. I have no clue what Ted is doing. Get back to me. Thanks, Mark. I owe you."

"You owe me your life, you crud," Mark said as he put a checkmark on his desk calendar under Jack's name. "By the way, I might be getting married. I'm going to be expecting one hell of a kick-ass present."

"No shit! Who would be dumb enough to marry you, Mark?"

"They're standing in line, big guy. When you taught me everything you knew, I paid attention, and now women drop at my feet. Her name is April Free and she looks like an angel."

All Jack could think of to say was to repeat his previous comment, "No shit!" before he closed his cell phone.

"Gather round, ladies, I have something to tell you," Jack said to the little group watching him.

Mitch Riley stood in his office, his eyes glazed as he tried to comprehend how seven stupid women could do what had just been done to him. As of this minute, he was the fucking acting director of the FBI. The fine print that said the position was only temporary didn't register with him at all. He knew in his gut he could still save this somehow. He *had* to save it or he was going to be flushed down a sewer. He didn't believe for a moment that it could happen. Not to him. He'd given his life to the FBI. He'd ruined his marriage for the Bureau.

Riley marched around his office, cow dung dripping from his clothing. How the hell did the damn vigilantes get into his house and where the fuck was that crazy wife of his? He walked over to look at the Medeco lock on the door. Not a scratch to be seen. How the hell did those damn vigilantes get a key? Even Alice didn't have a key. Was it possible Alice found the duplicate key? No way, the key was in the office, locked away in one of his desk drawers.

Riley knew his blood pressure had to be sky-high, so he sat down . . . and immediately regretted it. Now his chair would stink like cow shit. He hopped off but the damage was done. He needed to think. Think. A soothing shower almost always worked for him, enabling him to think, to plan, without intrusions. Maybe it would work today.

In the shower, cursing under his breath, Riley poured shampoo over his hair and body. He used a back scrubber and ran it over every inch of his body until his skin tingled. He rinsed off and did it again and then again. Satisfied that he'd washed the stink off himself, he climbed out of the shower and briskly towel-dried himself. He was about to brush his teeth when the house phone rang in the bathroom. "This better be good news," he muttered under his breath.

Fully expecting his wife to be on the other end of the phone, he snarled, "Alice, I need to talk to you."

Riley heard someone clearing his throat. "Sorry, boss, it's Tomaso. I wasn't able to pick up Jack Emery or Harry Wong. I went to both their homes, to Wong's dojo and no one has seen either one of them since the day before yesterday. What do you want me to do, boss?"

Riley clenched his teeth. "I want you to find their fucking asses and bring them to the Hoover Building. I don't want to see your face unless you have them on a leash. Do you hear me, Tomaso?"

"Yes, boss."

Riley was hopping around on one foot while he yanked at his jockey shorts when the phone rang again. This time it was Massey explaining that Judge Easter and her four cats were AWOL. He went on to explain that her bodyguard said she hadn't left the premises since he dropped her off on Friday evening after work. "He's right, boss, the keypad hasn't been activated, but I searched the house from top to bottom. The judge is gone."

Riley was still hopping around, trying to put one leg in his trousers while he juggled the phone on his shoulder. "Let me clue you in on something, Massey. If she's gone, then so are you. She's a fucking little old lady. She's probably hiding in the attic or the cellar. Goddamn it, find her. She didn't fly out of there. I want to see you and the judge in my office within the hour. Tell me you heard what I just said, Massey."

Massey sighed. "I heard you, boss."

Riley finished dressing. He marveled at how tingly he felt after his shower. Nothing like a good, hot shower after falling in a pile of cow dung. He proceeded to tie his tie. A Windsor knot. He loved Windsor knots. The phone rang again. He knew it was Dennis. Son of a fucking bitch! "Yeah!"

"It's Dennis, sir. Miss Fox isn't home. I called around to some of her hangouts and she hasn't been seen. The inside of the house is neat and tidy. Food in the fridge, bed made, no dirty laundry. No sign of her leaving in a hurry. She just isn't home. Her car is in the garage. It looks to me like she just went out, maybe with a friend, and is coming back. Do you want me to wait it out?"

"What the hell does that tell you, Dennis? For Christ's sake, you're a federal agent. If the car is in the garage, someone picked her up or else she walked away under her own power. She isn't coming back. If you were her and knew what was going on, would you go back? Do I have to think for you, too?"

"I just said that, sir. Except the part about her not coming back."

"Find her, Dennis. Your job is on the line. Bear that in mind."

Still tingling and admiring his Windsor knot, Riley slipped into his suit jacket. He peered into the long mirror hanging on the bedroom door. He thought he looked every inch the way the director of the Federal Bureau of Investigation should look.

Forgetting his immediate troubles for the moment, he looked around the room he'd once shared with his wife. It still looked the same—satin and lace and froufrous all over the place. When was the last time he'd had sex with his wife? At least four years, maybe longer. Since he really didn't care, he tossed the thought away. He picked up his keys and his cell phone that he was never without and jammed them into his pockets.

"Where the hell are you, Alice? When I find you, and I will find you, you are going to pay for this. I know you're behind this. For all I know you're now one of those damn vigilantes."

Riley was halfway down the stairs when his cell phone chirped in his pocket. He snapped off a greeting. It was Frank Peeps, who said he had spotted Maggie Spritzer in a taxi and was about to pick her up and take her to the Hoover Building. "Lupinski has Ted Robinson."

"You know what to do, Peeps. Don't let those two reporters talk to one another. I should be back in the office in forty minutes."

Riley looked out the window before he opened the door. It was still raining heavily. He reached for an umbrella in the stand by the front door. No sense in ruining two suits in one day. He eyed the huge pile of manure and decided to walk across the front lawn instead of trying to skirt the pile of dung. The worst thing that would happen was that his new wingtips would get wet.

Riley was about to get in his sedan when his neighbor, the guy he had often referred to as a half-blind, cranky curmudgeon, approached him with his golden retriever on a leash. "Good afternoon, Mr. Riley, or should I be calling you Director Riley?" he asked with a wide smile.

"Mr. Riley will do just fine," Riley said in what he hoped was a civil tone. He couldn't remember if he'd ever spoken to this guy or not. Maybe Alice had told him he was a cranky curmudgeon. Alice was the one who talked to the neighbors in the interest of promoting goodwill. He didn't give a good rat's ass about neighborly goodwill.

"Lots of activity at your house this morning, Mr. Riley, but then I guess you already know that. I wanted to call your office but Margaret said we shouldn't stick our noses into your business. I can't help but say we were both worried about your wife. She seemed . . . in such a rush when she got home. Then she left in a bigger rush with your daughter. We thought maybe something happened. Are they all right?"

"They're just fine. Thank you for your concern."

"Then there was this big fight out in the middle of the road. One of the biggest men I've ever seen was trying to intimidate a taxi driver and a young lady. The young lady ran after your wife as she was driving away in a strange car. A really big vehicle. Then the truck came with the manure. They just backed up and dumped it. Then it started to rain. One of your people arrived, at least Margaret said it was one of your people. She sees better than I do. Margaret said she's seen him on other occasions."

Riley digested all the information. A big man. A taxi driver and a young woman. He thanked his neighbor, smiled at the dog, who started to bark, and climbed in his car where he called his secretary. "Tell Morgan to find out which taxi company had a car in my neighborhood this morning. Bring in the driver. I want to know who his fare was. I should be in the office in forty minutes, maybe sooner, depending on this damn rain."

Riley broke every driving law in the book in his haste to reach the Hoover Building.

He was still marveling at the way his body was tingling from his invigorating shower. He took a moment to wonder why his armpits were itching. The deodorant must be old, he decided.

Chapter 26

Nikki looked into the rearview mirror to see Harry and Yoko holding hands. She wished Jack was here with her. Would they ever truly be together? Was a family in their future? The house with the white picket fence, the three kids, the dog and two cats? For a moment tears blurred her vision because she knew that particular dream wasn't going to happen anytime soon. Maybe never. She swiped at her wet eyes with the back of her hand.

"Turn here, park and let's talk this out before we make a move," Harry said. "I want to go on record as saying I think this is one dumb move."

Nikki pulled the SUV into the lot by the Vietnam Memorial. She stretched her neck to look at The Wall. Chills ran up and down her spine. The same thing had happened when she came here the first time with Jack. Both of them had walked away with tears streaming down their cheeks.

Nikki parked the car and turned off the engine. She was relieved that Harry had screwed on a new license plate to the SUV. By now someone, somewhere, had run the plates that were on it while it was parked in Riley's driveway. She squirmed around to look at Yoko and Harry. They were still holding hands.

Harry met her gaze. "What? We just go up and snatch her? Right in public? Don't you think someone might notice? I don't like this."

"You already said that, Harry. Our orders are to pick her up. You're our backup. Yoko and I will do whatever we have to do. I need to make sure you understand that."

Harry mumbled something neither woman could understand. He was probably cursing in his own language, Nikki thought. He did that a lot.

"I don't think a snatch per se is what's going to happen. We're simply going to invite Maggie to join us in this fine vehicle. To give her our story. Knowing what I know about her, she'll come willingly. With reporters, it's all about the scoop, the byline, getting your story *above* the fold. Maggie Spritzer lives for that. So does Ted but in a different way. Ted is pretty much by the book, while Maggie flies by the seat of her pants, and that's not necessarily a bad thing.

"When Isabelle called Spritzer to set up this meet, Maggie told her she's traveling in a taxi, a green and white one, so she'll be easy to spot. I think I see the taxi now, in row four. I'm going to move this rig, which will put me as close to the taxi as I'm comfortable with. Yoko goes with me. Harry, you stay in the truck, and keep us in your sights. The rain is in our favor so keep a sharp eye on all of us."

Anyone watching would see a mother and a little girl climb out of the SUV. Ignoring Nikki's orders, Harry got out of the truck and trailed behind them, a father bringing up the rear, to those watching.

Inside the taxi, whose meter was still ticking, Maggie watched closely, then slid out of the cab when she saw the trio approach the green and white taxi. She pulled the hood of her windbreaker over her head and advanced a few steps. She narrowed her gaze. It was all she could do to quell the gasp of shock she was feeling. *Mrs. Riley and her daughter.* Then she squinted to see through the rain. *Harry Wong.* Her adrenaline shot up to an all-time high, the closer she got to them. So high, she felt lightheaded. *Mrs. Riley, my ass.* She stopped in her tracks when Nikki said, "If you want your story, you have to come with me, Maggie."

"I knew it! I knew it! You were at the Riley house. You fooled them all. I'll be damned. How do I know I can trust you?"

"You don't," Nikki said. "It's your choice. We've been standing here too long already. Make up your mind, Maggie. If you need an incentive, one of us is talking to Ted right now, this very minute. You know what they say, the first one there gets the scoop."

"Okay, okay. Let me get my backpack."

As Nikki turned to walk away, she saw a man appear from between two parked cars. She heard a voice address Maggie.

"Ms. Spritzer, Frank Peeps, FBI. I need to talk to you." A badge flashed.

Maggie was stunned. A show of bravado was definitely called for. "So talk," she said as she grappled with her backpack while she rummaged for money to pay the driver. Suddenly she felt sick to her stomach. She whirled around to see the trio; they were just about out of sight, safe for the moment.

"Who were you talking to, Ms. Spritzer?"

"You writing a book or something?" Her heart was beating so fast Maggie thought it was going to pop right up her throat and out her mouth.

"I asked you a question, Ms. Spritzer. You don't want to mess with the FBI. What are you doing here and who were those people?"

Maggie weighed her options, which were no options at all. She shifted the backpack on her shoulders for a more comfortable fit. "Look, you tadpole, I'm here to do a story on the Memorial and how people come out to see it rain, snow or shine. How the hell do I know who those people are? They asked for directions to the Lincoln Memorial. In other words, tadpole, they're tourists. Go ask them yourself. Do I look like an information operator?"

"Director Riley wants to talk to you. I'm to take you in." It was hard not to miss the sarcasm in the agent's voice. "If you cause a disturbance, I'll have to cuff you and make a scene. What's it going to be?"

Maggie risked a glance at the SUV that was backing out of its parking spot. This was where the rubber met the road. She made an instant decision. The vigilantes would know she'd tried to cooperate. If she kept her mouth shut, they might give her another chance. She turned her back and with her right hand behind her, made fluttering motions to indicate to the trio that they should move out *NOW*. "Sure, why not? It beats standing out here in the rain."

As Nikki swerved out onto the boulevard, Harry

leaned forward. "What the hell happened back there?"

"As unbelievable as it sounds, I think Maggie Spritzer just saved our asses," Nikki said through clenched teeth. "Yoko, call the house and alert the others. I have to pay attention to the road and the traffic. Tell them we should be home in about thirty minutes."

Harry continued to mumble and mutter in the backseat. Yoko told him to shut up in no uncertain terms. In English. While she punched in the numbers, she turned to look at her love and said, "This is why we do what we do and you do what you do. I still love you so do not worry about it." Harry continued to mutter and mumble.

The steady, hard-driving rain continued as Nikki maneuvered the SUV through the heavy Washington traffic.

When Yoko ended the call, she leaned forward. "There is other news. Jack's friend Mark called him and said Mr. Riley also sent out agents to pick up the judge, Lizzie, Ted, Jack and Harry. They came up dry except for Maggie. I told them what just happened. Myra said she didn't know if Ted Robinson was picked up or not. Jack was going to call him to give him a heads-up. That is all I know."

"Five more minutes and we're home," Nikki said. In the rearview mirror she could see Harry's grim face. He was not holding Yoko's hand.

The task force was waiting outside Riley's office. He walked right past them, his face stormy, and then doubled back. "I want you all to spend the next hour polishing up your excuses because I am in no mood to listen to anything negative. I want written reports. In your hands, then to my hands. I want facts. I want to know how that house or cabin, whatever the hell it is, in Montana came to Jack Emery. How can he afford a vacation home? I think it's just a tad too convenient for him to be fishing, or whatever the hell he was doing out there in the wilds, when all this crap went down. That whole scenario smells big time. I want to know how those vigilantes got back into this country. If you can't give me information that I can use I want your resignations on my desk. You've had ten fucking months with no results."

Riley stomped off, glad he was out of their sight so he could scratch his various itches. He looked in both conference rooms, trying to decide who he wanted to tackle first, Robinson or Spritzer. He remembered the single-digit salute the female reporter had offered up to him when he'd had her hauled in for questioning ten months ago. He scratched his testicles and was instantly sorry. Now they itched even worse. Maybe the water company had put new chemicals in the water or something. Spritzer first, he decided. If there was one thing he excelled at, it was intimidating women. He banged open the door, his expression murderous.

"Good afternoon, Ms. Spritzer."

It took a lot to intimidate Maggie Spritzer and this clown with the red face certainly wasn't going to cow her. "What's good about it, Mr. Riley? It's pouring rain. I'm soaked to the skin. You haul me in here and don't even tell me why. You take my cell phone and my backpack. I want a lawyer."

Riley tried to be unobtrusive as he scratched his

backside. "Did you do something that requires the services of an attorney?"

"No, that's why I want one. This is the second time I'm asking for an attorney. Why did you bring me here?"

Riley looked down at Agent Nolan's report. "What were you doing at my home this morning and why were you fighting with a big man in the middle of the road?"

Maggie decided to bluster. "Is that what this is all about? I went out to your house to interview your wife but she left before I could talk to her. Some big sumo wrestler type picked a fight with my taxi driver and I was trying to break it up. My driver didn't speak English very well. The big guy was jabbering in another language, too. It was like a circus. Now can I go?"

"Not yet. What were you doing at the Vietnam Memorial?"

"Since I blew the interview with your wife I decided to do the Memorial. You know how people go there rain, snow or shine. It's called human interest. I want a lawyer. That's three times I'm asking for a lawyer. My paper isn't going to like this."

Riley needed to scratch his crotch so bad he thought he was going to scream. He turned around, his hand digging into his testicles. The temporary relief was so exquisite he thought he would swoon. He turned back around to face the reporter. "Who were you talking to in the parking lot?"

The lie came to her lips at the speed of light. "Some family who was asking directions to the Lincoln Memorial. I didn't ask their names. I want a lawyer. This is my fourth request."

"Yes, I know. All in good time." Riley reached up to scratch his neck.

"What's wrong with your face? Looks to me like an allergic reaction to something. Maybe it's hives. Stress will do that to you. I know because I did an article on hives and the people who get them. Stress. Stress can kill you. You should think about practicing yoga. It's all about communing with yourself and serenity. I can see this is probably a stressful job for you. Denying me my right to have an attorney present only adds to the stress factor," Maggie babbled. She was so out of breath from babbling that she had to gulp for air.

In spite of himself, Riley's hand went to his face. It felt hot to his touch. He wished there was a mirror in the room. "Don't worry about my face or yoga or your attorney. We're talking about you. I think you're lying. Because I think you're lying, I'm going to let you sit in here to think about all the lies you just told me. I want you to think about what I can do to you. Now I'm going to talk to your partner. For both your sakes I hope his story matches yours."

"Wait just a damn minute. My partner does things differently than I do. He has his snitches, his sources, just like I have mine. We work on different things. Just because we sleep together doesn't mean we work together. We're competitors. This is my fifth request for a lawyer."

"So you say." He had to get out of here and into the men's room before he went out of his mind. "I'll be back," he said ominously.

Maggie waited until the director's back was turned before she offered up her famous single-digit salute. "Screw you, Riley."

Chapter 27

Mitch Riley raced into the men's room and stared at himself in the mirror. What the hell was wrong with him? He dug at himself, scratching as fast as he could with both hands while he watched his left eye swell shut. He stopped scratching long enough to try to pull his eyelid upward. "Fuck," he cursed as he left the room, still scratching, to run to the gym where he ripped off his clothes and headed for the shower. The lukewarm water felt like a balm to his red, itchy body. He lathered up and rinsed, experiencing moments of relief, and then the itch returned immediately. Christ Almighty, he couldn't stay in here forever. He had to run the FBI. What the hell was happening to him?

Ten minutes later, Riley stepped out of the shower, dressed and left the gym, still itching. He did his best to ignore the agents who stared at him as he made his way to the room where Ted Robinson was waiting for him. He heard someone say, "Maybe he has poison ivy?" Yeah, yeah, that's probably what it was. From the manure in his driveway.

Well, they should be able to give him a shot for something like that. Maybe some pills. A lot of pills.

Ted Robinson gasped when Riley slammed into the room. On his worst day, Godzilla looked better. He cowered in his seat when Riley snarled, "Talk to me, Robinson, and don't leave anything out. We have your sex partner down the hall, and she's singing like the proverbial canary."

Maggie singing like a canary? The Maggie he knew could not even sing off-key, much less like a canary. Lie number one. "That's your problem, Riley. She sounds like a frog when she sings. What do you want? Why'd you drag me in here? I think I want a lawyer before everyone starts getting pissy. Are you sure you're all right, Mr. Riley? Your face looks like . . . like it's getting *bigger.*" Ted tried to lean farther back in his chair but there was no place else to go. He could smell Riley's coffee breath, that's how close he was.

Riley wanted to rip the skin off his body. It took every ounce of willpower not to scratch. "I told you to talk. As you can see, I'm not in a very good mood."

"Yeah, well, I said I wanted a lawyer. You gonna get the rubber hoses out or what? I thought you FBI types were civilized. You know, the college degrees, the suits, the shades, the badges, the whole ball of wax. What is it you want?"

"I want to know where the vigilantes are. You and your girlfriend know something and I want to know what it is, and I want to know *now!*"

"Yeah, well I want to know a lot of things myself, Mr. Riley. Like what the hell is wrong with you? Are you contagious? I don't want you breathing on me. God, you look like you're going to explode!" To make his point, Ted leaped off his chair and backed himself into a corner as he bellowed at the top of his lungs. "Get me the hell out of here! This guy is going to explode!"

Riley couldn't take it one more second. He pressed a button on the wall. "I need a doctor right now! Send someone in here *STAT!*"

To Ted, he said, "You're here until I see a doctor. One wrong move and I'll toss you in the goddamn shredder all by myself. Remember this: whichever one of you talks first gets the lawyer." Riley was afraid he was going to black out any second. It was all he could do to stand erect. Scratching himself from head to toe wasn't helping.

"Are you shitting me, Riley? You drag me in here because I started a stupid *rumor*? The last time I checked this was a free country. A rumor is a rumor. So, okay, I'm sorry I said the vigilantes were back in town. It was a slow news day. I wanted to get a rise out of everyone. Hey, man, it worked. Everyone has been chasing their tails for a week now. It got reams of press and hours on television. That's what it's all about, you know."

Riley did his best to keep his wits about him. A rumor! This guy was saying he started a goddamn *rumor*? Then who broke into his home office and left the message with the seven stick figures? Alice? She was too stupid to pull off something like that. "You're lying," he managed to gasp.

"Well, back then I was but now it's not a lie. They *are* here. They called me. Personally. They wanted to set up a meeting. You guys blew it when you hauled me in here. I was on my way to the meeting. *They're here, Riley!*" Ted sing-songed. "And I bet you my next week's salary, they got to you. Think about it, Director. Did you have . . . this allergic reaction or rash thing, or whatever it is you have, *before*? It just cropped up, right? It ain't poison ivy, either. I get poison ivy so I know what it looks like. Blame the vigilantes and then blame yourself for hauling me in here. Can I go now?"

"Shut up, Robinson. You know damn well I can hold you for seventy-two hours. Let me get this straight. You started a rumor the vigilantes were in town because it was a slow news day and then by magic, the vigilantes are suddenly *here*? Is that what you want me to believe?" Where the hell was the goddamn doctor?

"Well, yeah, that's about it. Incredible timing, wouldn't you say? Who knew I had such amazing power?" Ted smirked as he threw his hands in the air.

The door opened suddenly and a potbellied little man with gray hair entered carrying a bulging medical bag.

Ted went into his act, screaming and yelling that Riley had the plague or maybe worse and he wanted out of the room. "I want a mask. Give me some kind of shot of something. I want a lawyer," he bellowed as an afterthought.

Two agents appeared out of nowhere. They did their best to avoid looking at Director Riley, who was digging at his beet red face and neck.

"I've called for an ambulance, Director Riley. I'm going to need to run some tests that can only be done in the hospital," the doctor said.

Riley stopped scratching long enough to issue orders. He fought with himself, with every ounce of willpower he had, not to black out. To the female agent, he said, "File the press releases on my desk immediately." To the male agent he said, "Lock this guy up and don't let him near a lawyer until I say so. The same goes for Spritzer. Where's the task force?"

The two agents looked everywhere but at Riley as they shuffled from one foot to another. Finally, the female agent said, "Their resignations are on your desk. They cleaned out their desks and are out of the building."

Riley wanted to cry but his eyes felt like they were glued shut. It was a relief when he was helped onto a gurney and wheeled out of the office.

Thirty-six hours later, Maggie Spritzer and Ted Robinson walked out of the Hoover Building to a bright, sunny day. Maggie turned around and offered up her single-digit salute. Ted grinned and did the same thing. They walked along, savoring the bright spring weather, their destination the *Post*, where Maggie was welcomed with open arms while their colleagues shied away from Ted.

Within minutes they learned that the acting director was in the hospital with a mystery illness that defied diagnosis. That was the good news. The bad news was Riley was conducting business as usual from his hospital room. They further learned that Judge Cornelia Easter, Attorney Elizabeth Fox, District Attorney Jack Emery and Harry Wong, a martial arts expert, were fugitives, with warrants issued for their arrest.

"We're the only paper in the District that didn't run with that story. We didn't print a word based on your calls, guys. I hope I'm not going to regret it," the city editor said in a voice that was somewhere between a purr and a snarl. "Tell me something I can print."

Maggie ignored her boss. "Did I get any calls while I was an unwilling guest of the FBI?" she asked casually as she settled herself in front of her computer. "I couldn't believe they wanted to keep my cell phone. I had to threaten them with the paper and my First Amendment rights. They finally turned it over."

Maggie rolled her chair backward until she was facing Ted's desk. Her voice was an angry hiss. "I can't believe you told Riley the vigilantes called you. I denied it. Why in the hell did you do that? You blew it and if they call me again, I'm not sharing. Jerk," she said before she rolled back to her desk.

Ted rolled his chair after her. "Are you kidding? Did you see that son of a bitch? I thought he was going to breathe on me and I was going to get what he had. Has," he corrected himself. "I didn't sell you out. I spoke only for myself. If the situation was reversed, I'd share with you. I even told them I started the rumor. It's not my fault they didn't believe me. Come on, Maggie, tell me you'll share."

Maggie gaped at her partner. "In a pig's eye you would. Go sell that to someone who cares. If the vigilantes call me again, I'm going to tell them you gave it up. Jerk!" she repeated.

Ted rolled his chair back to his desk. He felt lower than a snake's belly when he turned on his computer to bring up the front pages of the four newspapers that were the *Post*'s competition.

After he read the four articles he snorted in disgust and he rewrote the articles in his head. He could write circles around those guys. At best what he was reading was a slapdash job. He hoped that Judge Easter, Lizzie Fox, Jack and Harry Wong would sue the Bureau and all the papers along with the reporters who'd written the stories. Like Judge Easter or Lizzie would really put their professions on the line for the vigilantes. Jack, maybe. Nah, Jack had ethics. He realized he didn't know enough about Harry Wong to form an opinion as to what he would or wouldn't do.

Ted realized he didn't always think like this. The thirty-six hours in Bureau custody might have something to do with his switch up. Then again, maybe he was finally becoming realistic. It still baffled him that the vigilantes were in town. How weird was that? He started a rumor and voila! They appear. "I must be psychic," he muttered.

Walking past his desk, Maggie heard him. "You're not psychic. You're an asshole."

Ted's head jerked upright. "Where are you going?"

"Since when do I have to tell you where I'm going? I have to pee. Is that okay with you?"

"Do you need your backpack to go to the bathroom?" Ted asked suspiciously.

Maggie rolled her eyes. "Well, yeahhh," she drawled.

"You need to stop lying. Your nose is going to grow a foot long." Ted sniffed but he didn't take his eyes off his lover's retreating back.

Maggie knew he was watching her so she offered up her middle finger. Lately, she seemed to be doing that a lot.

Inside the bathroom, Maggie sat down on a stool to contemplate her options. She wished there was a way to call the vigilantes. But that was impossible

so she had to wait for them to contact her again.
And, she needed to come to terms with the snap
decision she'd made in the parking lot. All she would
have had to do was open her mouth, point out the
trio, and the FBI agent would have taken off after
the little group. Was it just the scoop? Was it because they had called her instead of some other reporter? Well, they did call Ted, but she knew that
was an afterthought. This was a woman-to-woman
thing. She felt it in her gut. Which brought her
back to the decision she'd made. She had let them
get away. She'd suffered through thirty-six hours of
grilling by FBI agents and she hadn't given up a
thing. Not a thing. She felt proud of herself for
not divulging anything that the Bureau could use
against her or the vigilantes.

Like Ted, she'd read the competition's articles
online. She liked the part where the three reporters
said Maggie Spritzer of the *Post* had denied knowing anything about the vigilantes, whereas Ted
Robinson, also of the *Post,* had said loud and clear
that the vigilantes had contacted him on his cell
phone. *That* would not play well with the other jour-
nalists in the area. Ted was going to be off-limits
for a very long time. Maybe forever, Maggie thought
gleefully. Maybe she would have to get a new partner.

Maggie stayed in the bathroom for a full hour
before she decided to leave. By now Ted should
have given up. Alas, he was waiting by the elevator
for her.

"You're tainted, big boy. I can't afford to be seen
with you. Now, that doesn't mean I won't sleep with
you, but I can't be seen in public with you. Shoo!
Scat! Beat it, Ted!"

Chapter 28

The vigilantes had cabin fever.

Kathryn was snapping and snarling as she paced the confines of the small living room. The others watched her with glum looks on their faces. "We're forty-eight hours over our time limit. How much longer will we be safe staying here? Well?" she bellowed when no one answered her.

Myra stood up and walked over to where the former long-distance truck driver stood. She wrapped her arms around the angry woman. "We came here to do a job, Kathryn. We can't abandon Nellie, Lizzie, Jack and Harry. I ask you to remember that they all helped us in our blackest hours. Please, take a deep breath and sit down."

Kathryn sat down, her eyes locking with those of Lizzie Fox. She could easily read the defiance, the intelligence in the lawyer's eyes. Then she looked at Judge Easter, who was smiling at her the way a mother smiles at her daughter. She returned a wan smile. Jack and Harry walked over to her to pat her shoulder. A sign that they recognized her impatience. A sign that they understood. A sign that something was about to happen.

"Look, I just hate inactivity. We should be doing *something*. We've been here too long already. This was supposed to be an in-and-out deal. Things are going wrong. Why aren't we going after Maggie Spritzer?" Kathryn swiped at a long strand of hair dropping over her forehead.

"Because, dear, we can't call her," Annie said. "It stands to reason the FBI confiscated her cell phone. I'm certain her home phone is bugged. There is no way to get in touch with her. We have to come up with something that will work for all of us, Maggie included."

"She has a tail, that's for certain," Nikki said. "Ted will have one, too. Just because Riley is in the hospital doesn't mean he isn't on top of all this. His career is hanging in the balance." As an afterthought, she added, "We're just as anxious as you are, Kathryn, but our first priority is to keep our friends safe and out of Riley's clutches. Let's kick it around and see what we come up with."

An hour later the only thing they had accomplished was to finish a pot of coffee.

Isabelle gathered up the cups and saucers. "We need to do something daring. Something that will put us on the front page of every newspaper in the country."

"To what end?" Yoko demanded.

"To show we're in charge. That we came out of hiding to bring down that bastard for framing our friends. Then we disappear," Isabelle responded, the cups and saucers clinking and clattering in her nervous hands.

"We could accomplish that by sending Riley's files to any newspaper," Nikki said.

"That's much too simple. Getting those files to Maggie Spritzer is a better method of going public," Annie said. "She didn't . . . uh . . . rat us out."

"Good point," Myra said.

"How do we get to Maggie?" Alexis asked.

"Boldly and brazenly," Kathryn said coldly.

Jack Emery looked at Harry Wong and punched him in the arm. "Now, this is where it's going to get interesting."

Harry sat down cross-legged on the floor. He was all ears and eyes as he listened to the women, who rattled off ideas and suggestions at the speed of light. He barely noticed a tray materialize containing a fresh pot of coffee with clean cups. To say he was fascinated, mesmerized as well as horrified, was to put it mildly.

Two hours later the plan was on the table. All they had to do was wait for Charles's approval.

Another two hours passed while they waited for Charles to fax them blueprints of the hospital where Director Riley was receiving treatment.

More hours passed while Alexis hauled out her red bag of magic tricks and went to work.

Kathryn raced into the room with a sheaf of papers in her hand. "Okay, Charles came through for us. Riley has two guards outside his room. Three nurses on duty plus one private-duty nurse who was just fired. One of us is going to be her replacement and, no, I don't know how Charles is going to work this out. There are no other patients on Riley's floor. They were all moved to other floors to safeguard him the day he was admitted. We go in during supper hour. Supper will be compliments of Alice Riley, although he doesn't know that. Supper that is loaded with a fast-acting drug that will incapacitate the nurses and the guards. We waltz Riley out of the hospital on the special elevator the FBI commandeered just for his use. Then we dump him on Maggie Spritzer, along with his files. We give Spritzer a good, say, thirty minutes, maybe forty, certainly no more than that, and then we call the Feds, the local police, the Capitol Police, every cop in town. Hell, let's toss in the CIA for good measure. They're gonna love seeing that guy go down.

"The thirty or forty minutes we're giving Spritzer is *our* thirty- or forty-minute window. We need to get to the airport and have wheels up before anyone arrives at Maggie's apartment. I realize this is the rough version and we have to fine-tune it but I love it. All in favor say aye," Kathryn said, her eyes sparkling with anticipation.

Hands shooting upward caused the air in the living room to stir.

Harry blinked, a dazed look on his face.

"Told you," Jack chortled, pride ringing in his voice. His ladies, and they were his ladies, could do anything.

Fresh coffee arrived along with some pecan cookies.

"All right, ladies, let's fine-tune this puppy," Annie said gleefully as she smacked her hands together in anticipation.

"See, Harry, the ladies have it going on," Jack said. "Just sit back and enjoy the ride."

* * *

Mitchell Riley sat on the edge of his hospital bed, his mind racing. He hated the stupid hospital gown he was forced to wear but had to admit it was easier for the nurses to apply the medicated lotions they bathed him in hourly. He was tired but refused to give in. He had things to do and places to go. And he was thirsty. He reached for the buzzer attached to his bed but his puffy fingers couldn't quite grasp the thin wire with the buzzer attached at the end. He heard it thud on the tile floor. He spent all of two seconds wondering if he could pick it up before he bellowed to the guard outside his room.

The door opened. "Yes, Director?"

"Where's that goddamn nurse? I thought a private-duty nurse was supposed to be in attendance every minute of the day. Fire her ass and get me someone who knows what they're doing. That's an order, Agent Simms."

"Sir, you told her to wait at the desk until you needed her. You said you couldn't stand her hovering around, listening to you on the phone. Then you told me to fire her. Which I did. Do you want me to hire a new nurse?"

Riley knew he was being unreasonable but he didn't care. "Yes. Tell them to send me someone who isn't as ugly as the last one. Get me some Gatorade. Orange."

"Yes, sir." The door closed.

Riley swung his legs back on the bed. He hated this place. Hated the bed, the smell, the bedding, the pillows. He hated that someone had to bathe him, to help him brush his teeth. More than anything he hated the urinal and the bedpan.

Riley bellowed again. Simms opened the door with the Gatorade in hand. "Is there any news on my family?"

"No, sir, I check in on the hour." The agent opened the bottle of Gatorade and poured it into a glass for the director. At the last second he added a straw. Riley had to hold the glass in both hands.

"Well, Simms, maybe that's good enough for you but it isn't good enough for me. Get my section chiefs in here ASAP. I want to know what happened to my family and what's being done to find them."

When the door closed behind his agent, Riley leaned back against the pillows, his eyes on the repeated clips of Josh Carpenter's funeral airing on the Fox Network. The event of the year, and he'd missed it. He'd watched it, paying careful attention to every detail. As far as he could tell, the only thing missing at the solemn ceremony was his presence. Well, he'd have to live with that. When he got out of this damn place, he'd make a personal pilgrimage to Carpenter's gravesite with flowers in hand. In his mind he rehearsed the scene he would play, right down to the tears trickling down his cheeks. NEW DIRECTOR LEAVES HOSPITAL SICK BED TO PAY HIS RESPECTS. It would play out for weeks in the media.

Suddenly, Riley's head jerked upright. Something was wrong. It took him a few minutes before he realized he wasn't itching. *He wasn't itching.* Maybe all those shots and pills were finally starting to work. Now, all he needed was a diagnosis to prove once and for all that those goddamn vigilantes hadn't gotten to him. There was no way on this

Earth that those stupid women could outsmart him or his beloved FBI.

Thank God there was nothing wrong with his mind. He was as sharp as he ever was, but right now that sharpness wasn't working for him. He needed to find his files, his family, and prove that the warrants he'd issued for Judge Easter, that slut Lizzie, Emery and Wong were being acted on. People don't just disappear into thin air. Somewhere, somehow, someone saw or witnessed something. All he had to do was find those witnesses. Right now, he had to believe Alice had his files and planned on using them to blackmail him for whatever it was she wanted. That he could live with. But if Alice didn't have the files, that had to mean the vigilantes had spirited her away after she turned the files over to them, then spirited the judge, the slut and the two jerks to some safe place. If that was the case, he was dead in the water and all his dreams would gurgle down the drain.

Riley grappled with his pillow to find his cell phone underneath. He punched in number after number and barked orders. "Get me the reports ASAP on all calls coming and going for the following cell phones"—he rattled off the numbers for Maggie Spritzer, Ted Robinson, Jack Emery and Harry Wong.

Riley closed his eyes and let his mind race. If things didn't work out, what was he going to do? He was well aware of what the Bureau would do to him if they could prove the files he'd collected were bogus. He felt a chill run down his arms.

He had to get out of here. He wasn't itching. Once he was out of here, he could slather on the lotion just the way the nurses had. How much talent did that take?

The knock on the door startled Riley. There was no privacy in a hospital. People just came in and out at will. He hated the lack of privacy more than anything else in this damn place. He looked up at the six men, all highly trained agents. "Talk, and you had better have good things to tell me."

To the agents he sounded meaner than a junkyard dog.

There was no shyness, no stammering, no shuffling of feet.

"It's zip, sir," the senior agent said in a voice that rang with anger. "There's no trail, no clues, nothing. The only thing we have is that your wife drove away from your house under her own power with your daughter in the backseat. A witness can attest to that but that's it. As for the others, it appears they just walked out of their respective houses and have not been seen or heard from. In essence, they dropped off the face of the Earth."

Riley wanted to scream out the rage he was feeling. He was starting to itch again. Stress. He forced himself to calm down, to speak slowly. "People do not disappear without leaving a clue of some kind. I want you all to backtrack, take some fresh eyes with you. Use as many agents as you need but bring me something I can sink my teeth into. This is giving the Bureau a black eye and I will not tolerate black eyes on my watch.

"I want a report by"—Riley looked at the oversized clock on the wall opposite the television—"by seven this evening. Don't disappoint me, gentlemen."

Riley closed his eyes again. Now he was exhausted. He knew he wouldn't go to sleep, simply because there was too much to do, too much to think about. The last thing he thought about before falling asleep was that he couldn't wait to go home to take a shower and sleep in his own bed.

Chapter 29

Charles Martin worked feverishly. He had one eye on the clock, his ears tuned to the 24-hour news channels while he scanned e-mails, reached for faxes, scanned photos and worked his encrypted cell phone, making call after call to the District of Columbia where the sisters were waiting for his input. So much to do, so little time. His thoughts were as feverish as his movements.

The six-hour time difference that he thought would be a problem was proving to be a blessing. So far he'd been able to reach everyone in his network—fellow retired covert spies eager to get back into the game, all excited to work again with Charles Martin, a legend in his own time.

Charles checked and then double-checked the papers he was about to send off via encrypted fax. Certain that all the bases were covered, he pressed the SEND button. He took time to marvel at the electronic age, wishing that just half the tools available to him today had been there for him when he was a special-operations agent active in the field of espionage under Her Majesty.

All he could do now was wait. Maybe he needed to go upstairs to the kitchen and cook something. He was always able to relax when he cooked. The only problem was there was no one here to eat the food but him. Still, he could bake a ham and roast a turkey, and have them available when the women returned to the mountaintop.

Charles was almost at the door when he remembered to pick up the two encrypted e-mails that had come through at dawn. He could decipher them over a cup of coffee in the kitchen. He took a moment to wonder why the deeply buried covert operatives of Interpol and Scotland Yard would be e-mailing him. In his heart of hearts, he knew why: both agencies wanted to hire the Sisterhood and him as well.

Charles filled the coffeepot and then walked around the spacious modern kitchen with the pink brick walls and stone floor. How lonely this place was without all the sisters! Oh, how he missed his beloved Myra. He missed all the women, who were like daughters to him. His eyes started to burn. He shook his head as he blinked away the tears that were about to flood his eyes.

The women were safe. He felt it in his heart. He'd done everything humanly possible, synchronized everything right down to the last sync. Still, things could go wrong. It didn't matter how perfect a plan was, the human element always made itself known in some way. He consoled himself with the knowledge that his girls were the best of the best. If they weren't, why did he receive the two e-mails this morning from Scotland Yard and Interpol?

Charles worked rapidly with the encrypted e-mails, the cheery sound of the coffee dripping into the pot the only noise in the kitchen. When he was finished, he leaned back and smiled. Two invitations for the Sisterhood to work undercover for Scotland Yard and Interpol. The RSVP acceptance said details would follow. Well, this was something he had to put before the Sisterhood for it to be voted on. He felt a little giddy at the mere thought.

Charles poured coffee, sipping it as he worked in the kitchen. No matter how he tried to hide his worry, it was still there. Would Nikki and Yoko return with the others? He simply didn't know. Myra had tried to prepare him for that possibility by saying affairs of the heart were the human element. Myra was worried, too, even though she had said she wasn't.

How long would life on this mountaintop appeal to the women? If they were working, possibly a very long time. If they remained idle, frittering away the days in the warm sunshine, not long. As Kathryn would say, sometimes life was a bitch.

Charles scored the ham before he stuck cloves into the corners. Later he would baste it with his special apricot-lime sauce. Myra loved his baked ham. He eyed the huge turkey that was defrosting. He poked at it, only to have it slide off the counter onto the floor just as his phone rang. He looked at the tile floor to see the large crack in the tile. He hoped there were spare tiles in the toolshed.

Charles listened to Myra's voice. He was nodding as she spoke before he realized she couldn't see him agreeing with her. He looked over at the clock on the range. "Check in with me, Myra, every fifteen minutes if possible. What am I doing? I'm baking a ham and trying to figure out how to replace a tile on the floor. Why? The turkey fell off the counter and cracked the tile. No, dear heart, I am not making this up to make you feel better. Good luck, my darling."

The moment the twenty-five-pound turkey in its wrapping was in the sink, Charles raced back to the war room where he settled himself behind the computer.

The sisters were on the move. With all his high-tech gadgetry he could chart their movements without any trouble. Childishly, he crossed his fingers.

The small living room was beyond crowded. Bug-eyed at what they were seeing, Judge Easter and Lizzie Fox moved to the side to allow Myra to hold court.

"Showtime, ladies. And, gentlemen," Myra said. She tried to hide her smile as Jack and Harry both flinched at her words. "Let's run through this one more time just to be on the safe side." She looked at Nikki and Yoko, who were still in the Alice Riley and daughter disguise. "You will show up at the hospital at exactly six o'clock. At four o'clock, I will call the hospital to ask to speak to the agent outside Mr. Riley's door. I will say that Mrs. Riley asked me to call to say she ordered dinner for the hospital staff as well as themselves. I'll have the agent tell the director that Mrs. Riley and her daughter will be there to dine with him. One of Harry's employees will deliver the dinner in a properly marked van. I'm sure one of the agents will check everything before it's allowed up to the director's floor. What we're hoping is that all the director will be thinking about is the return of his wife and daughter.

"All the action is taking place at six o'clock. Kathryn will be the new private-duty nurse. She will say she's been assigned the six-to-midnight shift. I'm sure the director will approve of her. She will be the one delivering the food trays and will be the one to lace them with . . . never mind, the less everyone knows, the better off they are."

Myra winked at the others as she pointed out Kathryn with the flaming red wig, the elaborate makeup with the facial-altering latex and the short white uniform. Her nylon-clad legs drew everyone's attention as Kathryn strutted around the room. The perky white cap, which nurses actually no longer wore, bobbed up and down as Kathryn pranced and danced. Everyone clapped. Kathryn bowed.

Alexis and Isabelle were made up to look like Washington tourists, complete with straw hats, flowered dresses and sandals. Each had a camera slung over her shoulder.

Myra pointed to the two women and said, "Alexis and Isabelle will meet up with Maggie Spritzer at the hospital parking lot to . . . uh . . . deliver the goods. So to speak. Jack and Harry will be busy tailing Ted Robinson so he doesn't interfere with Maggie reaching the hospital. Your window of time is forty minutes, not one minute more. At six-forty, a police car will arrive at the emergency entrance where you will all be waiting to be whisked to the airport, sirens blasting. Special Agent Bert Navarro will be your driver. Do not talk once you're inside the car."

"Hey, hold on here! Are you saying Special Agent Navarro is . . . *one of you?*" Lizzie Fox demanded.

"That's what we're saying," Annie said. "I hope you're impressed with our capabilities, dear."

Lizzie threw her hands in the air as she tried to grapple with what she'd just heard and what she was seeing with her own eyes. Finally, her eyes sparked as she realized she was now officially *one of them* but under a new director, Judge Cornelia Easter. She risked a glance at the judge, who brazenly winked at her. Lizzie tried to hide her laughter.

Jack Emery caught a glimpse of himself in the hallway mirror. He as well as Harry now looked like a spit-and-polished version of one of the Gold Shields he did battle with almost on a daily basis. They were ready to replace Director Riley's six-to-midnight agents but only after they tracked Ted Robinson to make sure he didn't become involved.

Myra looked at the little group, her eyes sad. "We have ten minutes before it's time to leave. That's another way of saying it's time to say good-bye." She felt like crying when she saw Nikki's and Yoko's tear-filled eyes. She turned to Judge Easter to hug her. "We have to go now, Nellie. By tomorrow evening you and Lizzie will be vindicated. Stay here until we send you word that you can surface. I will miss you, old friend." She turned to Lizzie Fox and said, "Take care of her." Lizzie nodded.

"Time to go," Isabelle said briskly. "Jack, you and Harry go first." She gave both men a fierce hug. "We'll be back. Go now and don't look back."

Jack bit down on his lower lip but he didn't look back. Harry, however, did look back and waved halfheartedly. Yoko looked straight ahead and didn't acknowledge the wave. Nikki turned to wipe the tears from her eyes.

"I wish I was going with them," Annie said.

"They don't need us, Annie."

"I know. Like Kathryn says, they have it going on. I like being in the loop instead of out of it. I guess being the second string isn't all that bad. Get your gear, Myra, and let's head for the airport."

At the door, Myra turned to the judge and said, "Be careful with your new recruit, Nellie. Lizzie, keep your eye on her and report in. Thanks for all your help. You're home free now."

Lizzie, never at a loss for words and never teary-eyed, ran to Myra and Annie to hug them. "Thanks for all the help. I won't let you down, Myra, so don't worry about me. From here on in, I have the perfect cover. Once Riley's story gets out there, the FBI will never give me or the judge a second look. Especially when we refuse to knock the Bureau. Go now, stick to the schedule. We'll see each other again."

"Count on it," Annie chirped as she headed for the garage.

They were nuns or, as Annie said, penguins on the march, as they climbed into the minivan. One of Harry's men turned the engine over as he rattled off a string of something, to which Annie replied, "If it works for you, it works for us."

Alarmed, Myra demanded to know what the man had said.

"I don't have a clue. That's why I said what I said. Oh, I wish we were with the girls. We're missing out on all the excitement." Annie's voice turned fretful. "It's going to work, isn't it, Myra?"

"In theory, yes. Annie, any number of things can

go wrong, as you well know. Let's just think positive and hope for the best."

"I think I'm worried," Annie confessed.

Myra wished her heart wasn't beating so fast. She tried for a calm voice but it came out jittery. "About what?"

"Kathryn and the reporter Maggie Spritzer. She wanted us to take her on, and what happens? We start to trust her based on what Nikki said. Kathryn was livid over that and even though she came around to siding with Nikki, I'm not sure she's—"

"Don't say it, Annie. If we start distrusting each other, this whole thing will fall apart. Kathryn's okay with it. She's the most verbal of all of us. If she wasn't okay with it, we'd know it. She'd be the one going to meet Maggie and not playing the nurse. Kathryn is not a fool."

"If you say so, Myra. I'm still going to worry. Damn, this habit itches. I can't wait to get out of it."

Myra agreed. "What time is it, Annie?"

"Nuns don't wear watches. We've only been gone ten minutes at the most."

"It seems like hours," Myra said as she stared out the window. "I don't think I could ever live in this city. I like the mountaintop. I really do."

"It won't work forever, Myra. The girls are too young to live like hermits on top of some damn mountain. It doesn't matter how wonderful, how serene it is. They all need to be in love, wanting to get married and making babies or adopting babies."

"I know. That's *my* worry."

"We're like two old mother hens, Myra. We need to stop stewing and fretting and let life take its own course. When we get back to Spain I am going to actively seek a partner of the opposite sex."

"Why?"

"Because I need to get laid, that's why."

Myra wasn't stupid. She knew when to leave well enough alone. "Uh-huh," was all she could think of to say.

Chapter 30

Maggie Spritzer stepped out of the steaming shower and struggled to towel-dry her hair and her body at the same time. Damn, how she hated this crappy shower with no fans or air vents in the confined space. She could barely make out the vanity with all the steam swirling about. She opened the door to let the steam escape, knowing Ted was sitting in the living room with his laptop. Not that she was shy about her naked body, but there was a time and a place for nakedness and this wasn't the time or the place.

Normally, she didn't shower at four in the afternoon, but she'd gone for a late-afternoon run and she was sweaty. With little going on in the newsroom, she had more off hours than on hours these past few days.

Maggie had just finished wrapping her flyaway hair in a towel turban-style when her cell phone rang. She quickly shut the door as she tried to find the little phone she'd left on the vanity. She'd brought the phone into the bathroom with her because sneaky Ted would answer it otherwise. She looked down to see the words WIRELESS CUSTOMER in the little window. Her heart skipped a beat and then another as she cautiously announced herself. "Maggie Spritzer."

"Maggie, this is Nikki Quinn. Can you talk?"

Did Ted hear the phone ring or not? She wasn't sure. "I'm not sure. I can listen."

Nikki's voice was clipped and professional. Maggie likened it to her courtroom voice. No crap, just the facts. "Be in the hospital parking lot in an hour. Just sit and wait and we'll find you. You know what I'm talking about, right?"

Hospital. There were dozens of hospitals in the DC area. "No, I don't. Oh, wait a minute, the one where the . . ."

"That's the one. Tell me I can trust you, Maggie."

Maggie took a deep breath. "You can." She gulped when she realized she truly meant what she'd just said. Trust was a powerful thing.

"I'm going to make your dream come true, Maggie. But if you screw us over we'll hunt you down like a mad dog. Do you understand?"

"I understand." Maggie swallowed hard at the promise she'd just made. She could see the panic on her face in the mirror now that the steam in the bathroom was evaporating.

"You play fair with us and the dream is yours. One hour. There is a dark green Honda parked in front of your building. The keys are under the floor mat. Once we hand over to you what you will need to make that dream come true, you are to go to the Willard Hotel where there is a prepaid reservation in the name of Nancy Anderson. The room key will be with the car keys under the floor mat.

Your room number is 812. Do I need to repeat any of this?"

"No, I understand." A nanosecond later the connection was broken. Maggie stared at the small appliance in her hand. Just like that, the most famous women in the world were going to make her dream come true. How wild and wicked was that? Damn wild and wicked, she decided. She felt like dancing a jig but she was too nervous.

How was she going to get out of the apartment without Ted getting suspicious? Hound dog that he was, he was going to *sense* something.

The knock on the bathroom door startled Maggie. She jumped a foot as she clutched the towel to her person. "What?" she bellowed. "Why can't I take a shower in peace? Do I bother you when you're taking a shower? No, I do not," Maggie babbled as she did her best to pull on her clothes over her damp body. "What?" she bellowed again.

"I thought I heard your phone ring. I was looking for it to answer it for you. You should never take a cell phone into a steamy room because it will rust the component parts."

Maggie jammed the cell phone into her jeans pocket as she threw open the door. "You are so full of it. You're spying on me, admit it!"

Ted guffawed as he peered into the steamy bathroom. "You always dress in the bedroom because the bathroom is too steamy and you say it's hard to get dressed. What are you hiding?"

"You know what, Ted? I think you think you know too much about me. I'm also thinking our sex life isn't worth you invading my privacy." She reached up to gather her long hair into a very wet ponytail. "I'm going to go out now and think about you and me. I might come back and I might not, so don't leave the porch light on."

Ted sniffed. "We don't have a porch light. We live in an apartment."

Maggie sniffed in return. "Whatever. I'm going out. Get a pizza or something. There's some leftover Chinese if you don't want pizza. See ya," she said, gathering up her backpack.

Maggie was pleading silently with Ted not to follow her. Her pleas went unanswered as Ted followed her out to the elevator. When she read his intentions, she opted for the steps. *Don't follow me. Don't follow me.* But Ted did follow her down two flights before he demanded to know where she was going.

Maggie turned around. She tried to whip some disgust into her voice. "I'm going to meet all seven vigilantes. They want me to join their cause. I'm going out of the country with them so we can wreak havoc on the world. You are not invited. I'm sorry if that's more than you need to know."

Ted's eyes narrowed. He heard the words, saw the manufactured disgust and knew his reporter's instincts were on target. Maggie was already a flight down ahead of him when he got his wits about him and galloped down the steps. He could tell Maggie was picking up speed as she tried to put distance between them.

Maggie was already in the green Honda, the key turning in the ignition, when Ted exited the building. She pulled into traffic, narrowly missing a shiny black town car. She risked a glance in her rearview mirror. There wasn't a taxi in sight. But . . . Who were those two guys approaching Ted? She had a bad moment, wondering if the two men carried gold shields. Oh, well, Ted was a big boy. Now she could relax and have a nervous breakdown.

Ted Robinson sensed the air around him stir as he committed the license plate on the green Honda to memory. He whirled around to see Jack Emery and Harry Wong. *What the hell?*

"Another tiff with your girlfriend, Ted?" Jack asked.

"What the hell are you two doing here? Get out of my way, Jack."

"Why?" Jack asked.

"Because I hate your guts, that's why. You played me, you son of a bitch. I have a long memory, buddy."

"Yeah, I have the same kind of memory. Don't think for one minute I've forgotten that little fiasco in California."

"Cut the crap, Emery. You're one of them and you aided and abetted those women. You know it and I know it. I'm going to nail you sooner or later."

"Yeah, well, sooner is gone and later is here right now. Go back inside like a good little reporter."

"Screw you, Jack!"

"See, now, you're just showing off for my friend here. Just in case you didn't hear me the first time, I told you to go inside. Inside and stay there!"

"Like you're going to make me!"

A posse of motorcycles roared down the street. None of the men paid attention as motorists honked their disapproval. Ted turned to walk down the street. Harry Wong reached for his arm to jerk him backward. "Mr. Robinson, Mr. Emery asked you nicely to go back inside your apartment. You need to listen to Mr. Emery."

"Oooh, oooh, look how I'm shaking in my shoes. Mr. Emery issued an order and I'm expected to do what he says. I don't think so. What are you going to do? Do one of those high-flying kicks and knock me senseless?"

"Yeah."

Ted blinked. Then he turned around and walked back to his apartment building. He didn't look back.

"Okay, Harry, let's go. Ted isn't going to go anywhere. There's no way he can track Maggie now. We're in the clear." He whistled sharply. Within seconds a black and white police car pulled to the curb. Both men piled in. The cruiser started to move before either man could close the doors. The siren started to wail immediately.

"Gentlemen," the driver said by way of greeting.

"Agent Navarro, nice to see you again," Jack said.

Isabelle drove around the hospital parking lot three times as she waited for the GPS tracker in the green Honda to tell her where Maggie Spritzer would park the car.

"She's entering the lot now. She's going to Zone 3," Alexis said. "Let's give her a few minutes to get her breath. She's probably nervous as hell. I know I would be. I hope to God we can trust her."

"It's too late now to change our plans. She's all we have going for us. Nikki said . . . Nikki said she's on our side so we have to believe what Nikki believes. Call Maggie now and tell her to find a spot with an empty space behind her so we can back in and unload from our trunk to hers," Isabelle said, her eyes on the GPS screen on the dashboard. Alexis made the call. They both watched as the reporter maneuvered the Honda to a suitable spot.

"This is a crazy place to be doing all this covert stuff," Isabelle grumbled as she backed the car she was driving into the space behind the green Honda. "This damn place is crawling with FBI agents."

Alexis looked at her watch. "Look," she whispered.

Isabelle turned to look out the back window at the scene being played out near the private hospital entrance leading to Director Riley's wing. She could see Jack and Harry being dropped off at the door by Special Agent Navarro. She continued to watch as he parked the police car to the left of the entrance and got out. Isabelle sighed. Three down.

Maggie Spritzer sat in the green Honda watching the entrance and marveling at the choreography of this little caper. She took a few seconds to congratulate herself on being part of it all.

"There goes Kathryn. She looks great! I bet the director's eyes pop right out of his head when he gets a gander at his new nurse," Alexis said and did her best not to giggle. She continued to watch as Nikki and Yoko, aka Alice Riley and daughter, stepped out of the same SUV they drove away from the Riley household.

"Here comes the catering van."

The newly appointed FBI agents, Emery and Wong, stepped up to the van along with the two agents going off duty. Behind them the pseudo Alice and Sally Riley watched the proceedings. "Alice" was talking nonstop as she waved her arms about. The little girl at her side, head down, scuffed the ground with her sandals

"So far, so good," Isabelle said breathlessly. She looked at the little clock on the dashboard. "We're on target."

Alexis had her own eyes glued to the sweeping hand on her watch. "It's time to load up Maggie's trunk." She adjusted her wide-brimmed straw hat as she climbed out of the car, careful to keep her camera within eye range for anyone interested enough to care, one way or the other, what she was doing. Isabelle also climbed out of the car. Her straw hat was just as wide-brimmed but a different color than Alexis's. She, too, held a camera as she let her gaze sweep around the parking lot. Both women started snapping pictures of cars, each other and the entrance to the hospital. They laughed, preened and postured before closing their cameras. Isabelle popped the trunk of the car and waited for Maggie Spritzer to do the same.

"What . . . What are you giving me?" Maggie asked. "What's in the boxes? Am I going to get arrested?"

Isabelle stared at the reporter. "Your Pulitzer, Ms. Spritzer. I don't know if you will get arrested or not. Be careful."

Maggie looked at the boxes sitting in her trunk. Was it possible the contents would really lead to a prize-winning story? She felt giddy at the mere thought. "Why me? I've given you all so much grief. Why did you pick me? Or, is this a setup? Please, I need to know."

Alexis smiled. "You're one of us even though you won't admit it. Here, Nikki said to give you this.

Read it when you get to the hotel. Then, shred or burn it. I want your promise as a journalist to follow the rules we set out for you."

Maggie nodded. "You have my promise."

"Your room at the Willard is yours for forty-eight hours. Do not leave the hotel until you have a concrete plan of action. The car is yours for a full week. Leave it in the parking lot at the Willard and it will be taken care of. There's a spare license plate and a screwdriver on the backseat. Change it before you leave here. Take the old plate with you into the hotel. If you have any questions, ask them now."

"Just the same question. Why me?"

"Nikki said you could have turned us in and you didn't. The real reason," Isabelle said, smiling, "is we need you. Right now, this minute, if you've been watching what's going on at the entrance over there, you have our lives in your hands. All it will take is one phone call and we're dead in the water. Is that going to happen, Ms. Spritzer?"

"No, it's not going to happen. I don't know what to say. Can I ask where you're going? Will you call me again? Should I leave now?"

Both women laughed as they turned to get in the car, leaving Maggie standing outside her car, her eyes still full of questions.

Her heart beating trip-hammer fast, Maggie watched as the car behind her kicked to life and sped out of the parking lot. One call was all it would take. One call and she would become, like the vigilantes, a household word. She could name her price. There would be a book deal, a movie deal. As she climbed into the green Honda she wondered why her finger wasn't itching to make that one call that would make her a household name. Suddenly, even the thought of a Pulitzer was losing its allure.

Maggie was about to turn the key in the ignition when she remembered she was supposed to change the license plates. She hopped out and did so with all good speed, and then she was on her way to town and the Willard. The cell phone that she'd tossed onto the passenger seat chirped all the way to the Willard. Ted. She leaned over and turned off the phone. Ted was the last person she wanted to talk to right now. Maybe never again.

What, she wondered, was going on inside the hospital? She burst out laughing. Something only the vigilantes could pull off, that was for sure. She could hardly wait to see the evening news to find out what it was.

Chapter 31

The special agent outside Director Riley's door knocked, waited and then opened the door when the director said he could enter. "Sir, Agent Melrose just called. I wanted to give you a heads-up since I know how worried you've been about your family. Your wife and daughter are downstairs and are coming up to have dinner with you. In fact, Mrs. Riley ordered dinner for the whole staff. And your new private-duty nurse is on her way up. She'll be in to check on you before they serve dinner."

Riley turned rigid at the agent's report. Dinner? Alice and his daughter? The new nurse? What was wrong with this picture? The only thing he could think of to say was, "Did anyone check the food, Hunter?" It would be just like his stupid wife to try and poison him.

"I'm sure someone did. Your wife ordered the dinners from the Occidental. For fine dining, it doesn't get any better than that, sir. The catering van is right outside the entrance. Dennison said he called the restaurant, right after your wife called, to make sure it was all legitimate, and they told him Mrs. Riley placed the order at four o'clock. She told the staff at the restaurant it was a celebration dinner. Is something wrong, sir?"

"It would be nice to know where the hell my wife and daughter have been all this time. Did anyone think to ask?"

"Yes, sir, we did ask. Your wife said she couldn't stand the smell of the manure in the driveway so she took her daughter to a hotel. She said she didn't know anyone was looking for her. It seems the hotel has tons of videos and your daughter loves watching them. Mrs. Riley said she didn't read any papers or watch any television. We did check it out, sir, and she was staying at the Willard."

"The Willard!" Riley barked. "Do you know what a room there costs? More than I make in a week."

"Sir, it wasn't a room, it was a suite. Mrs. Riley said she always wanted to stay at the Willard. Will there be anything else?"

"No. Send the goddamn nurse in here. I need another shot, I'm starting to itch again."

"Yes, sir!"

Agent Hunter closed the door and wiped at his perspiring brow. His partner grinned. "Another hour and the old man is someone else's headache. Wonder what's for dinner."

"Whatever it is, it will be better than the egg salad sandwiches we've been getting from the coffee shop. What time is the wife due up here?"

Hunter looked at his watch. "Momentarily."

Then, like all good FBI agents, Hunter proceeded to talk into his sleeve, his eyeballs rolling for his partner's benefit. "Food's here," he said, smacking his hands together. "Well, holy shit, would you look at what the director drew for his late-night-shift nurse!"

Hunter's partner eyeballed the long-legged, flame-haired beauty sashaying down the hall toward them.

"I don't think Mrs. Riley is going to like this very much," Hunter mumbled.

"Nope. But the director will," his partner smirked.

Kathryn Lucas, aka Nurse Evelyn Evans, stopped in front of the two agents, Director Riley's chart in one hand, a medical bag in the other. "Good evening, gentlemen. I'm the director's evening nurse. Do you need to . . . uh . . . frisk me or . . . something?"

"No, ma'am. Our detail cleared you on the first floor. The director is waiting. I believe he's got a severe itch."

Kathryn offered up a roguish wink. "So do I, Agent. I'll call you if I need you."

"I'll be here," Agent Hunter said with a sappy look on his face.

No you won't, you idiot. Two bites of your food and you'll be asleep for twenty-four hours. Better men than you have been brought down by a woman. Welcome to our little world.

Kathryn opened the door to Director Riley's room and offered up a megawatt smile. She tossed the flaming red hair as she strutted toward the bed, her hand outstretched. "Director, I'm Evelyn Evans, your night nurse. Now, tell me, what can I do for you? Your agent outside said you're experiencing some discomfort. Is the itch worse?"

Riley sucked in his breath. He wondered what he had done to deserve such a looker. His weakness had always been red hair, green eyes and milky-white skin. He marveled again that he had ever married Alice. But he knew why: because she fit the profile of an FBI agent's wife.

"At times it's worse. They still don't know what caused it. Does it say anything on that report?"

Kathryn wagged her finger. "No, no, none of that, Director. Only the doctor can speak to you on that. It says here you have another half hour to go before you get your next shot. That will work because your wife and daughter are on their way up to share dinner with you. By the time you're finished with your dinner it will be time for your shot. Is there anything else I can do for you before I tidy up the room?"

"No, no, I'm fine. Sit down. I like to talk to my nurses. You can tidy up later."

Kathryn walked over to the only chair in the room and sat down. Her short white skirt hiked up to midthigh. She knew in her gut Riley was likening her pose to the one Sharon Stone had made famous. "What would you like to talk about, Director?" she asked, looking at her watch.

Riley adjusted the sheet that covered his lower extremities. This was the first time since coming down with whatever the hell was wrong with him that he felt any kind of desire and he was rapidly getting a hard-on. He squirmed and settled on his side to hide his erection. "Do you have a family, Ms. Evans?"

"A mom and a dad, three brothers, all cops, and two sisters who are schoolteachers. I'm not married. I like to think I'm married to my career. I love being able to help sick people. It's so rewarding. And the money is very good."

Riley squirmed some more. "I didn't think nurses generally made much money."

"They don't. I specialize and make more."

"What's your specialty?" he asked curiously. Suddenly he felt uncomfortable at the way she was looking at him.

"Rich old men."

Riley's eyebrows shot upward. "Well, that's being honest. I'm not a rich old man so does that mean you're settling for me? The Bureau isn't known for its generosity."

"I know," Kathryn said sweetly. "The Bureau isn't paying me. It seems you have friends in the private sector willing to pay my fee. It is a fee, Director."

"You'll have to tell me who my generous benefactors are so I can properly thank them when I get out of here." For some reason his stomach suddenly felt like it was tied in a knot.

"I can't do that, Director. Oh, I think I hear your dinner arriving. That has to mean your family is here. I'll leave you alone for now but I'll be right outside if you need me."

"Before you leave, Ms. Evans, can you pick up my call button?"

"Well, I suppose I could but I really don't feel like it right now. Maybe when I get back I'll do it," she said, and then she left.

Riley drew back into his nest of pillows at his nurse's cool words. He leaned over and struggled to reach the wire that was flat on the floor. There was no way he could reach it.

Riley could hear conversation outside the room, but he couldn't distinguish the words. He couldn't wait to get his hands around his wife's scrawny neck. What the hell was going on out there? He noticed his erection was nothing but a memory. He bellowed his displeasure.

Kathryn poked her head in the door. "There will be none of that, Director Riley. You are to speak calmly and rationally to me. I will not tolerate blustering and bellowing. If you continue to displease me, that shot you're waiting for will be delayed. Do we understand each other, Director Riley?"

"Send my wife in here right now," Riley bellowed.

Kathryn looked over at the two agents who were doing their best to keep their eyes open as they balanced their food trays in their laps. Nikki grinned as she held up one finger, meaning another minute and both agents would be down for the count.

The women ignored Director Riley as they leaned against the wall and waited. Together the three women dragged both agents to the nurse's station around the corner. The two on-duty floor nurses were sleeping peacefully, their heads on the counter. Together, the women laid them all on the floor with pillows taken from the empty rooms under their heads. Yoko ran back to one of the rooms for blankets.

"They're comfortable," Kathryn said. "It will probably be the best sleep any of them have had in weeks. Well, time to beard the lion, ladies. By the way, everything you've heard about this guy is spot-on. He's a bastard. And, he's still itching." She shouldered the door so that Nikki, who was holding a tray of food, could go through first, Yoko right behind her.

"Hello, honey!" Nikki said.

"Hello, Daddy," Yoko said.

Riley bolted upright when Kathryn also entered

the room and closed the door behind her. He started to thrash around in the bed but Yoko hopped onto the bed and had his arms pinned within seconds. Nikki set down the tray on the floor while Kathryn whipped a hypodermic needle out of her pocket. She waved it around, a huge smile on her face.

"What the hell is going on here?" Riley blustered, his eyes never leaving the needle in Kathryn's hands. "You aren't my wife! Where is she? Oh, Christ, I know who you are! Hunter! Get your ass in here! Cooper!" The director's voice was so shrill, Kathryn covered her ears. She walked over to the bed and cuffed him on the side of the head. Riley cursed, his legs thrashing every which way. Yoko held tight to his wrists with her powerful hands.

Nikki raised her hand. "How's this for an off-hand guess? We're the vigilantes!"

"We have your files, Mister Director," Kathryn said. "As we speak, they are being viewed by a reporter from the *Post*. Think Deep Throat, Mister Director. I think you might make the news by this time tomorrow. Of course, you'll be in custody by then, so you might not appreciate it."

Rage, unlike anything the women had ever seen, erupted as Riley fought with Yoko. Nikki grabbed one leg, Kathryn the other, as he cursed, then bellowed like a bull, spittle foaming at the corners of his mouth.

"Why are you doing this to me? I'll see all of you in a federal penitentiary."

Kathryn bopped him on the side of his head again. "I thought I told you to be quiet. Why? You have the audacity to ask why? Because of those bogus files you had stored at your house. The files your wife turned over to us. You were more than willing to ruin hundreds of people's lives just so you could become director of the FBI. Judge Easter. Your old lover Lizzie Fox. District Attorney Emery and Harry Wong, to name just a few. Let's not forget Senator Donner and hundreds of others. The press is going to have a field day with you, Mister Director. The humiliation alone will be unbearable. You better hope there's some dumb lawyer out there who will be willing to take you on pro bono."

Nikki let loose of the director's leg and went into the bathroom for a washcloth. She stuffed it into his mouth. The sudden silence was deafening.

"Who's watching the time?" Yoko queried.

"I am and it's running out. Kathryn, get the tape," Nikki said. She quickly yanked up the bed rails as Kathryn removed two rolls of duct tape from her medical bag. Within minutes they had their prisoner taped to the rails of the bed.

Yoko hopped off the bed. "Three minutes. Do we wipe down everything?"

Nikki looked at Kathryn, who whipped out a can of Clorox Wipes. When they were finished wiping, she stuffed them back into the medical bag. She fished another one out when she noticed the food tray on the floor.

"What about the other food trays and the nurse's station? One minute."

"The food trays are gone. Jack and Harry were supposed to take care of the nurse's station and the door handles. We didn't touch anything else," Kathryn said.

"Wait! Mister Director, you wanted to know about your medical condition. It's fiberglass. We went to your house and rubbed it in all your clothes and on your towels. Don't thank us, it was our pleasure.

We penetrated the FBI's security of the director himself. I'd say we should get a gold star for that little feat, and we're the reason you're where you are right now."

"We're minus one minute," Yoko said. "The elevator is on hold. Hurry!"

The women ran down the hallway to the elevator where the doors stood open. A second later they were on their way to the ground level.

"Minus four minutes," Yoko said calmly as they ran through the hospital zones to reach the police car waiting outside. They skidded to a stop when Jack and Harry appeared. Tears flooded Nikki's eyes. Jack waved her on, his face miserable.

Yoko rushed forward to kiss Harry soundly before she sprinted forward.

The police cruiser, driven by Special Agent Bert Navarro, appeared, blue lights flashing, siren wailing.

Jack Emery, his eyes burning, looked around as though he expected something to happen. Nothing did.

"Buy you a beer, Harry?"

"I hate you, Jack."

"I know, Harry. I hate you, too. I'm buying."

Hands jammed in their pockets, the two men sauntered across the parking lot and out to the street where they hailed a cab. Neither man looked back.

"You think we'll get arrested, Jack?"

"Nah. Remember, we have friends in high places. Very high places. I'm thinking, Harry, maybe we should take a vacation and head for that little spread I own in Montana. Whatcha think?"

"Why?"

"Would it help you to make up your mind if I told you there will be two very lovely ladies waiting for us? I have here in my pocket two first-class tickets to Montana, compliments of one Charles Martin."

Harry sighed as he grinned from ear to ear. "It would definitely help a lot."

"Then let's go."

Miles away, at the airport, Kathryn, Nikki and Yoko raced toward a silver Gulfstream. On the opposite runway, a second sleek Gulfstream waited, jets roaring.

A man who none of the women recognized diverted Nikki and Yoko, motioning them toward the second waiting plane.

"Go! Go!" Myra and the others shouted so they could be heard above the roar of the jet's engines.

Nikki and Yoko looked startled but obeyed the instructions. "What happened? Why the diversion? What's going on?" Nikki gasped as she struggled to get her breath.

The unidentified man shouted, "This plane is going to Montana."

"All right!" Nikki and Yoko shouted at the same time as they galloped up the portable stairway.

The plane was taxiing down the runway just as the heavy door was locked into place. Kathyrn ran to board the jet holding her other sisters.

Minutes later, one Gulfstream was flying west, the other east.

The women aboard the first Gulfstream clapped their hands in approval.

Myra adjusted her seat belt. "Well done, girls.

Nikki and Yoko will be back with us on the mountain in seven days."

Kathryn looked around at the girls. "Damn straight, we did good. We beat out the FBI. I can't wait to read our reviews."

"Time to go home, ladies. Charles said he has a surprise for us," Myra said.

"I hope it's one of his special dinners. I'm sick and tired of eating crackers and jelly," Alexis said.

"Let's all take a nap. Wake us when we get home," Isabelle said.

"We will, dear. One more time, girls. You all did wonderfully. Charles said to tell you he's proud of you."

"I don't think they care, Myra. Look, they're already asleep."

"So, Annie, how did you like this little caper?"

"Loved it, just loved it. But I hope you and I have a more active role the next time."

"Count on it."

Epilogue

Two weeks later . . .

Considering that it was a command performance of sorts, Judge Easter thought the room and the courtesy being shown her and her little group were fitting. She ushered the group to a large, scarred table where coffee, pastries and juice were set out for them.

Nellie's voice dropped to a soft whisper. "Remember now, I do all the talking. We discussed this on the way in. Always remember, the less said, the better. I want us all to walk away free and clear with no interference in our lives. Lizzie, pour the coffee, please."

The door to the windowless room opened suddenly. The newly appointed FBI Director, with three men who looked like poster boys for the FBI, entered the room. "No, no, don't get up," Elias Cummings said.

He was a comfortable, capable-looking man with gray-white hair and steely eyes to match. He had wrinkles and a ruddy-looking complexion. He looked to be the same age as Judge Easter. Dressed casually, he was still a commanding presence.

Nellie eyeballed the director and gave a brief nod. She was a commanding presence herself and she knew it. Right now, she held all the cards, and the man standing in front of her knew it, too.

The director stepped over to the table. "Thank you all for coming. Let me say right off that the Bureau appreciates your cooperation. I want to assure you that what is said here today will never leave this room. For starters, we're off the record here. We're just a group of people discussing an unfortunate incident."

Nellie nodded in agreement as she rose to the occasion. "For now, Director." She wasn't sure but she thought the director flinched at those three little words. Good. This man needed to know right now that she and the others were not pushovers. FBI or not.

Nellie looked around. It looked to her like the director was turning over the floor to her. She stepped up to the plate. "Director Cummings, if we're laying all our cards on the table, I want to let you know that I have a copy of all those files that were turned over to you by the *Post* reporter. Those files could have ruined my life, my career and the lives and careers of Ms. Fox, Mr. Emery and Mr. Wong. Not to mention all the other people Riley was intent on destroying to achieve his goals.

"The four of us decided that the Bureau does not need to be undermined with this kind of garbage and that's why we've remained silent. We will continue to remain silent unless it behooves us to do otherwise."

"That sounds like a threat, Judge," the director said quietly. "You can't threaten the FBI."

Nellie smiled. She sipped coffee that was so bitter it made her eyes water. Her companions did the same thing, although their smiles were strained. She wagged her finger. "Off the record, remember?"

The director sighed. "I could force you to turn those files over to me."

Nellie continued to smile. "You could try. I surrendered them to others for safekeeping. At this time I don't even know where they are, other than that they're safe."

The director sighed again. "Judge, you're treading on thin ice here. Who has those files?"

Nellie didn't hesitate before she replied. She didn't even blink. The name slid off her tongue smooth as silk. "The vigilantes have them."

Limp as a rag doll, the director flopped down on the chair at the head of the table. "Are you telling me you aided and abetted those . . . those . . .women?"

Nellie clucked her tongue. "I don't remember saying anything of the sort. I did not *give* them the files. At their demand, I *surrendered* them. I'm way too old to fight that kind of fight. That's your job. I believe the vigilantes are the ones who turned the files over to the reporter. There's no other way the reporter could have gotten them. As to how they came into my possession . . . Let's just say they were delivered anonymously," the judge said, lying with a straight face. "However, the vigilantes did give me a message to give to you."

The director bounded to his feet. "And that would be . . . what?"

"To cease and desist. Leave them alone. They no longer reside in this country. They said to tell you if you persist in your endeavors, if you don't honor their request, *they'll come back*. They said if they have to come back, you'll be sorry. That's all I can tell you. Now, my colleagues and I want, in writing, a little cease and desist of our own. None of us want surveillance of any kind. We want to go on with our lives and put this whole unsavory mess behind us. This is a bad case of all of us being at the wrong place at the wrong time. All we want is to get on with our lives. You're in their crosshairs, Director Cummings."

"That's blackmail, Judge, and you damn well know it. I can lock you up right this minute."

Nellie stood up and gathered her purse and briefcase. "You can but you won't. We both know it. Besides, we're off the record." She whipped out a small tape recorder from her jacket pocket. The director groaned. "Now, have someone type up our agreement and we'll leave your lovely building."

Jack, Harry and Lizzie rose to follow the judge. The three agents at the door moved in, their hands inside their jackets.

Harry looked at Jack.

Jack looked at Harry and shrugged.

Two minutes later it was all over and Harry had his foot on the director's chest. The three agents were sleeping peacefully on the floor. Lizzie giggled at the director's dazed expression.

Jack dusted his hands together as he moved toward the door. "Our work here is done."

"Well?" Nellie asked.

Harry removed his foot from the director's chest to allow him to reach for his cell phone.

A young man with a spiky hairdo entered the office just as the director was struggling to his feet. Cummings spoke rapidly to the young man, who didn't even blink at the sight of the director getting up off the floor or the three sleeping agents. He was back in less than ten minutes with four sheets of paper in his hand. The director scanned them quickly, and then scrawled his signature before he handed them out.

The director's guests filed toward the door, the judge and the director the last to leave. Nellie turned around, winked and whispered, "You did good, Elias."

"My pleasure, Nellie. Maybe I should have been an actor. How about lunch next week?"

Nellie laughed. "Have your people call my people to set up a time and place."

Nellie could hear the director, an old and dear friend of hers, laugh as he encouraged his agents to get up off the floor.

As Jack had said, her work here was finished.

The hour was late. Pinewood, Myra Rutledge's estate in McLean, Virginia, blazed with light from top to bottom.

Had there been neighbors, nosy or otherwise, those neighbors might have wondered why, after so many months, the house was suddenly alive with activity and light. But, since the farmhouse was so secluded and there were no neighbors, there was no one to take notice.

Downstairs in the secret room where Charles Martin and the Sisterhood had held court, machines hummed as the small assembly of people gathered.

Judge Easter rose from the table. "Ladies and

gentlemen, welcome to Pinewood. Let me introduce everyone. Lizzie Fox, Jack Emery, Harry Wong,
Maggie Spritzer and Bert Navarro."

"What the judge is saying, without saying it, is
we're the second string," Jack said.

The others hooted and stamped their feet.

"Second string, my ass," Lizzie Fox said.

The judge held up her hand for silence. "It
doesn't matter. Let's just say we're an extended
group of the American persuasion. With all that's
gone on this past month, I think it's time for all of
us to take a vacation. We've been invited to head
abroad. It seems the . . . uh . . . first string can use
our help. All those in favor say aye."

Six hands shot upward as the ayes rocked the
underground room.

"The ayes have it. We leave one week from today."

"Where are we going?" Maggie Spritzer asked.

"To a beautiful mountaintop in Spain," the judge
said. "I think we're adjourned, ladies and gentlemen."

Please read on for an excerpt from *Santa & Co.*

In this sparkling new Christmas novel by #1 *New York Times* bestselling author Fern Michaels, four close friends get together for a skiing vacation filled with a few unexpected bumps—and lots of laughter . . .

When longtime friends Amy, Frankie, Rachael, and Nina reunited for a holiday singles cruise, it not only deepened their bond, it changed their lives. Now they're getting together for another adventure, and what better winter setting than a fabulous ski lodge? Crisp snow and fresh air by day, cozy fires and delicious food by night, capped off by meeting up with their significant others for a New Year's Eve celebration—it's perfect.

At least, it's perfect until Frankie decides to go snowshoeing alone. When she twists her ankle right after losing her phone in the snow, Frankie wonders how she'll be able to summon help—only to be rescued by a reclusive Grizzly Adams lookalike who lives nearby and introduces himself as Troy Manchester.

Troy saves the day by helping the injured Frankie back to the ski lodge, but in the process encounters a part of the L.A. life he's tried to leave behind. Nina, visiting the gift shop to buy magazines for a recuperating Frankie, is similarly shocked to glimpse someone to whom she was once connected.

Even in this unlikely spot, it seems there's no way to avoid their pasts. And as the mischievous Rachael and her sidekick Amy go to great lengths to patch up old friendships and spread the spirit of the season, the New Year may contain all kinds of new beginnings . . .

* * *

The instigator of the cruise, Francesca (Frankie) Cappella, discovered romance was right around the corner from her Manhattan apartment. Giovanni Lombardi, brother and partner at nearby Marco's Restaurant, offered to look after her cat Bandit while she was on the cruise. Across the sea and thousands of miles away, the universe was working behind the scenes to bring Frankie and Giovanni together upon her return.

For Frankie, it was a wonderfully comfortable relationship. For the most part, Giovanni was as married to the restaurant as Frankie was to her publishing career. Both appreciated the affection and attention of the other without the insecurities and demands other partners had put on them. Frankie knew the elephant in the room was the word *marriage*. Neither broached the subject, and their friends and family had the good sense to keep their lips zipped.

Rachael Newmark, the second member of the foursome, had the reputation of being a major flirt. "Boy crazy" was often used to describe her, despite her protestations. She was coming off a messy divorce followed by a string of unhappy relationships. But it was her passion for dancing that recharged her self-worth when she opened a dance studio in Ridgewood, New Jersey. Her talent was her introduction to Henry Dugan, a dance virtuoso who spent every year on the cruise ship raising money for his organization, Let's Dance, a program to enrich the lives of underprivileged children. He was more than a decade older than Rachael, but that seemed to be working for her.

Nina Hunter was starring in an extremely popular sitcom when she was told the series was canceled while she was aboard the ship. Fortunately, her writing talent caught the eye of a colleague, who opened a new and exciting opportunity for her. The stipulation was she had to move from LA to New York. It took two blinks, and she was ordering packing materials. She was ready for a big change. While she convinced herself she wasn't ready for romance, it, too, presented itself. What began with snarky banter at the opening cocktail party became the basis for interesting, deep, intellectual, and often hilarious conversations. They say the way to get into a woman's pants is through her brain. Make her laugh. Seal the deal.

Nina and Richard shared a similar interest in the arts, theatre, books, and music. He was an attorney in Philadelphia, which allowed them to continue their new relationship. He was only an hour drive or a train ride away.

Amy Blanchard was a brainiac. She worked as a bioengineer at a firm in Silicon Valley, but academia was her true love. She applied for a position at MIT as an associate professor. It would mean a major move across the continent and a decrease in her salary, but it was her dream job. Eventually she would figure out her finances with the help of Peter Sullivan, an accountant she met on the cruise. He lived in Connecticut, a much shorter commute than Northern California. In Peter, Amy found someone who loved solving math puzzles, whether they were business-related or for sheer entertainment. It was true nerd love.

Nina, Frankie, and Amy agreed they had almost perfect situations. No one was smothering them, yet it was comforting to know there was that one special person out there. As for Rachael? The jury was still out. No pun intended. Richard once referred to Rachael's relationships as "one mistrial after another." Sure, it sounded cruel. But Richard was a pragmatist. His assessment was remarkably close to the truth.

Amy's father, William Blanchard, had not been part of the original plan, but after his golfing buddies canceled their weekend in Florida, he decided as long as he was already there, he might as well take advantage of the opportunity to see a few sights, eat, drink, and socialize. A cruise sounded like just the ticket. His daughter was off with some friends, and his ex-wife? Well, who cared? He booked his ticket to the ocean air and relaxation.

The day the women boarded the ship, Amy thought she was having "dad sightings," but Frankie convinced her it was just guilt about leaving her father alone for the holidays. While on the ship, the four gal pals became acquainted with a slightly older woman named Marilyn. One evening, Marilyn canceled their dinner plans, saying she was "meeting someone." The women were concerned she might be seduced by a charming lothario looking for a rich widow, so Amy and Frankie stalked Marilyn, only to discover the "someone" was Amy's father. Surprise!

A year after the cruise, the five couples, including William and Marilyn, met for New Year's Eve at

The Ridgewood Country Club. As they reminisced, they agreed the trip had been a magical adventure, but one never to be repeated. And yet . . . "never say never" had always been one of Frankie's favorite expressions.

Visit our website at
KensingtonBooks.com
to sign up for our newsletters, read
more from your favorite authors, see
books by series, view reading group
guides, and more!

BOOK **CLUB**
BETWEEN THE CHAPTERS

Become a Part of Our
Between the Chapters Book Club
Community and Join the Conversation

Betweenthechapters.net

Submit your book review for a chance to win exclusive
Between the Chapters swag you can't get anywhere else!
https://www.kensingtonbooks.com/pages/review/